PUFFIN BOOKS

GREAT ESCAPE STORIES

Some of the most exciting stories ever written have had escape from the enemy as their theme. In this book Eric Williams has collected together the escape stories of twelve different men and women who were involved in the Second World War. You can read about André Devigny's escape by rope over the roof of Montluc military prison in Lyons, or about Lieutenant David James's escape from a naval internment camp near Bremen disguised as a Bulgarian naval officer, or about Airey Neave's escape from Colditz Castle (supposedly escape-proof and designed for persistent evaders) dressed in a 'home-made' Oberleutnant's uniform! Not all the stories are about actual escapes – some describe measures taken to evade the enemy over a number of years. Madame Brusselmans in occupied Brussels, for instance, risked her own and her family's lives every day to shelter members of the Allied forces, and Denys Teare, forced to bail out over occupied France, has some very near misses before he is given help from the French Resistance movement. Twelve very different experiences, but all have qualities in common – great ingenuity and daring and a terrific excitement and suspense which we believe will sustain the reader's interest to the end of the book.

Among other books by Eric Williams are *The Tunnel*, *The Wooden Horse*, *The Escapers*, *More Escapers* and *Great Air Battles*.

D0227462

GREAT
ESCAPE STORIES

Collected and introduced by

ERIC WILLIAMS

PUFFIN BOOKS

Puffin Books, Penguin Books Ltd, Harmondsworth, Middlesex, England
Penguin Books, 40 West 23rd Street, New York, New York 10010, U.S.A.
Penguin Books Australia Ltd, Ringwood, Victoria, Australia
Penguin Books Canada Ltd, 2801 John Street, Markham, Ontario, Canada L3R 1B4
Penguin Books (N.Z.) Ltd, 182–190 Wairau Road, Auckland 10, New Zealand

—

First published by Weidenfeld & Nicolson 1958
Published in Peacock Books 1963
Reprinted 1964, 1966, 1967, 1969, 1971, 1972, 1973, 1974, 1976
Reissued in Puffin Books 1977
Reprinted 1978, 1980 1981, 1983

—

Printed and bound in Great Britain by
Hazell Watson & Viney Ltd, Aylesbury, Bucks

Contents

Acknowledgements

I am indebted to the following for their permission to use copyright material: Messrs Hodder & Stoughton Ltd for the extract from *Evader* by T. D. G. Teare (THE EVADER); Messrs Ernest Benn Ltd for the extract from *Rendez-vous 127: the Diary of Madame Brusselmans*, M.B.E., transcribed by Denis Hornsey, D.F.C. (THE HELPER); Messrs Dobson Books Ltd for the extract from *Escape from Montluc* by André Devigny (CONDEMNED TO DEATH); Messrs Hollis & Carter Ltd for the extract from *A Prisoner's Progress* by David James (THE 'BULGARIAN' NAVAL OFFICER); Messrs Hodder & Stoughton Ltd for the extract from *They Have Their Exits* by Airey Neave (ESCAPE FROM COLDITZ CASTLE); Messrs William Heinemann Ltd for the extract from *Horned Pigeon* by George Millar (CROSSING THE BORDER); Messrs William Collins Sons & Co. Ltd for the extract from *Return Ticket* by Anthony Deane-Drummond (ESCAPE FROM HOSPITAL); Messrs Allan Wingate for the extract from *Dare to be Free* by W. B. Thomas (THE LAND OF YOU-NEVER-KNOW); Allan N. Medd Esq. for the extract from *The Long Walk Home* by Peter Medd, originally published by Messrs John Lehmann Ltd (JUMP FOR FREEDOM); Messrs Burton Publishing Company for the extract from *We Fought for Freedom* by Winton K. Sexton (THROUGH ENEMY LINES); Messrs Frederick Muller Ltd for the extract from *The Edge of the Sword* by Captain Anthony Farrar-Hockley, D.S.O., M.C. (ESCAPE IN KOREA); Messrs William Collins Sons & Co. Ltd for the extract from *I am Fifteen and I do not want to Die* by Christine Arnothy (THROUGH THE IRON CURTAIN).

CHAPTER ONE

The Will to be Free

SINCE the end of the Second World War many first-class escape books have been published. My problem in making this collection has been not to find twelve exciting stories but to decide which to use. To shorten the list I determined: (a) Each escaper must tell his own story for only from first-hand accounts can the reader learn what it was truly like to be that man in that situation at that time; and (b) each escaper must have been ultimately successful. I admit I have broken rule (b). To stick to it slavishly I should have to exclude the man who is perhaps the most invincible escaper in the book. I am confident that if the Korean War, in which he was taken prisoner, had lasted only a little longer, Captain Anthony Farrar-Hockley would somehow have got back to his own lines.

Not all these escapes are from actual imprisonment. Denys Teare, shot down over France, successfully evaded the Germans and is technically an 'evader'. Madame Brusselmans was never caught, but she spent four years dodging the dreaded Gestapo in Brussels. And the young Hungarian girl, Christine Arnothy, in breaking through the Iron Curtain, escaped not from a prison but from a whole country in captivity.

You will find here stories of escape by subterfuge, in disguise, by cutting barbed wire, climbing from windows, breaking through doors, jumping from trains – in fact twelve escape stories showing twelve men and women escaping in twelve different ways. I chose my twelve and then discovered that I had not included a tunnel. It is an extraordinary truth that tunnels, the most popular means of getting out of a prison camp, were not often successful. Beneath Stalag-Luft III, the 'escape-proof' camp built by the Germans especially to hold Allied aircrew, over one hundred tunnels were dug. Yet although many prisoners got outside the camp by this means only six tunnellers were lucky enough to get clean away. I think the main reasons why tunnels failed were: (i) The difficulty of disposing of the excavated earth; (ii) the length of time taken to dig one makes the danger of discovery proportionately greater; and (iii) the tunnels themselves were usually too big, involving too many people. When one broke, the Germans panicked at the thought of so many enemies at large and called out all police, troops, Home Guard and Hitler Youth to search for the escapers. When I was a prisoner I used to assess the chances of any tunnel in inverse proportion to the number of men who were engaged in its construction.

On the other hand, tunnels were popular because: (i) The escaper can choose his own time to leave and his departure can be unhurried and well prepared; (ii) he can leave the camp ready dressed as a foreign worker, merchant seaman or whomever he has decided to impersonate on his journey; (iii) he can take as much luggage as he can carry – which usually means food carefully hoarded from his share of the Red Cross parcels; (iv) he can seal the exit after him and his absence will not be immediately noticed; and (v) a number of prisoners can escape at the same time.

To give my readers an idea of what tunnelling was like, here is an extract from one of my own books called *The Tunnel*, which describes my attempts to evade capture and my first escape attempt. Peter (myself) and John (Michael Codner, M.C., with whom I eventually escaped from Stalag-Luft III through the *Wooden Horse* tunnel) have served their apprenticeship as 'stooges', keeping cave for other escapers. They have been invited to dig.

'The scene in the central cookhouse reminded Peter of the setting for a modern ballet. The four boilers, like enormous witches' cauldrons, stood side by side on an apron

of concrete against the farthest wall. Beneath the end
boiler, now dead, was the narrow entrance to the tunnel,
open; and by its side lay the trapdoor made from concrete
in a shallow wooden tray. In each of the side walls small
high windows threw their spotlights on to the figures of
the orderlies, who tended the boilers, and the early shift
of tunnellers, who had just come to the surface. The tunnellers were dressed in woollen undervests and long pants,
patched like harlequins, bright yellow from the puddled
clay. On their heads they wore woollen caps or handkerchiefs knotted at the corners and, dancer-like, they wore
no shoes.

'Tyson, already in his tunnelling clothes, was waiting
for them. "Hurry up, chaps," he said.

'Peter and John quickly took off their outer clothing and
joined the new shift, who were waiting to go below. It was
cold and they shivered as Tyson slid under the boiler and,
after much grunting and straining, disappeared from view.
Peter, following, found a hole in the floor about two feet
square. There was a rough ladder fixed to the side of the
shaft, at the bottom of which the flickering rays of a lamp
showed Tyson's legs as he crawled out of sight. Presently
his face appeared where his legs had been. "Go easy down
the ladder," he said.

'At the bottom of the shaft was a square chamber about
six feet by four in which a man crouched, working a crude
concertina-like air pump made from a canvas kit-bag. By
his side the goon lamp cast its lurid glow across his sweating face as he swung to the rhythm of the creaking pump.
The walls and ceilings of the chamber and the mouth of
the tunnel which opened from it were of solid wood, bed-
boards jammed together side by side; but the floor was
liquid clay.

'Tyson was crouching half in and half out of the tunnel.
In his hands he had two smoking lamps, one of which he
passed to Peter. "Follow me!" He spoke in a whisper, as
though he could be heard through twelve feet of solid
earth.

'The tunnel, once they had left the chamber, was no longer lined with wood. The walls and ceiling dripped with water which gathered in long puddles on the floor and, as he wriggled after Tyson into the blackness, Peter felt this water soak through his woollen vest and the cold grip him with its icy fingers.

'After crawling for about fifteen feet the light in front stopped moving, and when Peter caught up with it he found Tyson crouching over a hole in the tunnel floor, about three feet from where it came to an abrupt end. "It goes down another six feet," he whispered. "The real tunnel starts from the bottom of this shaft. The upper tunnel is only a dummy. We camouflage the trapdoor over this shaft whenever we leave it, and then if the goons discover the upper tunnel they'll think it ends here. They'll just fill in the top shaft and this bit of tunnel – and then when the flap's all over we can strike the lower tunnel from another shaft. That way we only lose the short upper tunnel, and save the lower one." He chuckled and climbed down the second ladder into the lower gallery.

'Peter, stifling his feeling of panic, followed. This was what he had wanted. He'd got the chance, and now he must go through with it.

'It seemed deep, deep down in the earth. Somehow the second shaft seemed a hundred times deeper than the first. It seemed completely beyond help from the surface. At intervals, where there had been a fall, patches of wooden shoring bulged ominously inwards. He had to fight hard to force himself to carry on.

'He seemed to have been crawling for about half an hour before he again caught up with Tyson, who had reached the end of the tunnel. "You work here," Tyson told him. "Here's a knife. Put the clay you dig out into this toboggan." He showed Peter a rough wooden trough about eighteen inches long by twelve inches wide. "When you pull the rope twice I'll haul it back to the lower shaft. I pass it up to the top tunnel, and John will send it back to the upper shaft in another toboggan. You see now why we need such a large team."

'When Tyson had left him there was silence; more complete silence than Peter had ever known. It seemed as though the eighteen feet of soil above his head was pressing down, pressing inwards. Then, in the silence, he heard the faint hiss of air pushed by the man at the pump through its life-line of jam tins joined end to end. This metal pipe, coming along the upper tunnel, down the shaft and along the wall of the lower tunnel, was his connexion with the outside world – that, and the rope which pulled the toboggan. He took the knife and began to hack away at the clay in front of him.

"An hour later Tyson called a halt. John took Peter's place at the head of the tunnel, while Peter pulled the clay back to the lower shaft. The rope, thinly plaited from the sisal string off the Red Cross parcels, cut deeply into his hands, and the strain of pulling the heavy toboggan through the thick sludge of the tunnel floor made his shoulders ache. He had blisters on the palms of his hands from the handle of the knife and, as he unloaded the clay into jam tins and passed them up to Tyson at the top of the shaft, he began to realize that there was more to tunnelling than he had thought.

'At the end of the two-hour shift they came to the surface. Peter now knew why the earlier tunnellers had staggered as they crossed the kitchen floor. He had been sweating for the last two hours, and his woollen underclothes were wringing wet with sweat and moisture from the tunnel.'

Only one of the escapers in this collection, André Devigny, would have been executed if he had sat back and twiddled his thumbs instead of trying to get away from his cell. Even a man held in safety and comparative comfort like David James, or wounded like W. B. Thomas, seized the first opportunity to escape. What is it that inspires weak and sometimes wounded men to jump into the darkness from a swiftly moving train, claw their way along the crumbling cornice of a building far above the ground, crawl under fences in the field of fire of enemy machine-guns – risk death in cold blood as the men in these stories do? They could have remained in the security, companionship and spartan comfort of the prison camp; yet they preferred the dangers and certain discomfort and loneliness of the apparently forlorn hope. These men were not fanatics. Their stories are told with humour, tolerance and an eye to the other fellow's point of view. Why did they try to escape?

The answer lies, I think, in their independence of spirit. They had been caught: that was bad enough. They were going to do something about it themselves and not wait to be liberated. And they objected to being kicked around.

Escaping is essentially a lonely business and an escaper must be able to dispense with companionship. His mental wholeness, or integrity, is more important than complete physical fitness.

He needs, then, independence of spirit and the ability to think and act alone. Above all, he needs luck.

In the Second World War there were prisoners who spent the whole term of their captivity, whether five years or one, in persistent attempts to escape. Many of them succeeded in getting out of their camps time and again only to have the bad luck to meet an extra-suspicious ticket-collector, a sharp-eyed youngster, or a too-friendly waitress.

Not all the lucky escapers were lucky enough to survive the war. One of the greatest of all, the Luftwaffe fighter-pilot Franz von Werra, was afterwards killed flying. Twice he had escaped from prison camps in England; the second time he nearly succeeded in stealing one of the latest Hurricanes from the Rolls-Royce testing field. The third time he was lucky as well as resourceful and courageous: he dived from the window of a moving train in Canada

THE WILL TO BE FREE

in mid-winter and staggered to freedom in then-neutral America across the ice-bound St Lawrence river.

Von Werra escaped each time in enemy territory and knew that he could count on no help from the civilian population. In Europe most Allied evaders and escaping prisoners made straight for one of the enemy-occupied countries and sought help from civilians. Unless the fugitive was unlucky enough to approach a quisling collaborating with the conquerors he rarely asked help in vain. The men, women and children of the occupied countries, and of Italy too, succoured him because they valued the same ideals of liberty, respect for the individual and human charity for which he was fighting.

The escaper would only lose his liberty if he were caught. The civilians who helped him risked interrogation, torture, incarceration under bestial conditions in concentration camps and execution. After the war the nations agreed that as civilians are nowadays inevitably involved in war they should have the same rights as combatants.

The rights of combatants were agreed at the Geneva Convention of 1906. The principal clauses affecting a prisoner-of-war are: (1) He is the captive of the Government of the enemy country and not of the individual who has captured him. (In olden days a general could dispose of the prisoners taken by his army. They were usually sold, kept as slaves or exchanged for ransom.) (2) He must be protected by his captors from violence, insults and public curiosity. (It had been the custom to march prisoners in chains through the streets to prove to the public that a victory had been won.) (3) When interrogated, he is obliged to reveal only his name, rank and serial number; and no pressure may be brought to bear to force him to give any other information. (Torture was used by the Japanese in the Second World War against military prisoners, and by the Germans against captured members of the Resistance movements and British agents captured in civilian clothes.) (4) His permanent place of captivity must not be in a district which is unhealthy, nor in an area where he will be exposed to the fire of the fighting zone. He may be reasonably restrained but he must not be strictly confined except under absolute necessity. He must be properly housed and his dormitory accommodation and food must be the same as for depot troops of the captors' army. (In the Second World War the Japanese ignored all these requirements, and the Germans, although they usually obeyed the letter of the law, manacled some prisoners after the Canadian raid on Dieppe in 1942.) (5) He must be given freedom of religious worship. (6) He must be treated with due regard to his rank and age. If he is an officer he cannot be obliged to work, and, if an n.c.o., can be obliged to work only in a supervisory capacity. A working prisoner must not be made to work longer hours than a soldier of his captors' army and must be paid the same rate of wages. He cannot be required to do work which is directly concerned with the captors' war effort. (Again, the Japanese ignored these rules, and the Germans only adhered to them when convenient.) (7) He must be allowed to correspond with home and to receive parcels of food, clothing and books. (Few prisoners of the Japanese received letters or parcels. In German prison camps the books were rigorously censored, and these and other gifts from home were often torn to pieces by the guards in their search for hidden maps and messages. In fairness to my German guards, I must admit that the parcels often contained things that no law-abiding prisoner would need!) (8) Attempts to escape shall be punished only by disciplinary action – usually a spell of solitary confinement. All forms of corporal punishment, confinement in cells not illuminated by daylight, and all other forms of cruelty whatsoever are prohibited as disciplinary punishment; nor may the prisoner be deprived of his rank.

Once the Geneva Convention had been ratified, escape from captivity became a game with set rules and forfeits for breaking them. Once a fighting man had been captured he both gained and lost certain rights and obligations. Before capture he could kill an enemy in uniform and, if subsequently captured, could not be punished for this. After capture he lost his status of 'combatant' and became subject to the civil law of the enemy country. If during an escape attempt he killed a guard he committed the civilian crime of murder and expected to pay the penalty.

On the other hand, since he had lost his combatant status by being captured, the escaping prisoner could disguise himself in civilian clothes without running the risk of execution as a spy – unless it could be proved he did spy during his escape. (Recaptured escapers often had difficulty in clearing themselves of a charge of espionage.)

It was a step in the right direction to agree to these humane rules. It would be real progress if the nations would abide by them. Individual men are not often, by themselves, brutal and sadistic. Bullies always lack courage. They like to have the excuse of 'authority' behind them. The Japanese guards who beat helpless prisoners or chopped off their heads acted in the name of an all-powerful Emperor. The Gestapo men who beat up André Devigny, and those who shot in cold blood fifty recaptured prisoners after the big tunnel break from Stalag-Luft III, had the approval of the tyrannical Nazi régime. The young major who tortured Captain Anthony Farrar-Hockley in Korea had the backing of a system of government which declares that any brutality or injustice against any individual is good if it is done in the name of Communism. This is the difference between democracies and dictatorships. In a democracy the individual counts: the State is his servant. In a dictatorship the individual does not count: he is the servant of the State.

The Communists have added a new hazard to those faced in the past by the prisoner-of-war. They do not shrink from physical torture: they also attack a man's mind. They are not content to feed and clothe and keep him out of action: they must convert. They attempt by subtle means to destroy his self-respect so that they can replace it with their ideal of men as cogs in a mass machine.

Today individual freedom and integrity are threatened more than ever before. No one knows when he or she may have to meet a situation similar to the one which faced the heroes and the heroines of this book. Here are twelve vivid accounts by twelve individualists of the moment in their lives when they made their private choice and refused to accept defeat. Often single-handed, they licked the enemy. It is the unconquerable spirit of these men and women that wins wars. It is the spirit also that refuses in peacetime to bow to a dictator – the spirit that by fighting for individual freedom guarantees the freedom of peoples.

Each of these twelve stories is an account of its author's escape from captivity whether it be captivity in a prison or in a country. Each one is an escape from oppression, whether oppression by an alien enemy or by a Government imposed by force. Each story is an adventure because the greatest adventure of all is the adventure of taking one's life into one's own hands and depending on one's own resources.

CHAPTER TWO

The Evader

THE best way to escape is not to get caught. In the Second World War a great number of our airmen who were shot down over enemy territory managed to get back to England without being captured. These men who evaded capture were officially known as 'evaders'.

That they were successful was very often due not only to their own courage and resourcefulness but to the bravery of the civilian population among whom they fell. Denys Teare, bomb-aimer in a Lancaster, made his last raid on Germany on 5 September 1943. Although the aircraft was badly hit by 'flak' over the target, the pilot managed to keep the machine in the air until they were over Occupied France. Then ...

*   *   *

... 'Bale out! Bale out!' came the urgent order over the intercom, and I knew that a moment far more exciting and dangerous than anything I had yet experienced was close at hand. The crippled bomber was plunging down towards the inky blackness of enemy territory below.

At dusk on 5 September 1943 we had crossed the North Sea at twenty thousand feet, but after making our way through the reception thrown up by the coastal defences, we had only three engines intact.

Although losing height, we reached our target, Mannheim, and found the Pathfinders had already dropped their green flares to indicate the target area. While making our run with bomb doors open, I could see the familiar pattern made by tons of explosives dropping all over the town. There were clusters of tiny white lights which kept appearing as the incendiaries landed, and amongst them the huge orange flashes made by the four-thousand-pound cookies'.

As the centre of the blazing inferno slid below my bomb sight, I pressed the release button, and the slight upward lift of the aircraft told me that my own deadly load was on its way.

Closing the bomb doors, we altered course for home, but as fast as missiles descended from the five hundred or so aircraft in the darkness around us, so also were hundreds of shells coming up from the ground and bursting dangerously near. Being by now a mile below the rest of our compatriots, we soon began to receive far more than our share of hot shrapnel.

Suddenly the starboard engine, which had been pulling so well on its own, was hit, coughed and died out. The situation was now rather grim; we plunged about the sky while Bob, the pilot, wrestled with the controls to stop the wounded monster from rolling on its back. We struggled gamely along through 'flak' and fields of waving searchlights, losing height all the time. At first we thought that perhaps we would just reach the Channel; then one of the remaining two engines began to misfire.

A microphone switched on with a click and a voice came over the cracking intercom: 'Whereabouts are we Tommy?'

'About thirty miles from Luxemburg, I think,' replied the navigator. Tommy was a born gambler, but I could tell by the tone of his voice that he did not like the heavy odds against him.

'Is everyone O.K.?' asked the pilot. Each man in turn switched on and answered – rear gunner, mid-upper gunner, wireless operator, engineer, navigator, and myself. At least no one had been wounded, which was something to be thankful for.

'She won't maintain height,' Bob continued. 'We'll probably have to jump soon, chaps.'

No one had the chance to reply, for just then the spluttering engine caught fire, the aircraft lurched dangerously and hurtled downwards. With a last gallant effort Bob straightened her out once more, but she was still sinking. He pressed the button operating the fire-extinguishers in the port-side inner engine without effect; in a few seconds the whole wing would be ablaze.

We had practised the 'abandon aircraft' routine dozens of times on the ground, so when the order was given each man knew exactly what to do. I had often wondered what my reactions would be on an occasion of extreme emergency such as this. As soon as Bob's words reached me, both hands started to work mechanically, first snatching off my flying-helmet with its electrical leads and oxygen-pipe attached, lest they foul the silken cords upon which my life was about to depend, then jumping to my feet astride the rubber pads I had been lying on behind the bomb sights, and then bending down to tug at the release handle. Up came the hatch itself, helped by the pressure outside; wind rushed into the aircraft and I felt maps swirling round my legs. My parachute was already clipped in position on my chest, so all that remained to do was dive head first through the square opening in the floor.

I felt the cold rush of night air as I somersaulted through the slipstream. On the first revolution I got a glimpse of the underside and tail of the plane silhouetted against the moon, but on the second the moon alone.

In the course of various lectures attended during training, I had learned the number of strands of wire used in the manufacture of a parachute rip-cord, the strength of each strand, and the tests to which the completed object was subjected before coming into use. This instruction certainly increased the confidence of the pupil, but in my case I was left with the impression that the wire was made so strong in order to withstand the heavy tug required to release the parachute. In consequence, a few seconds after leaving the aircraft, I gave a terrific wrench on the chromium handle, knowing my life depended on it, and was horrified to feel it come away with no noticeable resistance whatsoever.

For a ghastly split second nothing happened and I continued to drop like a stone. Then something flashed past my face and a mighty jolt on the harness shook every bone in my body.

I had stopped falling and seemed to be standing still in mid-air. I gathered my senses together and began to take stock of my surroundings. I was alive, my parachute was above my head forming a big round dome lowering me to Mother Earth. I looked down past my dangling legs, saw that there was still a long way to drop and felt very sick.

During the previous four hours I had heard the incessant roar of engines in my ears, but now there was a peaceful quietness, broken only by the sound of one single aircraft going away in the distance. Just then another thought flashed into my mind. Had the rest of the crew baled out, or had I misunderstood the words spoken over the intercom? Perhaps the boys would be back in England at dawn; similar instances had happened in Bomber Command. A huge sheet of flame lit up the countryside a couple of miles away, then the sound reached me of a sickening crash and explosion. The silence was now unbroken, and I knew that old S for Sugar would definitely not see England in the morning.

Although I was slightly relieved to think I had not made a *faux pas*, I wondered if all seven of us were now drifting to earth, or whether anyone were dying in the wreckage below. I peered in all directions but saw nobody.

My descent probably lasted only two or three minutes, but during the time I hung in mid-air it seemed very much longer. The ground below still looked black and threatening. Gradually the landscape became clearer and in the moonlight I could see a wood directly beneath me and a small town at one side. The aircraft seemed to have crashed into a hillside. Quite suddenly everything became much clearer. I could see the little houses in the town, and the church, and then the trees seemed to rush towards me. I closed my eyes, covered my face with my arms, and curled up into a ball.

Crash! Branches rushed past me, then came another jerk on my harness as my parachute got caught in the tree-tops and I found myself still suspended in mid-air. After swinging about in all directions for several minutes, I finally wrapped my arms and legs tightly round nearby branches. Assuring myself that they were strong enough to take my weight, I gingerly released the buckle of the parachute harness and cautiously climbed down. With immense relief I felt my feet touch solid earth. One fist was clenched tightly and, looking down, I saw that my shaking hand still gripped the rip-cord handle.

I did not know whether I was in Germany, Nazi-occupied France, or Luxemburg. Wherever I was, the procedure was the same. I tried to dislodge my parachute in order to bury it, together with my flying-kit, but struggling in the pitch darkness of the forest I found it a task far easier said than done. After wasting a quarter of an hour in a vain attempt to cut it away or shake it down, I abandoned the job. The few hours before daylight were too precious to be lost. Emptying the pockets, I regretfully threw my flying-kit and Mae West in a heap on the ground. The trees were very dense, and there was a chance, unless a thorough search were made, that even the parachute might remain unseen indefinitely. Forcing my way in the darkness through the bushes, I kept in a straight line, aided by glimpses of the moon through the thick foliage, and eventually reached open fields.

In the clear moonlight I took stock of my possessions. My celluloid escape-pack was still inside my battledress, but when I opened it I found that the tube of condensed milk had been spilt, turning the Horlicks tablets, miniature compasses, matches, and energy tablets into one sticky mess. Licking a compass clean, I tried to read the tiny dial, but being unable to do so in the moonlight I stepped back into the wood in order to use the light from a match. Not one of the whole box would strike. I knew I would have to rely on the stars until the dawn.

I always carried a sheath knife on operational flights,

and used it now to cut off the tops of my sheepskin flying-boots, remove my brevet and sergeant's stripes. At the squadron I had been issued with a revolver, but had left it in the billet before taking off. My only other possessions were maps and Continental money in a waterproof packet which I would open in daylight.

From now onwards I was an 'evader'.

I knew that my best direction lay to the south-west, and who knew – perhaps a few weeks' cross-country running would bring me to the Spanish border, and eventually to the British Embassy in Madrid. Setting off at a jog-trot along the rough track by the edge of the trees, I pulled up suddenly as I heard a church clock strike one. Remembering the small town I had seen from above I realized that it lay directly in my path. Leaving the track I circled to the left across the field, avoiding the town.

Half an hour of hard running over potato drills, across fields, through hedges and barbed wire brought me to a wood even denser than the one I had left. Finding it impossible to make any headway, I retraced my steps and tried to get round to the other side of the town. Here again I found more dense woodland and also a kind of cliff which appeared to form the edge of the town.

The streets were dark and deserted, so I cautiously made my way directly across the town. Reaching the first of the buildings I was surprised to find them derelict; tiptoeing silently along I found two streets of shattered houses with no windows, doors or roofs. I learned later that this town had been almost completely destroyed during the First World War, and a new one erected at its side; of course, I had entered the ruined town first.

Leaving the scene of destruction behind me, I slid stealthily through the inhabited streets, keeping to the shadows. In what appeared to be the main street I came across a route indicator, on which I read in the moonlight the distances to Metz, Strasbourg and Nancy. I was thus able to establish my position fairly accurately, and was relieved to find that I was actually over the border in Occupied France.

While I was looking at the indicator, I heard a motor approaching and had just time to dive behind a pile of wood before it swung round the bend. Peeping out after it had passed, I got my first glimpse of enemy troops; the two uniformed occupants had probably been aroused to investigate the burning aircraft near by.

Gliding silently along the walls, I continued my journey, passing little cafés and shops with their various advertisements. Throughout the town I did not see a single window without shutters across it. The French people seemed to have a distinct dislike for fresh air, but this was perhaps an advantage to me, otherwise some sleepless person might have heard a slight footfall, seen a dark figure flitting from shadow to shadow and given the alarm. The dogs knew something unusual was happening, however, and I could hear them howling from miles around.

Reaching open country once more, I heard the clock behind me strike three times, and realized that it would soon be daylight. I was still not far from the aircraft, and the German troops would be searching for her crew, so I went into a steady trot which I hoped to keep up without tiring too quickly.

I plodded along for two hours, but my feet had become so sore that I went into a wood, crawled under a bush and rested. The soles of my feet were like pieces of raw meat, for I had left off an extra pair of socks thinking I might be too warm, and my feet had been slipping up and down in the big flying-boots, causing blisters which had burst and re-formed. After bathing my feet in a stream, washing my hands and face and filling my rubber water-bag, I lay down to sleep.

*

When I awoke it was about six o'clock and I felt very refreshed. It was a beautiful September morning, the sun was shining and the birds were singing. It reminded me of pre-war camping days, and I would have thoroughly enjoyed a breakfast of bacon and eggs cooked over a wood fire.

My dreams stopped abruptly when I heard the sound of snapping twigs. Someone else was in the wood only a few yards away. I did not wait to see who it was, but I could vividly imagine a German soldier prodding his bayonet in the bushes, looking for the late occupants of the burnt-out Lancaster. (I learned afterwards that it was Bill Millburn, another member of our crew.) I squirmed along on my elbows for a hundred yards, then ran in a crouched position, keeping under cover as much as possible.

With the aid of my compass I kept in the same direction through the woods, seeing evidence of the First World War in the overgrown trenches I jumped over, which were still littered with rusty remains of barbed wire and steel helmets. A mile farther on I came across some more recently laid barbed wire entanglements and a notice-board with large red printing on it in French and German. I could not make out what it meant, my knowledge of both languages being slight, and I thought it probably referred to the property being private, so I crawled under the wire. I went at a jog-trot among the undergrowth until I came to where the ground was dotted with holes. I then realized what the notice was – I was running over a German artillery range! Luckily no firing was taking place that morning, but when I reached the other side safely I promised myself to walk round all red notices in future.

I was now into open country and, running along the hedges, headed in the direction of a smaller wood. Reaching this, I penetrated a few yards, then came upon a sheer drop of about fifty feet covered densely with brambles and bushes. From where I stood I could see the River Meuse twisting its way through the fields. At the foot of the cliff ran a road which made an 'S' bend, then crossed the river by a concrete bridge.

I realized that to continue in a straight line I would have to cross the bridge or swim the river. I could just faintly see two figures on the bridge, so I decided to descend the cliff and get as near as possible to see if they were guards or road workers.

A narrow footpath zigzagged steeply downwards through the bushes. I took this, but soon the steepness and loose shingle turned my cautious walk into an uncontrollable slide. Half-way down, on rounding a bush, I crashed right into a man trying to half-carry, half-push a bicycle up the pathway. I don't know who was more surprised, he or I.

I helped him to his feet and judged from his clothes that he was a wood-cutter on his way to work. Letting my handkerchief fall to earth several times, I indicated that I had descended by parachute. He understood, looked anxiously in all directions, and was obviously scared lest anyone saw him talking to me. He glanced down once or twice, probably realizing he would perhaps be thrown down the rest of the cliff if I thought he would betray me.

He hurriedly went through his pockets and offered me some money, which I refused, showing him the French notes in my R.A.F. emergency kit. I looked at his shoes, but they were not worth exchanging; they should have been in the dustbin long ago. So with a handshake and a smile we separated.

Reaching the foot of the cliff I left the bushes to walk along the road. My feet had become worse and walking on the smooth roadway after the shingle gave me unimaginable relief. Hardly had I enjoyed this pleasure for ten yards when I heard the sound of motors approaching, and round the bend of the road came an army lorry full of German soldiers, and across the bridge came a second one. In a flash I dived back into the bushes and lay there perfectly still, only a few feet from the road.

In each lorry were about twenty fully armed men dressed in green uniform, half of them armed with rifles and bayonets and the other half with sub-machine guns. I realized that they were part of the search-party turned out to look for the crew of the Lancaster.

When they had disappeared in the distance I crept out and went towards the bridge to get a closer look at the two men. They were both in civilian clothes, so I walked past them with my hands in my pockets, whistling *Alouette* and trying to look unconcerned, as if I had lived there all my life. Even though my dress looked a bit queer, I could hardly be described as having a military appearance. I wore no hat, no brass buttons, no badges and no chevrons. I needed a shave and a hair-cut and did not expect the French would recognize the colour of my battledress. However, these two men, as I knew later, had lived there all their lives and regarded me with suspicion while I was still a hundred yards away. Drawing level, I nodded my head and gave a slight grunt as if in greeting, but they just gaped at me in amazement. Walking right past them and over the bridge, I did not turn until I was two hundred yards on the other side. They were both peering in my direction; apparently I looked anything but a local inhabitant!

On either side of the road stretched potato and turnip fields, and instead of the hedges one sees in England, there grew apple and pear trees every fifty yards or so. They were laden with fruit and, needless to say, I helped myself. I hoped to sight an isolated farm which I might approach without being seen, explain with signs and drawings who I was, and hope that the occupants would be patriotic and give me assistance.

After trudging along the dusty road for a couple of miles I saw a car approaching. There was no cover at hand, so I ran quickly into the turnip field and knelt there pulling up weeds as if I were a farm worker. The vehicle passed by unheeding, so I continued on my way. For three more miles I walked wearily along without seeing a single house, but I was obliged to resort to pulling weeds on two other occasions, first for a cyclist, and next for a motor-cyclist. On my right were a railway line and a canal, both gradually converging on to the road. Eventually I reached the point where they crossed; there I sat down and bathed my feet in the canal. It was here that I met Pierrot and M. Pierre, who were guarding the bridge.

In Occupied France every bridge of even the least importance was guarded, the main ones by German troops, those of lesser importance by local Frenchmen conscripted for the work. At certain times during the day and night, each bridge was visited by German patrols, and if they found a Frenchman absent or not alert, he was punished. Although these men were unarmed, they were expected to resist attempts by saboteurs or paratroops, and if the bridge was wrecked they were held responsible. In some cases their families had been taken as hostages. The two men I had passed on the first bridge must have been on duty.

Pierrot was a very different person from the labourer I had met earlier in the morning. I will never forget the excitement in his dark eyes when he realized who I was. He danced round shaking my hand again and again, hardly believing that here was a real live *aviateur anglais*. He was crazy about aeroplanes; night after night he listened to the deep roar of our heavy bombers and in the daylight strained his eyes into the sky searching for the American Fortresses, usually flying so high that they were almost out of sight. He had wished time and time again that he could see a parachutist come down and help him to escape. And now before him stood an Englishman. At eight o'clock that morning he had been along to see the smoking ruins of my aircraft before mounting guard on the bridge.

His companion was a small, middle-aged man, very shabbily dressed, with an unlit cigarette drooping from his lips. He badly needed a shave, and the bottom row of his dirty, tobacco-stained teeth overlapped the top.

Alongside the bridge was a stone cabin, into which they motioned me. It was used as a guard-room-cum-sentry-box, and in one corner a wood fire was burning, the smoke going out through a hole in the roof. The only furniture was a wooden bench, and on the floor was a straw-filled palliasse. An earnest discussion took place between the two men. There was obviously a difference of opinion, and it looked as though the elder wanted to give me some food and let me wander off, while Pierrot wished to take me to his home. At length a decision seemed to have been reached. Pierrot thrust a couple of apples in my hand, then dashed off on his bicycle down the towpath.

When I was alone with M. Pierre he seemed very uneasy in case anyone approached, but from his pocket he produced a piece of dark bread and a small slice of raw bacon. As he handed me the two together, his fingers trembled and the bacon fell on to the earth floor. Muttering curses he picked it up, scraped it with his penknife and rebalanced it on the bread. This was my first taste of black bread, and although the bacon was now rather dirty, and smaller than a matchbox, I was hungry enough to be extremely grateful for it. From another pocket my host took out half a bottle of wine, from which he filled a small glass and handed it to me. It tasted rather sour, but I found it quite refreshing; twice I emptied the glass and twice M. Pierre offered me more, trying to tell me it was good stuff.

Unfolding my small escape maps and using signs, I asked M. Pierre to indicate where I was, pointing in the direction by which I had arrived. He repeated 'Saint Mihiel' several times, until I gathered that this was the name of the town through which I had passed in the darkness. I had found two handkerchiefs in my waterproof escape-packet, one printed with the map of Germany on one side and Northern France on the reverse side, the other one with maps of Italy and Southern France. Searching through the German towns, my companion put his finger on Berlin, and, making whistling noises and indicating with his hands the dropping of bombs, looked questioningly into my face. I nodded my head and he shook my hand with great approval. I pointed out other German towns I had bombed, and managed to make him understand that I had never dropped a single bomb on any target in France. He grinned approval, spat on the floor and babbled some incomprehensible phrase, which ended in the word 'Hitler'.

Fingering the map of Italy, he repeated his sign-language question. Pointing first to Turin and then Milan, with the accompanying sound effects, I gave my answer. He appeared slightly perturbed and said a lot more in French that I did not understand. Then he tried German, to which I shook my head and said 'nix', whereupon he changed to a third language which I believed was either Italian or Spanish, but still I could not understand him. At that moment young Pierrot returned on his bicycle with a sack over his shoulder. He spoke to the older man, then turning to me and using the words *Mama, Papa, Babba*, gave me to understand that M. Pierre was an Italian, born in Turin, and that the rest of his family still lived there. Noticing my worried expression, M. Pierre indicated his attitude towards the war by spitting on the floor, banging his fist on the bench, and disgustedly muttering, '*Boche*' and '*C'est la guerre*'. I learned later that he had never declared his true nationality when the Germans over-ran France, but continued to live as a Frenchman, proprietor of a little café in a village near by, where he lived with his wife and twenty-two-year-old daughter.

Opening the sack, Pierrot produced some civilian clothes and a note written in English which read: 'Follow the boy, he will lead you to friends.' ...

* * *

... From that moment onwards, until France was liberated by the advancing Allied armies, Denys Teare was sheltered by French Resistance workers. At first, unable to speak the language and helpless in a strange land, he was passed on from one French family to another. Gradually as his command of the language grew and he found his way to the more active centre of Resistance, his life became more and more exciting until towards the end he was a fully fledged member of a band of *maquisards*. *Maquisards* originally were men who took to the *maquis*, a thorny bush covering scrub country in wild parts of France. From this shelter they harassed the German invaders. Later the term *maquis* was used for all Resistance workers.

CHAPTER THREE

The Helper

FOR the thousands of our airmen who were shot down over enemy-occupied territory and for the even greater number of our soldiers who had been overrun by the *Blitzkrieg* ('lightning war') of the advancing German armies in 1940, the only hope of returning to their own country was through the help of the civilian population. The penalty for giving such help was death.

In September 1940 Madame Anne Brusselmans, a Belgian mother of two young children, was visited in her Brussels flat by the local clergyman. 'There are British soldiers hidden in the city,' he told her. 'Will you help?'

From that September morning until the liberation of Brussels by our troops four years later, Madame Brusselmans and her family risked their lives every day to hide, feed and finally to pass on to safety the 'charges' who came to her flat for sanctuary. At first her charges were soldiers overrun by the *Wehrmacht* in their victorious advance; then there were R.A.F. pilots shot down in dog-fights over occupied territory, followed by increasing numbers of aircrew shot down on their way to and from targets far inside Germany; towards the end there were the Americans, floating down in their dozens from the daylight bombers which, hard pressed by German fighters, fought their way across the sky.

Madame Brusselmans and her husband Julien became important links in the famous *Comète* Line, an escape organization which extended from Belgium, across France and over the Pyrenees to neutral Spain and Portugal. At the same time as she assisted evaders, Madame Brusselmans gathered information about German troops and military establishments to pass on to England.

The following extract from a diary this brave woman

kept during these exciting years gives a vivid impression
of the uncertainty and terror of her chosen way of fighting. ...

* * *

... *10 September*

The other night I had to fetch in two Americans, Hank
and Martin.

Hank hails from Chicago but is far from looking like a
gangster. Mart comes from Ohio.

Martin still bears the marks of the heavy burns he sus-
tained when he jumped out of his plane in full daylight.
All his clothes were on fire. Everything he had on was
burning except his parachute.

The two Americans landed near a river, which Hank
helped Mart to cross by swimming beside him. He then
took him to shelter amongst the bulrushes. Meanwhile, the
Germans had seen the men come down and were searching the countryside for them, so they hid in this swamp
for nine hours. At night they were helped out of their
uncomfortable hiding-place by members of the Belgian
underground movement who, in a boat rowed by the
young son of the local farmer, brought a doctor and a
nurse with them to give Mart morphia and attend to his
burns before taking them both off to the nearby farm.

After staying in the district until Martin's burns were
healed, the two men came to Brussels. There was then
the usual procedure first, at Mr P's house, where it was
decided that as it was late Martin should stay the night
but that I would take Hank to stay at my house.

It is now dark, and as we walk part of the way home we
stumble, for we can't see very much. The Brussels streets
have cobbles which date back to the sixteenth century, or
at least they feel as if they do. I know the way pretty well,
as I have done this journey often in the heavy black-out,
but Hank, poor man, I pity him.

Hank, however, has given me some good advice. At
least, he *says* it's good, or rather, good for the eyesight.

'Eat as many raw carrots as you can,' he says. 'They are good for night vision.'

Well, I'm not fond of carrots, either cooked or raw, but as they are about the only thing the Germans are leaving us I shall have a go at eating them raw, as he advises. But, oh, for a nice juicy steak!

Half-way home we took a tram and it so happened that the two carriages were filled with Germans. I jumped in first and saw Hank hesitate, just for a second. Then he got on after me. We were the only civilians in this tram. Hank's face was most expressive.

There was no hesitation, however, when I went to get off. Hank jumped up double quick and followed me at once. He heaved a sigh of relief, and, as a matter of fact, so did I. If those Germans had only known what a bundle of medals they were missing.

The following day I took Hank down town again to have his photo taken for his French identity card.

*

12 September

This journey passed off without incident, but on another one that night I really found myself in a tight corner. Two more Americans having arrived, I went off to fetch them in, and as we got on the tram one of the men took out his cigarette-case and offered cigarettes around.

Now, since the Germans have tumbled to a habit the Belgians have of burning soldiers' uniforms with their lighted cigarettes, smoking on trams is forbidden, although of course the Belgians soon found another way of annoying their oppressors. (Now they pour a few drops of acid on the uniforms instead, and then get off the tram.)

However, this was not the time to tell this story, so before the men had time to light up their cigarettes I gave them the wink and hastily got off the tram. They looked surprised to have to leave the car after so short a journey, but were even more surprised when I told them how nearly they had given themselves away. Of course, it is my fault, for I should have thought of warning them about this before. Funny how these small and quite innocent daily habits may lead us all to face a firing squad.

Arriving about half past nine at Mlle C's house I have a funny feeling, though I don't know why, that the house is not safe any more. So I ask the boys to stand by and watch. 'If I flash my torch,' I tell them, 'everything is in order. But if I walk into the house without signalling, walk to the top of the street and wait for me there.'

Then I walk up alone to the house and ring the bell. There is a short wait, then Mlle C comes to the door and opens it. Everything was all right, after all.

We go in, and there they are all congregated, all laughing and joking. With those in there already, there are now twelve of them, and it is good to see them, and to hear them talk and make fun of their foreign civilian clothes. The Americans don't like the long-tailed shirts that men wear in Belgium; it's a lot of wasted material, they say. The British don't like the style of men's hats. As for the Canadians, they don't seem to care: all they long for is a good, strong drink. One tall American has wider interests – he wants to know if the use of peroxide is unknown in Belgium, for he has not seen a nice young blonde since he came here.

I returned home with the last tram to find Julien getting anxious. I suppose it is worse for those who are waiting at home than for those who are out on the road. But I could not resist staying with the boys to listen to all the latest news from England. All are anxious to get back to take part in the big invasion, but after their description of the amount of planes and bombs they are accumulating on the other side of the Channel in preparation for this, I felt more like running away.

It's no use pretending otherwise, I do feel sometimes like nothing on earth. This continuous strain is getting me down. Yet I must keep on. I know that by now the Allies are counting on us. Again and again I remind myself that each man we send back is a man of experience, and that the mere fact they do go back is good for the morale of those who, day after day, night after night, go out into the skies to face and meet death. And what a death! Burned alive or machine-gunned as they come down by parachute. Yes, we must keep on.

Word has come through to expect three more Americans. One is badly wounded, with a bullet in the leg. This happened ten days ago and he cannot be moved from where he is because the Germans have encircled the village and are patrolling all the roads. The wounded man is hiding at a priest's house and as soon as all is clear will be brought into Brussels, where Mlle C will take him in, for he must be sheltered where there are no children. Our doctor friend has been warned, for he will be needed. And so we are all standing by. Meanwhile, the wounded man is being nursed by a Belgian nurse who belongs to the underground movement in the district where the man is hiding.

This week Julien took Hank to visit the bombed area. As Julien is in the A.R.P. he has a special pass and arm-band which enables him to enter the forbidden zone, so he got an extra arm-band for Hank and off they went.

When they came back Hank was speechless. It is one thing to be in a plane and drop bombs; quite another to be the target. Hank says he does not want to be in Belgium when the invasion starts (after seeing this). This sounds joyful to us. It looks as if we are going to have a tough time. Well, let it come. The sooner the better.

*

Hank has left. I took him down town at 8 p.m. He will stay one night with Mart and then leave for Paris. Thrilled at the idea of seeing 'gay Paree' he has made up his mind to buy some perfume for his wife – *Soir de Paris,* he wants.

In their place I have four more men to fetch. I shall get two in the morning and two in the afternoon. If these airmen keep coming in at the rate they are doing now we shall soon see them walk down the streets four abreast.

The Germans are getting a nuisance on these journeys. They have started the same little game as in 1914–18, stopping the trams and searching civilians. For this the men must get off the tram and stand facing the walls with their hands up over their heads, while the Germans feel in their pockets, around their bodies, arms and legs, and then check their identity papers. After this is done they are allowed to re-enter the tram.

When the Germans decide to search the women, they take with them a German woman (a 'Grey Mouse', as we call her) and she searches them and any children as well. It is useless to try to run away. Each patrol consists of twelve to sixteen men, two of whom stand in front of the tram, two at the back, and two on either side, while the rest do the searching. If one tries to run away, they shoot; and if arms or underground papers are found in the trams, an army truck is sent for and all the passengers are taken away to the *Kommandantur* to be questioned.

Men aged between eighteen and fifty-five are made to go and work in Germany, unless they can prove they are working for a public concern, such as the police or the post office, or that they are employed by public undertakings like the gas and electricity associations or tramways. In that case they have to produce special papers issued by the Germans and giving the name and address of employer and employee. It looks as if we shall badly need some of these papers very soon.

*

The wounded American has arrived and I have been to see him. He comes from Virginia, so I call him 'The Rebel'. Poor fellow, he is not looking very well, although he seemed better on my next visit after the doctor had extracted the bullet – or what we thought was a bullet – from his wound. (It turned out to be a piece of the plane.)

What we need now are bandages, iodine and ether, and we can only get these things with a doctor's prescription. As it is a risky thing for a doctor to prescribe all this without being able to produce a patient in case of an inquiry, I went to see my neighbour the chemist to see what I could do on my own account.

'Mr V,' I said, 'I need bandages fifteen centimetres wide, iodine and ether, cotton-wool, and sterilized lint, and all this without a doctor's prescription.'

He looked at me for a second.

'All right,' he said, and a few moments later produced a neat little parcel.

'How much do I owe you?'

'Nothing.'

I thanked him, and walked away.

'If you need any more come back and see me,' he called after me.

He had guessed, of course, why I needed these things, but as a very wise man asked me no questions and saved me telling stories.

Michou has been in with a letter from Hank,* who says that he and Mart have had their journey postponed at the last minute. One of the guides has been arrested and Hank is worried. He says members of another organization have been in to see them, and have promised to repatriate them at once, but he and Mart are suspicious of this and want me to take them away as quickly as possible.

*

I immediately went off to get Hank and Mart, but arrived too late. The woman sheltering them had let them go with these other people. I'm simply furious at this. It is the first time anything like this has happened to me. Who are these people, I wonder? We must find these two men, but why

* *Letter to Madame Brusselmans:*

Hi You All,

There seems to be another organization in operation at this house where we are staying. Don't know what to do. I don't feel safe and my companion shares my feelings. Please get in touch with me at once.

As ever,
HANK (Sarnow)

have they left? I had warned them not to leave with
strangers. Really, they are worse than children.

*

Meanwhile, I had been to say good-bye to Stanley and his
friends – two Americans – who are leaving tonight. I asked
them to drink our health on Christmas Eve and they
promise they will do so.

Well, with all this journeying about, there is no getting
out of it. We must steal or forge some of these *Werbestelle*
papers, for with the Germans stopping and searching civilians at any time of the day or night it is getting a risky
thing to take these men out if they are not in possession
of these documents.

*

The men are now leaving at the rate of ten a week. Not
bad! I hope it keeps up, and it no doubt will, for I have
received a letter from the south of Belgium saying that
fifty more men are waiting their turn to come up. However, we are still busy evacuating men from the north of
Belgium who are arriving from the Holland area.

But with all these other men coming along, I am still
preoccupied about Hank and Mart. There is no news of
them, though their names and descriptions have been
given to every underground movement with which we are
in contact.

There were two more men to get today, but I feel like
taking a rest. I'm nervous. I don't know why, but I have a
funny feeling again. I still feel that Mlle C's house is not
safe any more. Too many people seem to know its address.
However, no more men are to come to Brussels until all
those we have here have left, and I must use this opportunity to look for Hank and Mart.

*

Hank and Mart have been found! Five weeks after they
left. On learning the news, I insist they come back here,

and that they must get priority on the departure list.

They have now arrived back in the flat.

I met them in the hall and said – 'Well?'

They both lifted up their shoulders and answered – 'Well?'

Then Hank spoke up.

'I was never so pleased to see a house as when I recognized this one.'

At this I am afraid I lost my temper and was giving them both a piece of my mind at their stupidity when Mart stopped me.

'Don't forget, Anne, we sweated this thing out.'

He was right. It must have been no fun for them to be stranded in a strange house for five weeks on end with no hope of getting away. So we closed the subject by mutual consent.

It was worrying, all the same, for nobody ever found out what had gone wrong; the message which led to Hank and Mart being discovered had arrived by roundabout means, and the people who had taken them away remained discreetly under cover.

Just after Hank and Mart returned, the wife of the doctor who had to leave Belgium in 1942 came to see me. She had heard at last the message which her husband had promised to send her through the Belgian programme on the B.B.C. Every morning at nine o'clock, personal messages are broadcast. This one told her that her husband is safe in England – the message which she has been awaiting for over a year now. She would like to let her husband know too that she is well, but personal messages are not allowed on our underground transmitters unless they are very important ones. I thought the best way to help her would be for her to ask Hank and Mart to try to find the doctor when they get back to England. This she did, and they promised to do what they could to get a message to her husband.

Hank and Mart are leaving us. They must go at 6 a.m.,

which is an awkward hour for me, as the nuns living next door go to mass at that time. I wonder what they would say if they saw me smuggling two men out of the house at this hour of the day?

I have been out to buy an overcoat for each of the two men. But Hank is so tall, and all I can find for him is an Austrian type of coat called a *Loden*. But I got a thick overcoat which fitted Mart quite well.

Clothes and food are getting terribly scarce now, and can only be bought on the black market. Money is just as scarce, too, and I never see any come our way.

*

Mart and Hank started on their journey with Hank still determined to buy his *Soir de Paris*.

I got up at half past four and made some coffee. Luckily, I have a big store of this, for the Americans prefer coffee to tea. Then I go to wake the two men and they start getting ready, putting on clean shirts and collars for the occasion. Mart seems to have some difficulty with these, and is airing some of his strong Air Force language. After a quick breakfast, I tuck some sandwiches into their coat pockets and get them to repeat their Belgian names and supposed date and place of birth, and to show me what they must hand out if the Germans ask for their passport and what they must produce if the French ask if they are in possession of any foreign currency.

Then, a last look over the balcony to see the nuns go off to church, and as soon as the nuns have turned the corner we all leave, having said all our good-byes before leaving the house.

We are the only three people in this important street and the sound of our footsteps seems to fill it.

'Well, here we are again,' whispers Hank, 'Anne and her two henchmen.'

'Yes, Hank, and don't forget you owe me five francs for all the spots you made on my tablecloth,' I whispered back.

(I make the children pay a franc for each spot they make on the cloth, just to make them careful, so naturally Hank and Mart had to do the same.)

And so we try to make light conversation, not that we feel in a joyful mood, but rather to hide our feelings. After all, the three of us are trying our best to escape from a ruthless enemy, with the odds against us.

At the station we are met by the guide and here, with a casual handshake and knowing wink, they are gone. So, day after day, men not knowing a word of French go out to try their luck with fate, knowing full well the price they will pay if they fail.

Will this ever end? I wonder sometimes. Will next spring bring us the big event we all dread yet are longing for? Time will tell, and meanwhile we are facing another winter and another war Christmas.

The children miss Hank. They gave him the name of Scaramouche, for he started to read a book of this title when he first came here and finished it before he left.

I shan't take in any more men for a few days, if possible, for we need a rest. I notice that every time the lift comes up my small son Jacques runs to the sitting-room to close the door if the men are in that room. He does not know these men are airmen, yet he seems to sense the danger when they are in the house. He also knows they are not to be seen by visitors.

To add to my feeling of disquiet I have just read in *Le Soir* about the death and shooting of some of our friends.

This gives me an icy feeling down my back and I lay awake at night thinking of them.

What were their thoughts as they were being taken to the shooting squad? Could they see the streets and the avenues they knew so well, on their way? Avenues and streets which they were now seeing for the last time. ... Were they frightened or was death a relief to them after their ill-treatment?

These questions kept running through my mind and I wonder if at their last ordeal they were thinking of their families who were probably then still asleep at home, not knowing that the last hour had come for those they loved.

If this happened to me, how would I take it, I wonder?

At this thought I shiver, and feel sure I would not be brave. I can visualize the whole scene. The grey dawn, the last cigarette, and the waiting around, perhaps, while the first batch of prisoners are shot. The last few words with the priest, while the sound of the volleys which are just being fired still ring out. Then, marching up to the execution post, and incredibly, that last word heard on this earth as the officer shouts out, 'Fire!'

I see this scene over and over again in my mind until at last I cannot stand it any more and I get up. My eyes fall on a book, *The Pilgrim's Progress*, by John Bunyan. Opening it at random to glance through it, hardly knowing what it is I am doing but just, I suppose, to try to divert my thoughts into less gloomy channels, this is the first thing that I see: 'Death is not welcome to nature, though by it we pass out of this world into glory.'

I hope this is true. But, if the time comes, will the hope of it mean anything at all to me – and did it to them?

*

Last night I had a telephone call from Michou. Could I take two puppies at once? The mother is ill and one of the puppies has a bad paw. Do I mind? I answer, no, I don't mind and shall ask for a vet if it is at all necessary. Of course, I know what this means. Two men are to be transferred at once, for someone was arrested who was looking after them, and one man is wounded.

At 10 p.m. there is the conventional ring at the door – dot, dot, dot, bar. The V-sign in Morse code. I open the door and find Michou there with the two men. She tells me in French that she does not know what is wrong with these two, one of whom is English and the other American.

'They have not stopped laughing since I met them!'

The two men then greet me in French, and I answer

them in the same language. They do not know I speak English.

Motioning them to the lift, I take them up in it and as we pass the first and second floor the long, white-painted corridors leading to the company's offices can be seen. The two men stop laughing for a moment on seeing this and then the tall American stoops down to the Englishman, and mutters into his ear.

'Say, brother, this looks just like an asylum!'

'Yes, it will certainly sound like one, too, if you both don't stop all this laughing.'

At my saying this, amazement spreads over their faces.

'Good heavens, are you English?' they ask in astonishment. This, however, is a question which is best left unanswered.

Bud, the American, and Lorne, the Englishman, soon make themselves at home in the flat. Lorne has a bad foot and has to have it massaged. He also suffers with terrible pains in the head, for he had a bad fall when he landed. Bud is very helpful. He helps by looking after the central heating, getting the coal, and peeling the potatoes. I am glad of a little help, for every day I have to bake two loaves and every week three more loaves for friends who are in prison. This baking keeps me busy. After the war I shall never bake any more.

The shop bread is too bad, the children would rather go hungry than eat it. We cannot get used to all this *ersatz* stuff. Luckily Mrs H sends me flour and keeps me provided with potatoes and ham. I don't know what I would do without her.

December 1943

On the 15 December we had a narrow shave from an unexpected source.

It was a lovely clear day, and at 10 a.m. a Messerschmitt 109 came flying over the house; no doubt on a practice flight in the early morning sunshine, I thought. But all of a sudden there was the sound of machine-gun fire, and I

rushed out on to the terrace to see seven Allied fighters
having a go at this Me 109. All the office clerks came rushing out too from below to watch the fight from the terrace.
Just then, something prompted me to turn my head away
to look back at my flat windows, and who should I see
there, still wearing their pyjamas, and shouting and yel-
ling at the top of their voices, but Bud and Lorne. I
dashed in, pulled them both from the window, and then
explained patiently why I had done so. I then went out
once more to see the finish of the fight from the terrace.
But no one noticed the two men. Everyone was far too
busy watching the Me 109 being brought down by the
seven fighters, which flew away like white butterflies
when they had finished what they had set out to do.

The day after this I went out with Michou and J to get
six airmen.

Three days later Michou came in to see me late in the
evening and asked to use my telephone. Before we quite
understood what was happening, she asked for a trunk
call, and to speak to Jeanne. I could see that Julien was
uneasy at this. He did not like the idea of a trunk call
from our house at nine o'clock at night. Then, as I listened
to the conversation, I gathered that Jeanne had been
arrested the day before, also the two airmen staying with
her.

Her uncle had been arrested as well, but the aunt had
been left free and it was she who was giving all these
details on the telephone. Well, I thought, if the Germans
have tapped their telephone line, we've had it. ... As for
Julien, he is furious, but it's no use just being angry about
it, for the harm's done now; the main thing is, what are
we going to do?

It's too late to move Bud and Lorne out of here now,
and as Jeanne knows Michou's address and also Mlle C's,
I suggest that Michou moves out with all her belongings
at once. Bob – the Rebel staying at Mademoiselle's house
– also has now got to be moved. He should have left some
time ago, and would have done but for a minor attack of

appendicitis. As for us, Julien and I decide to stay up all night, and the two men stay on their beds fully dressed, all ready to clear out quick if the Gestapo pay us an early morning visit.

It is 2 a.m. We are still all on the alert, with our nerves tense, at the least noise from the street, when we hear the sound of a car coming down the street. It stops, and then the door bell rings. At this, we all jump up, the men making ready to get out of the kitchen window. Only Germans can circulate at this time of the night. Julien goes to the inner door, opens it, and gets into the lift, which he takes down to the hall below. We hear the lift descending, but before he is half-way down the door bell rings again, five or six rings. There is no doubt now. These are Germans, and they are in a hurry.

The lift reaches the bottom floor. We hear the lift gates open, and then there is a pause as Julien goes to the main door. He opens it, and immediately there is the sound of loud German voices, shouting out. 'Why didn't you open up sooner?' a voice yells.

I can hear Julien arguing with the soldiers. The door closes, and there is the sound of footsteps in the hall downstairs.

They are Julien's, I think.

The lift comes up. Julien is alone in it, as I had presumed.

We all sit down and heave a sigh of relief. There was a light showing through the window next door and the German police thought it was from our building – and that's all it was, Julien tells us.

Yet the German net is closing in, even if it missed us this time. Because of this the journey to Liège that we planned has fallen through, so Bud and Lorne must wait. The escape route is blocked, and the Gestapo seems poised ready to strike.

*

Things are happening quickly. Mlle C was arrested the day before yesterday. So, either the house has been

watched, or Jeanne has been forced to give the address.
Well, for a long time now I had a feeling the place was
not safe any more.

Michou has been in. She has been followed, she says,
but managed to lose her follower. I think it is high time
for her to leave Belgium. The fact that the Gestapo
is having her watched means they have their reasons
for doing so. They don't waste their time following innocent people; not that I mean by this that we are
criminals.

Meanwhile, I want a new contact to take her place, for
the men keep on coming in at regular intervals and it is
now about time for Bud and Lorne to be on their way.
They have been staying one month with us, and are getting restless, especially after the events of the last few
days.

Before leaving with the two men for the station I had
to buy a suit for Bud, and what a job it was. Why are
these Americans so tall? It is so hard to find clothes to fit
them. As for getting ten men like this one in a B 17 it looks
to me that they must have to be folded in half before
entering the plane. Yet they say they are very comfortable
inside.

The usual preparations begin as the time approaches
for them to leave. First, I see that all their identity discs
(or dog tags as they call them) are securely in their
clothes, for if they are caught they must be able to prove
they are airmen trying to escape and are not spies. Lorne
has a cigarette-lighter which his mother gave him as a
twenty-first birthday present. It has his name and address
on it, so we have to find a safe place to hide this for he
won't leave it behind. These men are superstitious about
such things – a feeling I know well.

Afterwards, we walk down town, for the Germans are
intensifying their searches and it is easier to miss a search
when walking than when in a tram.

It is 3.30 p.m. We have to walk slowly, for Lorne's foot

is still a little painful. He is trying his best not to limp, however, so as not to attract attention.

On our way we have to pass in front of the building where the Luftwaffe question and condemn people for helping Allied airmen. Two German soldiers are mounting guard outside, and we pass right by them. They don't even look at us, and so much the better. 'If I fly again, my first bomb will be for this place,' Lorne whispers. Then we get to the station and it is good-bye once more. A discreet V-sign, with the first two fingers of the hand, and two more gallant men are on their way.

Before the men left they helped me make a Christmas tree but we are running out of decorations for it. However, the bombers drop a lot of aluminium strips to jam the German radar screens, and we are making do with this for decorating the tree.

This is our fourth war Christmas and the children won't believe us now when we tell them it will be the last one. I have been going round the shops to see if I can find a few toys for Jacques. He is eight years old. Yvonne is twelve, and she has to understand it is impossible to give her Christmas presents. She is very reasonable about this and it makes it easier for us to tell her, but it squashes any hope she may have had. After visiting all the shops, all I could find were a few tin soldiers dressed in German uniforms, or German tanks, and German machine-guns, all marked with the German iron cross and swastika. I just will not give such toys as these to my son to play with. I would rather see him disappointed once more. But I have made up my mind that when this war is ended he and Yvonne will have all the toys they long for, even if it means I have to work until the end of my life to get them.

And so another Christmas day comes and passes in wartime. I hope it is the last one.

*

I still need a new contact to take Michou's place. One

young girl, about eighteen years old, who volunteered to go on a journey to Paris with two men to see how she would manage, was followed in Paris, so she won't do. Someone else has to be found.

Michou left on the fifth for the south. It is high time, for the Gestapo seems to be on her trail, but I must somehow get in touch with the rest of the helpers. I know there are about one hundred men waiting to be evacuated now. They are scattered about in different houses all over Belgium, waiting their turn to leave.

I have contacted Rio. He is the link with the north-west of Belgium, and he would like me to interrogate eight Americans from his sector. I have made arrangements to meet them in a school the day after tomorrow. I shall also have to have a photographer ready to have their photos taken, for it is getting dangerous to go down town for this. Hitherto I have been to the Bon Marché and other big stores to have the men photographed, but always going to these shops with different men, I am afraid now of being recognized.

*

I was at the meeting-place at 9.30 a.m. as arranged, but there was no Rio to be seen. I walked round the block of houses, looking in all the empty shop windows, then returned to the meeting-place. Still no Rio.

At this, I decide to go on to the photographer's house. First, however, I inspect the house and the street. There is a man walking slowly down the road. Is he also watching, I wonder? I had better let him go by and see. No, he was waiting for his wife, who had gone into a shop. Reassured, I ring the bell of the first floor, though I know the photographer lives on the floor above that. A lady opens the door then, and I ask for Mrs Jean, the photographer's wife.

'Mrs J lives on the second floor,' answers the lady.

Of course, I know this. However, I apologize, and ask if Mrs J is in, does the lady know?

'Yes. I heard her walking about in the flat just now.'

Good, I think, with a sigh of relief. So far, nothing is
wrong here. Then, going up to the second floor I see Mrs
J there and tell her about the appointment with R and
her husband.

R was arrested yesterday at midday in a café. No, this
was all the news Mrs J could give me.

I left, after telling her it would be a good thing for her
husband to get a change of air, and went to our 'postal
box' near by – in this case a grocer's shop. For I want to
know what has happened, and also try to find the eight
airmen. But as I am approaching the grocer's I see the
Gestapo coming out with a civilian whom at first I think
to be the grocer. After waiting about for a few minutes I
walk into the shop, however, and the grocer comes up to
me with his face all bruised. I ask for two boxes of cleaning powder and, on paying for these and making sure
there are no more Gestapo still in the house, give him the
password and ask for news.

Bad news, is the answer.

'They are all arrested – five altogether – and I have just
felt the weight of the Gestapo's fist,' he says, adjusting his
tie back into position nervously.

'One of the arrested men has been made to talk. They
have just been in with him.'

His eyes, as he was speaking, had a withdrawn, far-
away look, and I did not press him for details. They
generally turn your stomach, and I needed all my guts to
face this new situation. For now I knew I was alone, on
my own in Brussels, with no one to help me.

There was nothing I could do for this man, but I told
him to clear out as quickly as possible. He is afraid, however, that if he does this the Gestapo will take his wife
and child as hostages, and it is difficult to find accommodation for three at such short notice. ...

*   *   *

... The grocer was arrested that same night. He was shot

before the end of the year. Time and again Madame
Brusselmans' fellow-helpers were caught, tortured and
shot; and the escape organization was disorganized.
Patiently and with the utmost courage she would piece it
together again until the evaders were once more on their
way to safety. She was a cool and careful planner and
always managed to keep one jump ahead of her adver-
saries.

The diary was written at the time of the events it describes and, hidden under the floorboards, behind a loose
brick or in the dustbin of the flat, survived three searches
by the Gestapo who, although they suspected her, never
found proof.

Madame Brusselmans was appointed a Member of the
Order of the British Empire and awarded high Belgian
and American decorations for her bravery. Above all she
earned the gratitude of one hundred and eighty airmen
for whose safe return to England she was personally responsible.

CHAPTER FOUR

Condemned to Death

NOT all resistance fighters were as lucky as Madame Brusselmans. André Devigny was a member of the French Underground operating in Nice. On 17 April 1943 he was arrested by the Gestapo and taken to Montluc military prison in Lyons, where he was brutally beaten up, condemned to death, handcuffed and placed in solitary confinement awaiting execution.

At first the small cell with its solid oak door seemed to offer no opportunities for escape. Then, with a pin given to him by one of his fellow-prisoners, Devigny learned how to pick the lock on his handcuffs so that he could take them off and put them on at will. This gave him freedom within the confines of his cell.

Next he noticed that although the door was constructed of thick oak boards these were fastened together by tongues of softer wood. By grinding the handle of his iron spoon on the stone of the cell floor the prisoner managed to make himself a joiner's chisel with which, after many days of patient work, he was able to remove first one, then several of the boards. This gave him access to the corridor outside, but he was still far from free. He knew that his cell was high up in the building and that his only escape route lay upwards to the roof.

With infinite patience Devigny began to twist himself a rope from strips torn from his bedding and reinforced with wire taken from his mattress. When his supply was exhausted he used his clothing – everything he could lay hands on. At last he had made sixty-five feet of rope.

Devigny's plan was to climb through a skylight in the ceiling of the corridor outside his cell, cross the roof of the building and lower himself to an inner courtyard. From here he would climb to the roof of another building, cross this and throw his rope to the outer wall of the prison. To make this feat possible he needed grappling-irons on the end of the rope. These he made from the metal frame which surrounded the electric light in his cell.

Just as Devigny was ready to make his attempt another prisoner named Gimenez was put in to share his cell. Devigny knew that should he escape and leave Gimenez behind in the cell the boy, only eighteen years of age, would be shot for not giving the alarm. The only thing was to take him along too. ...

*   *   *

... Gimenez took the boards from me one after the other and stacked them away. In the half-light we could just see the faint, barred outline of the gallery rails; it was too dark to make out the cell doors on the other side. I put out my head and listened. Only the creaking of beds as sleepers turned over, and occasionally a bucket scraping along the floor, broke the silence – that hostile silence against which we had to struggle for what seemed like a century.

For two long minutes I remained motionless. Then I pushed one arm out into the corridor, turned on one side, and crawled forward like a snake. I stood up cautiously. The light was on down below; but, as usual, its feeble rays were swallowed up in the vast gloom of the hall.

Gimenez passed me the light rope, which I at once took over to the latrines. It was followed by the rest of our equipment. I went back to the cell door to help Gimenez. We both stood there for a moment, listening. All was still. Slowly we moved towards our starting-point.

I tied one end of the light rope round my waist – the end, that is, which had no grappling-iron attached to it. Three steps, and we were standing by the metal rod. The rope would pay out as I climbed; I left it coiled loosely on the ground. Gimenez braced himself against the wall and gave me a leg up. I stood on his shoulders, both hands gripping the rod, and tried to reach the edge of the skylight. I pulled myself up slowly, with all the strength I had. But it proved too much of an effort; I had to come down again.

The weeks of confinement I had undergone since my previous successful attempt must have sapped my strength more than I thought. We went back to the latrines to give me a few moments' rest. I inhaled deeply, waiting till I got my breath back before making a second attempt.

I had to get up there, whatever happened.

Jaws clenched, I began to climb. I got my feet from Gimenez's hands to his shoulders, and then to his head. My fingers gripped the metal rod convulsively. Somehow I went on, inch by inch; at last my fingers found the frame of the skylight, and I got my legs over the horizontal rod, which shook in its rings as my weight hung from it. I got round the ratchet supporting the skylight without touching it. I was sweating and panting like a man struggling out of a quicksand, or a shipwrecked sailor clinging desperately to a reef. Eyes dilated, every muscle cracking, I gradually worked my way through the opening. Then I stopped for a minute to get my strength back. I had managed to preserve absolute silence from start to finish.

A few lights twinkled in the distance. The fresh night air cooled my damp face. It was very still. Slowly my breathing became normal again. Carefully I put out one hand on to the gritty surface of the flat roof, taking care to avoid touching the fragile glass in the skylight itself; this done, I hauled myself up a little farther and got my other hand into a similar position. With a final effort I completed the operation, and found myself standing upright on the roof, dazed by the clear splendour of the night sky. The silence drummed in my ears.

For a moment I remained motionless. Then I knelt down and slowly pulled up the rope. The shoes were dangling in their bundle at the end of it. I let it down again and brought up our coats. The third time I salvaged the big rope; it was a difficult job to squeeze it through the narrow opening.

Go slowly, I thought. Don't hurry. You've got plenty of time.

I unhooked the parcel and put it aside. Then I paid out the rope once more. We had agreed that Gimenez should tie it round his waist so that I could take up the slack and make his ascent easier. I waited a little, and then felt a gentle tug. I pulled steadily, hand over hand, taking care not to let the rope bear heavily on the metal edge of the skylight. We could not risk any noise. I heard the rods creaking under his weight; then, a moment later, two hands came up and got a grip on the sill. Slowly Gimenez's face and shoulders appeared.

I bent down and whispered: 'Don't hurry. Take a rest.' He breathed in the fresh air, gulping and panting.

My mouth still close to his ear, I said: 'Be careful how you pull yourself up. Don't put your hands on the glass.'

He seemed as exhausted as I was.

I untied the rope from my waist, and he followed suit. I coiled it up carefully, took a piece of string out of my pocket, and ran a bowline round the middle of the coil.

There we both stood, side by side, in absolute silence. Gradually my breathing slowed down to its normal rate, and I began to recover my strength. It was hard to get used to this immense, seemingly limitless space all around me. The glass penthouse (of which the skylight formed a part) stood out from the roof and vanished in darkness only a few feet away. I made out one or two small chimney-cowls here and there. The courtyard and the perimeter were hidden from us by the parapet. We could walk upright without being seen.

I felt the shingle grit under my feet at the least move I made.

I took a coil of rope in each hand and picked them up with great care. Gimenez did the same with the shoes and coats. We stood there waiting for a train: it was five, perhaps even ten minutes coming.

Gimenez became impatient. I was just about to move when the sound of a locomotive reached us from the distance. It grew louder and louder; presently the train steamed past on the nearby track. We managed to get ten feet forward before it vanished into the distance again. The stretch of line which runs past Montluc joins the two main stations of Lyons. As a result it carries very heavy traffic, which had hardly slackened off even at this stage of the war.

We had nearly reached the middle of the roof now. We found ourselves standing by the far end of the penthouse. A little farther on a second penthouse appeared, which stretched away towards the other side of the roof. My eyes were beginning to get accustomed to the dark. I could see the large glass dome above the penthouse; that meant we were standing above the central well. I thought then for a moment of our friends below in their cells: some asleep, lost in wonderful dreams; others, who knew of our plan, awake, waiting in frightful suspense, ears straining for any suspicious noises.

We had advanced with extreme care, putting each foot down as lightly as possible, bent double as if the weight of our apprehension and of the dangers we had to face was too heavy to be supported. Gimenez kept close behind me. I could hear his slow, regular breathing, and glimpse his dark silhouette against the night sky. We had to wait some time before another train came to our assistance. But this time it was a slow goods train. It enabled us to reach our objective – the side of the roof opposite the infirmary – in one quick move.

We put down our various packages. I turned back and whispered to Gimenez: 'Lie down and wait for me here. Don't move.'

'Where are you going?'

'To see what's happening.'

Gimenez obediently dropped to his knees, and remained as motionless as the equipment stacked round him. I crept slowly round the corner of the roof, raised myself cautiously, and peered over the parapet. Below me I could see the stretch of the perimeter which flanked the Rue du Dauphiné. I lifted my head a little farther, and quickly drew it back again at the sight of a sentry. He was standing in one corner near the wash-house. I had known he would be there; yet in my present situation he scared me nearly out of my wits.

Of course, he could not see me. I told myself not to be a fool.

I pressed my cheek against the rough concrete surface and slowly raised my head once more. Unfortunately, the wide shelf outside the parapet cut off my view of the part of the courtyard immediately below. As this was where we would have to climb down, it was essential to find a better observation-post.

But before moving I took another quick look at the soldier in the far corner. He seemed very wide awake. Soon a second sentry walked over to join him – probably the one who guarded the wooden barrack-block on the other side. I saw the glowing tips of their cigarettes. The lamps in the courtyard gave off so weak a light that the men themselves were mere shadows against the surrounding gloom.

Occasionally a twinkling reflection from buckle or bayonet hinted at their movements. I knew that the best way of remaining unseen was to keep absolutely still. If I had to move, it must be done as slowly as possible, with long and frequent pauses. It took me some time to get back to Gimenez, tell him to stay put, climb over the parapet, and crawl along the outer cat-walk till I was once more opposite the infirmary. A train passed by at exactly the right moment; I scrambled along as fast as I could to the corner of the wall. A loose piece of shingle, even a little sand going over the edge would have given me away. I would feel ahead with my hands, then slowly pull myself forward like a slug, breathing through my mouth.

In front of me the perimeter was clearly visible. Beyond

it the tobacco factory and the buildings of the military court formed a broken outline against the horizon. Above them the stars shone out in a moonless sky. After a little I could just make out the roof of the covered gallery over which we had to pass. Gradually our whole route became visible. I spotted a familiar landmark – the fanlight of my old cell – and then, on the left, the workshop and women's quarters. Close by was the low wall between the infirmary and the courtyard. Soon, I thought, we should be climbing that wall. One room in the infirmary was still lit up; the light shone behind the wall in the direction of the covered gallery. I was, I realized, directly above cell 45, where my first few weeks of detention had been spent.

I wriggled forward inch by inch, so as to reach the outer edge of the cat-walk and get into a position from which I could observe the whole area of the courtyard. The two sentries were now out of sight round the corner of the block, smoking and chatting. I could see no one below me. The way was clear. My heart beat excitedly. A little farther and I would be certain. My face against the rough surface, I peered cautiously over the edge.

I was horrified at the gulf stretching down below me; I could not help feeling that my rope must be too short.

Nothing was stirring. I examined every danger-point in turn – the shadowy corners by the wash-house and workshop, the women's quarters, the alley between the infirmary wall and the main block, the half-open doors leading from court to court, every conceivable hole or corner where a sentry might be lurking. Nothing. The cell windows were patterned on the façade like black squares in a crossword puzzle. Occasionally the sound of a cough drifted out from one or other of them. This, and the recurrent trains, alone broke the silence. Farther down, on the left, some of the windows seemed to be open. The stillness was almost tangible.

Still I scrutinized the courtyard with minute care. Suddenly a dark shape caught my eye, in a corner near the door of the main block. I stared closely at it. After a moment I realized it was a sentry, asleep on the steps. The weight of this alarming discovery filled me with a sudden vast depression. How on earth were we to get past him? How could we even be certain he was asleep? How – in the last resort – could we surprise him without being seen?

At this point the sentry sat up and lit a cigarette. The flame from his lighter gave me a quick glimpse of his steel helmet and the sub-machine gun he carried. He got up, walked a little way in the direction of the infirmary, and then came back again.

Midnight struck.

It must have been the time when the guard was changed. The soldier passed directly beneath me, between the infirmary and the main block, and vanished in the direction of the guard-house. Four or five minutes later his relief appeared. His footsteps crunched grimly over the cobbles.

A frightful inner conflict racked me as I studied his every movement, like a wild beast stalking its prey. We could not retreat. The way had to be cleared.

The sentry's beat took him away into the shadows at the far end of the court, then back to the main door, where the lamp shone for a moment on his helmet and the barrel of his sub-machine gun.

I watched him for a whole hour, memorizing the pattern of his movements. Then I raised myself on knees and elbows, climbed quietly over the parapet, and returned to Gimenez.

He was asleep. I woke him gently. 'Time to move on,' I said.

He got up without making any noise. I was busy untying the knot of the string lashed round the big rope.

'All set now,' I whispered. 'As soon as a train comes, we'll lower the rope.'

I stood with one foot on the roof and the other on the cat-walk, the low parapet between my legs. This way I could control the rope with both hands and pay it out without it touching the edge. I left Gimenez to control the coil and see the rope was free from entanglements.

An eternity of time seemed to pass before the train came. At the first distant panting of the engine I began to lower away, slowly at first, then with increasing speed. When I felt the reinforced stretch near the end passing through my fingers I stopped, and lowered the rope on to the concrete. Then I hooked the grappling-iron on to the inner side of the parapet. It seemed to hold firm enough. The rope stretched away into the darkness below us.

Gimenez would sling the parcels containing our shoes and coats round his neck, and follow me down when I gave him the signal. I knew that the moment I swung out from the roof into open space the last irrevocable decision would have been taken. By so doing I would either clinch my victory or sign my own death-warrant. While I remained on the roof it was still possible to return to my cell. Once I had begun the descent there was no way back. Despite the cool night air, my face and shirt were soaked with sweat.

'Hold on to the grappling-iron while I'm going down,' I told Gimenez. I took hold of his hands and set them in position.

Then I crouched down on the outer ledge, facing him, ready to go down the rope at the first possible moment, and waited for a train to pass. Gimenez leant over and hissed nervously in my ear: 'There's someone down below!'

'Don't worry.'

Then I looked at the sky and the stars and prayed that the rope might be strong enough, that the German sentry would not come round the corner at the wrong moment, that I would not make any accidental noise.

The waiting strained my nerves horribly. Once I began my descent there would be no more hesitation, I knew; but dear God, I thought, let that train come quickly, let me begin my descent into the abyss now, at once, before my strength fails me.

The stroke of one o'clock cut through the stillness like an axe.

Had an hour passed so quickly? The sentries' footsteps, echoing up to us with monotonous regularity, seemed to be counting out the seconds. There could not be so very many trains at this time of night.

Gimenez was showing signs of impatience. I told him to keep still. The words were hardly out of my mouth when a distant whistle broke the silence. Quickly it swelled in volume.

'This is it,' I said.

I shuffled back towards the edge of the cat-walk. Then, holding my breath, I slid myself over, gripping the rope between my knees, and holding the ledge with both hands to steady myself. At last I let go. The rope whirred upwards under my feet, the wire binding tore at my hands. I went down as fast as I could, not even using my legs.

As soon as I touched the ground I grabbed the parcel containing the second rope, and doubled across the court-yard to the low wall. I released the rope, swung the grappling-iron up, hauled myself over, and dropped down on the other side, behind the doorway, leaving the rope behind for Gimenez.

The train was fading away into the distance now, towards the station. The drumming of its wheels seemed to be echoed in my heaving chest. I opened my mouth and breathed deeply to ease the pressure on my lungs. Above me I saw the dark swinging line of rope, and the sharp outline of the roof against the sky.

I stood motionless, getting my breath back and accustoming my eyes to the darkness. The sentry's footsteps rang out behind the wall, scarcely six feet away. They passed on, only to return a moment later. I pressed both hands against my beating heart. When all was quiet again I worked round to the doorway, and flattened myself against it. I felt all my human reactions being swallowed up by pure animal instinct, the instinct for self-preservation which quickens the reflexes and gives one fresh reserves of strength.

It was my life or his.

As his footsteps approached I tried to press myself into the wood against which my back was resting. Then, when I heard him change direction, I risked a quick glance out of my hiding-place to see exactly where he was.

He did exactly the same thing twice, and still I waited.

I got a good grip on the ground with my heels; I could not afford to slip. The footsteps moved in my direction, grew louder. The sentry began to turn. ...

I sprang out of my recess like a panther, and got my hands round his throat in a deadly grip. With frantic violence I began to throttle him. I was no longer a man, but a wild animal. I squeezed and squeezed, with the terrible strength of desperation. My teeth were gritting against each other, my eyes bursting out of my head. I threw back my head to exert extra pressure, and felt my fingers bite deep into his neck. Already half-strangled, the muscles of his throat torn and engorged, only held upright by my vice-like grip, the sentry still feebly raised his arms as if to defend himself; but an instant later they fell back, inert. But this did not make me let go. For perhaps three minutes longer I maintained my pressure on his throat, as if afraid that one last cry, or even the death-rattle, might give me away. Then, slowly, I loosened my blood-stained fingers, ready to close them again at the least movement; but the body remained slack and lifeless. I lowered it gently to the ground.

I stared down at the steel helmet which, fortunately perhaps, concealed the sentry's face; at the dark hunched shape of the body itself, at the sub-machine gun and the bayonet. I thought for a moment, then quickly drew the bayonet from its scabbard, gripped it by the hilt in both hands, and plunged it down with one straight, hard stroke into the sentry's back.

I raised my head, and saw that I was standing immediately below the window of cell 45. Old memories fire-
worked up in my mind: hunger and thirst, the beatings I
had suffered, the handcuffs, the condemned man in the
next cell, Fränzel spitting in my face.

I went back to the doorway, near the infirmary, and
whistled twice, very softly. A dark shape slid down the
rope. It creaked under his weight. I went to meet him.
Gimenez climbed the low wall, detached the light rope
with its grappling-iron, passed them down to me, and
jumped. In his excitement, or nervousness, he had left our
coats and shoes on the roof. At the time I said nothing
about this. Clearly his long wait had depressed him; he
was shivering all over. He gave a violent start when he
saw the corpse stretched out near our feet.

I clapped him on the back. 'You'll really have something to shiver about in a moment. Come on, quick.'

Our troubles had only begun. We still had to cross the
courtyard in order to reach the wall between it and the
infirmary. Then there was the roof of the covered gallery
to surmount, and, finally, the crossing of the perimeter
walls.

I carried the rope and the fixed grappling iron; Gimenez
had the loose one. We doubled across to the wall. It was
essential for us to get up here as quickly as possible. The
light left on in the infirmary was shining in our direction,
and a guard could easily have spotted us from a first-floor
window of the central block as we made our way towards
the inner wall of the perimeter.

Gimenez gave me a leg up, and I managed to reach the
top of the wall and hang on. But I was quite incapable
by now of pulling myself up; all my strength had drained
away. I came down again, wiped my forehead and regained my breath. If I had been alone I should in all
probability have stuck at this point. As it was, I bent down
against the wall in my turn, and Gimenez got up without
any trouble. I undid the bundle of rope and passed him
the end with the grappling-iron attached. He fixed it

securely. Then I tried again, with the rope to help me this time. Somehow I scrambled up, using hands, knees and feet, thrusting and straining in one last desperate effort. Gimenez lay down flat on his belly to give himself more purchase, and managed to grasp me under the arms. Eventually I made it.

My heart was hammering against my ribs and my chest felt as if it was going to burst. My shirt clung damply to my body. But there was not a minute to lose. We coiled up the rope again and crawled along to the covered gallery. From here it was a short climb up the tiles to the ridge of the roof. We had to hurry because of that damned light; once we had got over the other side of the roof we were in shadow again.

Unfortunately I made a noise. Two tiles knocked against each other under the sliding pressure of my knee. Gimenez reproved me sharply.

'For God's sake take care what you're doing!' he hissed.

'It wasn't my fault –'

'I haven't the least desire to be caught, even if you have!'

Since this was a sloping roof, we only needed to climb a little way down the far side to be completely hidden. If we stood upright we could easily see over the wall. Soon we were both crouching in position at the end of the covered gallery, our equipment beside us.

I was not acquainted with the exact details of the patrols in the perimeter. When I went out to be interrogated, I had observed a sentry-box in each corner, but these were always unoccupied. Perhaps the guards used them at night, however: it was vital to find out. We already knew that one guard rode round and round the whole time on a bicycle; he passed us every two or three minutes, his pedals squeaking.

We listened carefully, Gimenez was just saying that the cyclist must be alone, when the sound of voices reached us. We had to think again.

Perhaps there was a sentry posted at each corner of the

square, in the angle formed by the outer wall. If this turned out to be so, it would be extremely difficult to get across; nothing but complete darkness would give us a chance. That meant we must cut the electric cable, which ran about two feet below the top of the inner wall, on the perimeter side.

I half-rose from my cramped position and took a quick look. The walls seemed much higher from here, and the lighting system enhanced this impression. A wave of despair swept over me. Surely we could never surmount this obstacle?

From the roof it had all looked very different. The yawning gulf had been hidden. But the perimeter was well lit, and the sight of it – deep as hell and bright as daylight – almost crushed my exhausted determination.

I craned forward a little farther. The sentry-box below on our left was empty. I ducked back quickly as the cyclist approached. He ground round the corner and started another circuit. A moment later I was enormously relieved to hear him talking to himself; it was this curious monologue we had intercepted a moment earlier. He was alone, after all.

Behind us rose the dark shape of the main block. We had come a long way since ten o'clock. Another six yards, and we were free. Yet what risks still remained to be run!

Little by little determination flowed back into me. One more effort would do it. Don't look back, I thought. Keep your eyes in front of you till it's all over.

Bitter experience had taught me that over-hastiness could be fatal; that every precipitate action was liable to bring disaster in its train. Gimenez was eager to get on and finish the operation, but I firmly held him back. I was as well aware as he was of the dangers that threatened us; I knew that every moment we delayed increased our risk of recapture. I thought of the open cell, the rope we had left hanging from the wall, the dead sentry in the courtyard, the possibility of his body being discovered by a patrol or his relief. Nevertheless, I spent more than a quarter of an hour watching that cyclist. Every four or five circuits he turned round and went the other way. We were well placed in our corner: he was busy taking the bend, and never looked up. We were additionally protected by the three shaded lights fixed on each wall. All their radiance was thrown down into the perimeter itself, leaving us in shadow. We could watch him without fear of discovery.

Three o'clock.

Gimenez was becoming desperate. At last I decided to move. Holding the end of the rope firmly in one hand, I coiled it across my left arm like a lasso. With the other hand I grasped the grappling-iron. As soon as the sentry had pedalled past, I threw the line as hard as I could towards the opposite wall. The rope snaked up and out, and the grappling-iron fell behind the parapet. I tugged very gently on it, trying to let it find a natural anchorage. Apparently I had been successful; it held firm. A strand of barbed wire, which I had not previously noticed, rattled alarmingly as the rope jerked over it. After a little, however, it was pressed down to the level of the wall.

I gave one violent pull, but the rope did not budge. It had caught first time. I breathed again.

'Give me the other hook,' I muttered to Gimenez. I could feel him trembling.

The cyclist was coming round again now. I froze abruptly. For the first time he passed actually under the rope. When he had gone I threaded the rope through the wire loop and we pulled it as tight as we could. While Gimenez held it firm to prevent it slipping, I knotted it tightly, and fixed the grappling-iron in a crevice on the near side of the parapet. In my fear of running things too fine I had actually over-calculated the amount of rope necessary; over six feet were left trailing loose on the roof. That thin line stretching across the perimeter looked hardly less fragile than the telephone-wires which followed a similar route a few yards away.

I made several further tests when the cyclist was round

the other side. I unanchored the grappling-iron on our side, and then we both of us pulled on the rope as hard as we could to try out its strength.

If the truth must be told, I was horribly afraid that it would snap, and I would be left crippled in the perimeter. When I pulled on it with all my strength I could feel it stretch. One last little effort and the whole thing would be over; but I had reached the absolute end of my courage, physical endurance, and will-power alike. All the time the cyclist continued to ride round beneath us.

Four o'clock struck.

In the distance, towards the station, the red lights on the railway line still shone out. But the first glimmer of dawn was already creeping up over the horizon, and the lights showed less bright every moment. We could wait no longer.

'Over you go, Gimenez. You're lighter than I am.'

'No. You go first.'

'It's your turn.'

'I won't.'

'Go on, it's up to you.'

'No,' he said desperately, 'I can't do it.'

The cyclist turned the corner again. I shook Gimenez desperately, my fingers itching to hit him.

'Are you going, yes or no?'

'No,' he cried, 'no, no!'

'Shut up, for God's sake!' I said. I could not conquer his fear; I said no more. Still the German pedalled round his beat. Once he stopped almost directly beneath us, got off his machine, and urinated against the wall. It was at once a comic and terrifying sight. As time passed and the dawn approached, our chances of success grew steadily less. I knew it, yet I still hesitated. Gimenez shivered in silence.

Abruptly, as the sentry passed us yet again, I stooped forward, gripped the rope with both hands, swung out into space, and got my legs up into position. Hand over hand, my back hanging exposed above the void, I pulled myself across with desperate speed. I reached the far wall, got one arm over it, and scrambled up.

I had done it. I had escaped.

A delirious feeling of triumph swept over me. I forgot how exhausted I was; I almost forgot Gimenez, who was still waiting for the sentry to pass under him again before following me. I was oblivious to my thudding heart and hoarse breath; my knees might tremble, my face be dripping with sweat, my hands scored and bleeding, my throat choked, my head bursting, but I neither knew nor cared. All I was conscious of was the smell of life, the freedom I had won against such desperate odds. I uttered a quick and thankful prayer to God for bringing me through safely.

I moved along the top of the wall towards the court-house buildings, where it lost height considerably. I stopped just short of a small gateway. Workmen were going past in the street outside, and I waited a few moments before jumping down. This gave Gimenez time to catch up with me.

At five o'clock we were walking down the street in our socks and shirt-sleeves – free men. ...

* * *

... André Devigny had escaped from Montluc prison and in doing so escaped certain death. He made his way via Switzerland to Spain and from there to Algeria where he trained as a Commando. With the Allied invasion of Europe he was back in France, fighting for her liberation.

Now Lieutenant-Colonel André Devigny, a professional soldier, is fighting again – this time in Algeria. He has been awarded many decorations, among them Commandeur de la Légion d'Honneur, Compagnon de la Libération, Croix de Guerre, Military Cross, Officer de l'Ordre de la Couronne Belge avec Palme and Croix de Guerre Belge avec Palme.

CHAPTER FIVE

The 'Bulgarian' Naval Officer

LIEUTENANT DAVID JAMES, M.B.E., D.S.C., R.N.V.R., was not a professional sailor. He was one of the many young men who on the outbreak of war dropped whatever they were doing to fight for their country in her hour of need. David James elected to do his fighting in motor gun-boats.

On the night of 28 February 1943 David James's boat was sunk by the Germans in the North Sea and after spending some time in the water he was picked up by the enemy and taken prisoner.

For the next year almost to the day (by which time he was a free man again in Sweden) David James thought of little else but getting home to fight again. The escape attempt I have included here is not his final successful break but an earlier effort which for sheer good spirits and humour alone comes high in the annals of escape.

The scene is the naval internment camp of Marlag-und-Milag Nord near Bremen. Once weekly the prisoners are marched to a bath-house outside the main wire of the camp for a hot shower. David James has conceived the idea of climbing out through the window of the bath-house while the other prisoners are undressing. He has decided to make his way to the Baltic coast in the hope of stowing away in a ship bound for neutral Sweden. To help him in his plans he consults Lieutenant Jackson, a member of the Escape Committee. . . .

* * *

. . . When it came to a character-part for my journey, I naturally consulted the ingenious Jackson. He made the good point that the best possible guise in which to tour seaports was that of a seaman. As I possessed a naval uniform, this was easy. He suggested that I go as a Bulgarian naval officer, since Bulgaria was a monarchy, which would account for the Royal Crown on my buttons, and their Navy had only about three ships anyway, so I was unlikely to meet anyone who would know how they really dressed.

His final inspiration lay in the choice of my name. It was highly important that this should be easy to remember, because in the event of cross-examination it is the one thing over which one cannot afford to falter. Under the eagle eye of a Gestapo official it would be easy to forget a name like Vladimir Solokov, or Serge Filov. I therefore became Lieutenant Ivan Bagerov of the Royal Bulgarian Navy. (You may pronounce my name as you please. It is properly said like a well-known 'term of endearment used among sailors'. I ought to know; after all, there are none like it in the Sofia Telephone Directory!)

This choice of character touches on another most important point of escape technique – it was essential to choose an *unusual* type. Any German official worth his pay would know the proper papers for German civilians, French 'forced' workmen, and others that they saw every day. But a Bulgarian naval officer or an Irish groom would only come their way at most once or twice a year, so any papers, provided they were sufficiently imposing, would suffice.

Mine consisted of a Bulgarian naval identity card and an open letter of introduction. The former was an approximate copy of our own naval cards. For a photograph we used the picture of a German E-boat hero, cut out of an illustrated paper. He did not look much like me, but it is a curious commentary on the gullibility of human nature that, provided there is a photo and it has a stamp on it, it is most rare for the police or customs of any country to look and see whether it resembles the bearer. In any case to minimize this risk we put much of the stamp over the face.

There is a great art in writing bogus letters of introduction. They must be concise, yet contain a complete story, to save the escaper from answering too many questions. They must be vague enough to cover a wide range of possible activity, and they must be imposing without committing themselves to anything definite. In short, they must closely resemble answers to Parliamentary questions.

Jackson composed me a masterpiece. It said: 'Lieutenant Bagerov is engaged in liaison duties of a technical nature which involve him in much travel. Since he speaks very little German, the usual benevolent assistance of all German officials is confidently solicited on his behalf.'

Besides an official Bulgarian stamp – invented in the camp because we had no idea what the real one looked like – this letter was endorsed by three German stamps. One simply stated 'Heartily approved', and was countersigned by some mythical official of the German Foreign Office. Another, apparently from the Chief of Staff at Wilhelmshaven, said: 'Permission to enter dock installations Nos. 9, 10, 11, 12, and 13 from 1st to 8th December.' This was so that as soon as I arrived in Bremen I could imply that I had just come from the west and not from the east. The third read, 'Identity checked by telephone from Berlin', and was signed by the Chief of Police at Cologne, whose name we had found in a German daily paper. This was to suggest that I had once previously been falsely arrested and had been released as soon as they discovered the mistake.

Most of the hard work for an escape lies in the preparations. Mine took almost three weeks and were very complete, for I was determined to enter as thoroughly into the character as I could. Bulgarians cannot pronounce the 'eu' sounds in words like *deutsch*. Instead of saying it like the 'oy' in boy, they pronounce it like the 'ye' in bye. To acquire this habit I used to read out aloud the leaders from the *DAZ* and *Das Reich* '*à la bulgare*'. The Bulgar also uses Russian characters in writing, so in order to be able to make a signature similar to that on my identity card I had to spend ten minutes every day practising it.

I resolved to take a small case with food and a change

of clothing. Every article of wear was marked with my new name, and I scraped the name of the maker off my soap and put a Bulgarian hieroglyphic on instead. There were two Greek officers in the camp, and, as the nearest possible thing, I asked them for their tailors' tabs and sewed them in my uniform and cap. By the time I had finished there was nothing on my person or in my case to suggest that I was English. I even carried in my pocket a series of 'love letters' written in off-Russian by Jackson in a very feminine hand.

It is most desirable to have something about one to distract the attention of any searcher from his job. I had the perfect thing to hand. One of my interests has always been the ballet, and when I was captured a friend very kindly sent me out some very fine half-plate photographs of the Sadler's Wells. One of these was a lovely full-face portrait of Margot Fonteyn in ballroom dress, from the ballet *Apparitions*. With her dark colouring and exotic beauty, this was just what I wanted. A short inscription in Russian was added, and she became 'my fiancée at the German Legation ball in Sofia'. The only time my case was ever searched, this picture occasioned far more interest than all the rest of the contents put together.

A number of articles I sewed into my clothing. There was a pocket in my trouser-leg in which I carried a recent letter from home to prove my identity to any neutrals or other potential helpers. My tally [identity disc] was sewn under one armpit and a spare sum of money under the other.

The only alteration or, rather, addition to my uniform was a five-letter flash – gold on a blue ground – on my left shoulder, standing for the initial letters of 'Kralov Bulgrski Voyenno-Mrskoi Flot', or Royal Bulgarian Navy.

And now, just when I thought I had everything prepared, I found a weakness in my scheme. One day a group of prisoners were taken by train into Bremen to see the oculist. This meant that my uniform would be recognized on the local line. I was therefore forced to adopt an entirely different character-part for the first part of the journey.

I decided that I would travel into Bremen as a Danish electrician. My story would be that my nerves had been severely shattered in a recent raid, I had been spending a week in the country to recuperate, and was on my way back for medical survey. For papers I had a temporary identity card (*Vorläufiger Ausweis*) and a note from the hospital (written, in fact, by Johnny Pryor) telling me to report there p.m. 8 December.

For my quick change at the bath-house I meant to go up in uniform with a greatcoat on, and with grey flannel trousers over my blues, but rolled up above the knee so that they shouldn't show. I had a check scarf well tucked down underneath my coat collar and a cloth cap made out of a blanket in one pocket. My shoulder-straps and belt were on hooks, so that they were readily detachable. The front buttons of my coat I covered with black silk, so that at a casual glance they looked like civilian buttons. To change then, all I had to do was rip off the belt and shoulder-straps, roll down my trousers, pull up my scarf, and don the cap. I practised this operation a number of times, till ultimately it took me less than thirty seconds.

All was now set. My final plan was to go up with the bath party, change, and drop out of the window, then walk down the road for about half a mile to where there was a small coppice. Here I proposed to kill half an hour putting on a few bandages and otherwise altering my appearance before walking to the station just in time to catch the 11.50 train. This train was scheduled to arrive at Bremen at 1.20 p.m. and start on its return journey ten minutes later. There would be such a crowd on arrival that I hoped to pass unobserved into the station lavatory. There I would discard my civilian clothes, and, once the train had left, emerge on to an empty platform as a Bulgarian. From then on my journey up to the Baltic ports should be fairly easy.

So many times had I rehearsed this scheme in my mind that I could almost believe I had done it. Only the play *Ten Minute Alibi*, performed in the camp a short time before, depressed me. For that showed only too well what a discrepancy there can be between the well-oiled plan of the imagination and its counterpart of obstinate fact.

The strange thing is that this one did run almost perfectly to schedule.

*

Thursday, 8 December, dawned cold and foggy. I awoke early and went to Mass; for I wanted to start with the blessing of God. After breakfast there was the usual last-minute rush to complete the preparations. The night before, I was sure that all was ready, but a whole series of last-minute details cropped up.

I had a small team of assistants for the job. There were Jackson and Bill Tillie to keep the guards talking and to persuade them that nobody was away should they find themselves one short. Johnny Pryor, the escape representative, and Roddy were to come as close support. Their job was to stand in the doorways leading in from the two changing-rooms and to start taking their greatcoats off as soon as the guards entered. This would act as a signal to let me know there were no guards left outside the building, and prevent them from seeing me as I got through the window.

But long before we started out there was plenty for them to do. It must have taken six men to get me dressed and ready. Where was I going to keep my Bulgarian papers while posing as a Dane? It would never do to get them muddled up. Somebody suggested strapping them to the inside of my thigh, and rushed off to the sick-bay for sticking-plaster. I had better take needles and thread, but at the last minute could not find my 'hussif' ... and so on. But at last my bag was packed. It had proved rather a squash getting all my food in, and my naval cap had to be jammed on top at the last moment.

The first bath party came back and reported that the

guards were being slacker than usual. The second party were now up having their shower, so just before 10.45 we began to form up in threes at the main gate. With Jackson and Johnny Pryor, I was in the second row. Roddy, who was looking more villainous than ever and thoroughly enjoying himself, had volunteered to carry up my case and was a few rows farther back.

As the second party came into view, streaming out from the bath-house, I was seized with a spasm of acute regret. The day was grim and misty, and there was a nice fire burning in our room. I was happy and busy in the camp. Why was I such a fool as to leave when the war was bound to end in a few months anyway? Why risk being shot for a hundred-to-one chance of freedom?

The second party came through the gate and I got a thumbs-up from Commander Beale, who had gone to see for himself how the guards were behaving. There was a horrid feeling in the pit of my stomach when we began to move forward. I was committed now, and there was no way out, but how I wished that the Kommandant would cancel the last bath, or the water run cold, or something occur to get me out of this foolish venture!

I heard laughter behind me and the column came to a halt. Looking back, I saw Roddy, surrounded by three guards, stooping down. Hell! the lock on the case had burst and my gear was spread all over the road. I could see a packet of sandwiches sitting disconsolately by the edge of a puddle. How could even German guards fail to regard this as an unusual aid to bathing? But Roddy stuffed everything back again and closed the case, just as though he always took chocolate and cheese to his bath.

We moved off again, this time everyone straggling according to plan, so as to increase the delay in getting into the changing-rooms to give me more time to change. Roddy sidled up alongside and whispered to me that in repacking my case he had put my cap in the other way round. The badge now faced the hinge and not the outside. I thanked him perfunctorily. I did not then know that had it not been for this, I would certainly never have got away. ...

As I went into the changing-room I was already rolling down my trousers. Thirty seconds later I was a civilian and passed through into the bathroom. Roddy was standing by the far bathroom door. As soon as he started to take his coat off, I knew that the guards were inside. Looking round, I found that Johnny Pryor was doing the same. With a quite unnecessary clatter, which would have given the game away to anyone less sleepy than our guards, I climbed through the window and dropped out. As I walked past the bath-house I heard the sound of footsteps running on the concrete. Was it one of the guards? Was he going to shoot? I didn't dare look back, but continued to shuffle off as speedily as was consistent with innocence. Behind me I heard a door slam, and then all was quiet. ...

At once a new danger loomed ahead. Up the hill from the camp there was coming Joseph, a German who knew me better than anyone. He was riding a bicycle, his head lowered, after the manner of one pedalling up an incline. I had to turn right to gain the main road, but Joseph and I were almost equidistant from the turning. Could I get there first, and would he or would he not look up and spot me? I could not afford to run, but I reached the turn with Joseph still ten feet away. He never gave me a glance.

Despite fog and drizzle, the main road, which was absolutely straight and without cover for over a mile, was unduly populous. Two Germans I knew by sight passed me without giving signs of recognition. There was, in any case, nothing I could do about it except to trudge on, looking as innocent as I could. Apart from the worry, I was beginning to enjoy myself. All the anticipations and regrets vanished the moment I dropped out of the window and saw freedom stretching ahead down that long road.

I was in this happy frame of mind when a tall figure in field-grey, passing on a bicycle, gave me a dirty look and called on me to stop.

This first investigation was a great test, and I could hardly control my nerves.

'Who are you?'

'Paul Hanson – a Dane.'

'Where are your papers?'

'Here,' said I, giving him my temporary pass, which was of imitation typewriting, in pencil.

'Where were you born?'

'Aarhus.' (Thank goodness I'd memorized all my details.)

'When were you born?'

'Fifth of October.' (My mother's birthday.)

'Is that your photograph?' said he, pointing at the small picture of a fair-haired man in golfing jacket, stuck on my pass.

With a nasty feeling in the pit of my stomach, I realized that I had grown a moustache, but had failed to add one to this photograph. Furthermore, he wore spectacles, and I had forgotten to take mine with me. Ignoring those discrepancies, I said, 'Of course,' in as pained a tone as I could. To my surprise he handed me back my pass without further comment.

'What are you doing here?'

'I am an employee of A.E.G., Bremen. I was wounded in the raid on 23 November and have been sent out for a week to rest my nerves. I'm now returning to the hospital for survey.' (This nerve story might discount any suspicion caused by my ill-concealed agitation.)

'Where have you been staying?'

'With the parson at Kirchtimke.' (There ought to be one at a place with a name like that.)

'Which one? What was he called?'

'I don't know his name. Everyone called him "*Pfarrer*" ("*Padre*"). The chap with grey hair, I mean.' (A fairly good bet that there wouldn't be any young ones left.)

'H'm. Where did he live?'

'In the little house by the church.' (That is the usual North German layout.)

'Let's see inside that case of yours.'

Now I was for it. Propping it on the seat of his bike, I opened the wretched thing up.

'H'm. Shirt, bread, cigarettes, jersey. What's in that paper parcel there?' (pointing to my chocolate wrapped in an old *DAZ*).

'More bread.'

'What's this?' (lifting the back of my cap. Thank goodness Roddy had turned it round.)

'My working cap.'

There was an ugly pause. He clearly had a residue of doubt lingering in his mind, which can hardly be wondered at, since he was the local policeman and we were still within half a mile of the camp. If he took me into custody I should be finished, for I could hardly survive a more searching cross-examination.

I produced my last trump card, Johnny Pryor's letter, purporting to be from the medical superintendent at Bremen Hospital, directing me to report back that afternoon. I gave it to him and the scales tipped in my favour. Pointing down, he said, 'Some of your cigarettes have fallen on the ground,' mounted his bicycle and was off. I stood in the middle of the road with my mouth open, clutching my case in both arms like a baby.

Continuing along the road, I dived into a wood, bandaged my head, and shaved off half my eyebrows. The fog was thicker, and I emerged on to the road again just behind a girl carrying a small suitcase. Evidently she was catching the train too, so I followed her to the station. It was later than I thought, and we had to run the last few hundred yards.

Buying the ticket presented no difficulty, and I climbed into a non-smoker full of typical German housewives. No one paid any attention to the sad-looking young man with a bandaged head, who sat by himself in a corner. The fat woman opposite was soon fast asleep. It was just as well. Half-way to Bremen I looked down and saw that the silk cover had fallen off one of my buttons. Nobody appeared to have noticed, so I hid it under my cap and then cut it off.

It was 1.15 when we arrived in Bremen, and there was a crowd on the platform waiting to go back to Tarmstedt on the 1.30 train. Together with several others, I went into the public lavatory. It was primitive and the light was shocking, but there was a bolt on the door. With great excitement, for the situation was becoming increasingly Edgar-Wallace-like, I removed my civilian trousers and stuffed the cap behind some pipes. Off with button covers and on with the greatcoat belt. I then blacked my moustache and darkened my eyes, as I had been taught by the theatrical make-up experts. Finally, with buttons uncovered, Bulgarian papers substituted for Danish in my wallet, and my cap, complete with badge, set at what I hoped was a suitably rakish Slav angle, I stepped out on to an empty and deserted platform.

From my journey to the camp nine months earlier I remembered my way to the main station. Arrived there, I was faced by a fresh problem. There were two entrances, civilian and military. Which should I use, and ought I to buy my ticket before or after entering? Eventually I decided to try the military way in, but was stopped at the barrier and asked for my papers and ticket. I played dumb – in the American sense – and merely handed in my letter of introduction, saying 'Nicht Deutsch'. The R.T.O. read it through, nodding his head and saying 'Ja' to himself. Finally, he decided that 'benevolent assistance' was indicated, and a minion was sent to help me. This worthy escorted me along to the booking-office, bought me a third-class ticket to Lübeck, found out the time and platform of departure of my train, and finally took me to the waiting-room and ordered me a beer!

I was so bewildered by these developments that it took me some time to calm down. I could not but be most encouraged. Evidently my papers were going to see me through most difficulties, while my uniform appeared to be causing no comment. As a final test, I went up to a

German sailor at the next table and asked him for the loan of a knife. He handed it to me without a word, and, German fashion, I brought a loaf of bread out of my case and cut off a large hunk.

Escaping is rather like that embarrassing social situation when you meet someone who evidently knows you well but whom you cannot place. Luckily, having a shocking memory for names and faces, I have had plenty of practice at pretending to know and then asking innocent leading questions, such as 'How long would it be since we last met?' until I get a clue. Travelling through an enemy country – and I had never been to Germany before – is like this on a vast scale. Without ever appearing ignorant, I had to learn the currency, what was and what wasn't rationed, whether one tipped the waiter, and lots of other points. Having so far paid for everything with a ten-mark note, I took my change along to the 'Gentlemen's' to see what the various coins were. Here another question arose. Should I put a penny in the slot or give it to the attendant? Eventually I did the latter, and spent the next half-hour learning which coin was which.

I caught the 4.17 train to Hamburg and arrived there without incident just after 6 p.m. Again ignorance led me into trouble. As one of the great junctions of the country and the main artery across the Elbe, Hamburg Station had some very sharp-eyed police about. It would have been possible for me to go from the Bremen to the Lübeck platform without going through a barrier at all, but not knowing the station layout, I left the platform at the wrong end and had to pass through three control points. One of these was a wicked place – a constriction in a passage, painted white and lighted by arc-lights, in which stood three Gestapo officials scrutinizing everyone who passed. I felt a lot better when I was through; for the fact that I was not stopped meant that I must have fitted in pretty well with my surroundings.

The waiting-room was packed, chiefly with soldiers on leave. I really felt quite sorry hanging my dear old naval

cap up beside the Nazi ones with their high, stiff brims.
It was like leaving a friend alone among thieves.

One could at that time still get a coupon-free dish in all
German restaurants at lunch- and dinner-time. This dish,
called the 'Stamm', was usually only a bowl of vegetable
soup, but for a few days I thought it should be sufficient
to keep my stomach full.

Sitting at the next table to me as I ate was a young soldier with an Afrika Korps flash on his shoulder. I suspect
that he had seen R.N.V.R. uniform before, for he kept on
looking at me very strangely. I returned his gaze, and he
evidently lacked the courage of his convictions, for he
never came up to me.

When I left to catch my 8 p.m. train for Lübeck, I was
stopped at the barrier and asked for my papers. The man
just looked at my identity card, said 'S'gut', and let me go
on. It struck me as rather amusing that he should accept
without question a document in Bulgarian lettering. Only
the serial number and the photograph were intelligible to
a Western European, and the latter bore very little resem-
blance to me.

In the compartment of the Lübeck train, which was
without light, a soldier and a civilian sat discussing the
bombing. I was surprised at the open way they spoke,
with a uniformed stranger in their midst, and soon after
we pulled out of Hamburg they asked for my views of the
situation. I explained that as a Bulgarian only recently
arrived in the country, I hardly felt entitled to an opinion,
and then took the opportunity to ask where there was a
good place in Lübeck to sleep; for I was due to arrive just
before midnight and did not fancy spending the night in
the open.

They explained with emphasis that it was not safe to
spend the night in any large German town in case of air
raids. Was I due to go on any farther? Yes, I intended
going to Stettin the following day. Without giving me a
chance to explain that I had business in Lübeck first, the
civilian said that he, too, was going to Stettin, and that he

would show me a very nice station waiting-room where he himself intended spending the night. Further, at the next stop he would see the guard and buy me a supplementary ticket. Feeling it better to let sleeping dogs lie than to embark on long and tedious explanations, I agreed to this.

We duly passed Lübeck, and an hour later arrived at Bad Kleinen, the junction stop for Wismar. Here my friend bade me get out and led me to what was a reasonably comfortable waiting-room, full of sleeping travellers. We found a vacant bench and sat down, but for me it was not to sleep. It had been an extraordinary day. Fourteen hours previously I had been in the camp; now I was the best part of two hundred miles away and on a coast full of promise. If I played my cards properly I should be home in a few weeks! ... or possibly even days. ...

At about 6 a.m. the next day I caught a train on to Stettin. It was fearfully crowded and ran very late. My compartment was full of soldiers of the young Nazi breed – swaggering and making far too much noise. At 9 a.m. there was a long halt just outside a place called Pasewalk. The carriage was getting stifling, but I looked at my watch with a certain sly satisfaction. Any minute now Tubby would be walking complacently to *Appell* [roll call] and the Feldwebel would go up and salute smartly and say : 'One man missing.' ...

It was after 1 p.m. when we finally reached Stettin and I was beginning to feel very hungry, but with only three hours of daylight left there was no time to waste, so I set off in search of ships. Stettin must be by far the ugliest of all the Baltic ports, but it was exciting to be there, and for a seaman it was enough just to be beside a river again, with tugs and ferry-boats bustling about. Moreover, I was convinced that at any moment I was going to find a Swedish ship that would take me to freedom.

A couple of hours' walking speedily changed this view. I could find no free harbour, as I had supposed, and what ships I could see were German and in inaccessible positions. Actually I know now that my search was incomplete. To find the docks in a large town without the aid of some map or plan is no easy task. I naturally searched the main river banks from the west (or railway station) side; I did not know that had I crossed the main bridge I should have found extensive free quays a couple of miles to the eastward, connecting with the main river farther down-stream.

As it grew dusk, therefore, my spirits fell and I became convinced that Stettin was no use. David Jolly – the only man I knew who had been there before – had drawn a blank and so had I. The one redeeming feature was that I had walked round the harbour for five hours without anyone commenting on my uniform. I became yet more confident in the disguise even though I despaired of finding a ship.

To cheer myself up, I went on a combined *Stamm* and pub crawl. At each of six water-front pubs I had a bowl of soup and a couple of half-litres of beer, at the same time keeping my ears open for any sound of Scandinavian being spoken.

A strange thing about some of these cafés was the little placard hung up in the bar saying, '*Wir grüssen hier mit Heil Hitler.*' Fancy an English pub having to display a notice saying, 'The motto of this house is God save the King'! In any case I took the hint and thoroughly enjoyed clicking my heels and saying, '*Heil Hitler*' with arm raised in every establishment I entered. By the time I reached the station I was taking a much brighter view of life, and even thought, as I had ample funds, of taking a train to Switzerland for a spot of ski-ing.

Finally, I resolved to try one more Baltic port, and took a second-class ticket to Lübeck. As the scheme of sleeping in a mid-way waiting-room had worked so well the previous night, I decided to try it again, and chose a place called Neu-Brandenburg, well known as a prison camp in the war of 1914–18. On alighting, I mingled with a crowd of naval ratings and made for the waiting-room. We were just trying to open the door when an R.T.O. came up and told us that there was better accommodation going for Servicemen in the *Wehrmachtsunterkunft* (the German equivalent of our Y.M.C.A. station canteens), and ushered us firmly along there.

The place was certainly pleasant enough. A buxom Red Cross sister gave us soup and coffee free; there was a fire and a number of comfortable chairs in which to sleep. But it was no place for a British naval officer. There was a German N.O. sitting at the next table, and with him were about a dozen ratings. It was all very well to get away with it in the street, but sitting opposite them all night was a very different matter. Still, I could not very well leave, so I had perforce to continue playing my part. As soon as one of them began to doze off I began to nod. Of course, any idea of sleep was out of the question, but it was the most convincing part to play. ... Crash! ... What was that? ... I looked at my watch. It was six o'clock and the last rating was going through the door. What extraordinary things occur! Entirely against my wishes I had spent a night in full uniform alongside an officer of the Kriegsmarine, and in official military accommodation too, and nobody had recognized me!

A few minutes later I was in the train rattling on towards Lübeck. By this time I was beginning to take rail travel for granted, but this was the one journey that caused me some embarrassment. A garrulous old man was sitting opposite, and he kept on quoting what sounded like proverbs or clichés at me in Low German. I could not understand a word he said, so smiled merrily and answered '*Ja*' or '*Nein*' as seemed best. Then I got up and gave my seat to an old lady. No sooner had I done so than I realized that it was not 'the thing to do'. People looked at me as though I were some creature from a strange world observing different customs. To make matters worse, I was jammed up against some little Hitler Jugends. I was always terrified of children. They are so quick-witted and observant. The ordinary man is not usually 'up' in types of aircraft, enemy uniforms, and the like, but it is just the sort of information on which little boys thrive. These lads only came up to my chest; I was frightened lest they should see the London stamp on the inner side of my Service buttons.

But the time passed, and shortly after 11 a.m. we arrived at Lübeck. My first need was for a shave, so by way of an experiment I went into a barber's shop and asked for one. It was an almost fatal blunder; for, as far as I could understand him, the man told me that with soap rationing there had been no shaves for about two years, and who was I to know so little about things anyway. Muttering 'Ach so,' I left hurriedly, followed by many a curious glance.

*

It is a strange fact that although all my time at large in Germany was during good weather, in retrospect it seems as though the sun never shone. Everything there was so dull and cheerless, I can only visualize it beneath skies of grey. Other escapers have returned with exactly the same impression.

Lübeck was the only exception. A charming little town, it seemed a sort of backwater from the main-stream of war – there was more in the shops, the people seemed better dressed and more cheerful, and – yes, the sun shone. Just over the bridge was a comfortable hotel, and to this I went for my shave. The porter's desk was empty, so I locked myself in a bathroom, had a good wash, and put on a clean shirt and collar. I felt much better after that, and went down to the restaurant for lunch.

This meal was notable for the well-dressed people there – one couple in particular could have been transported straight to the Berkeley – and also for a two-course *Stamm*, the only one I have ever heard of – a bowl of consommé, followed by a dry vegetable hash. This was the one trace of civilization I saw in the whole of Germany, and it made me long all the more for home.

Leaving my suitcase at the hotel, I started off on a

reconnaissance in high hopes. If the geography of Stettin
was hard, that of Lübeck was very easy, for here the river
was flanked on either side by quays and warehouses, and
these were the docks. Rather than walk down the verge
between the warehouses and the ships, where I might con-
ceivably have got picked up for taking too great an interest in the goings-on, I decided to use the road outside,
which was full of trucks, dockers, horses and carts, and
cover the opposite bank by peering through the occasional
gaps between the warehouses. Taking the east bank first,
I walked about two miles and, to my great excitement,
saw two Swedish ships. That meant that they were still
trading to Germany and were not shut in by Baltic ice, as
I was beginning to fear. On the other hand, they were
not of much use to me, since they were both auxiliary
schooners, with decks piled high with lumber, so that,
quite apart from the lack of good hiding room there is in
a sailing ship, they might be several days yet in discharg-
ing their cargoes.

Retracing my steps, therefore, to the main bridge over
the river, I started to walk down the west bank, looking
east.

Almost at once I saw just what I was after – two coasters
lying alongside, bow to stern, with Swedish flags painted
on their top-sides. For the first quarter-mile below the
bridge the river was divided into two by a long, narrow
spit or peninsula called the Halbinsel, and it was alongside this that they lay.

Without further ado I turned for the hotel to get my
bag. Since it was thirty-one hours since I had last been
challenged, and as a bold and forward policy had always
worked hitherto, I resolved to try to walk aboard in broad
daylight, trusting that an authoritative bearing and deci-
sive manner would prevent anyone from asking me my
business.

It was after three o'clock when I left the hotel, and I
was glad that things were going to be put to the test. I
was beginning to feel the lack of food and sleep; also, one

operates the whole time under certain nervous tension, and I wanted to get the matter settled one way or the other.

As I approached the Halbinsel I found that it was wired off with a gate and a sentry. This latter, however, had a beat nearly thirty yards long; for a road and a double railway track ran on to the peninsula through the gap he was guarding in the wire. Better still, there were some goods vans on one of the tracks, jutting out just beyond the line of his beat.

My line of approach lay along the main road and bridge, cutting across the Halbinsel, with the wire on my right hand. I adjusted my pace so that the sentry would have his back to me – i.e. be walking in the same direction as I – by the time I reached the goods wagons. When he turned at the near end of his beat I was just walking down the road, apparently interested in a girl on the pavement opposite; twelve paces later and I dodged down the track behind the goods vans.

I came on to the jetty, and there, ahead of me, lay the two Swedish ships. There were no sentries on the gangway, but I could not afford to hesitate. A quick glance – they both looked exactly the same – and I made for the nearer, which was loading coal. In a fever of excitement that can well be imagined I walked straight up the gangplank. In front of me lay a companionway, so I went down it. Below, I found myself in an alleyway with doors on either side. I saw one marked 'Steward', knocked, and went straight in.

A pleasant, sandy-haired individual looked up as I entered. 'Excuse me, I'm an escaped British officer and I'm in need of help. . . .' A pause. . . . He got up, went over and locked the door.

So far so good. I began to have dreams of home by Christmas. He produced a cigar and a drink and asked me how I had got there. I gave him the outline of my story, and asked in return why he had demanded no proof of my identity.

'Oh, I recognized your uniform. I spent the first two years of the war trading on the English coast. You're R.N.V.R., aren't you?'

After three days of furtive wandering, with nobody to talk to, it was a relief to be able to gossip quite freely with this man! The precious minutes began to slip by. . . .

'And now to business, Steward. I want to get to Sweden. Can you hide me away anywhere?'

'Sure. Just you wait here and I'll go and arrange it with the Chief Engineer.' A few minutes later he came back with a long face. 'It's no good. The Chief says that she is low on coal and due to bunker tomorrow. That means there will be stevedores crawling about the ship everywhere. Your best plan is to go to the ship astern. She's a motor-ship belonging to the same company, and she's due to sail today some time. Her steward is a good fellow – took some Russians to Gothenburg last trip. Offer to make it worth his while and he'll certainly hide you away.'

I argued the point. I felt so secure aboard this ship that I was loth to leave her, even for a fifty-yard walk down the jetty, but at length the steward persuaded me it was the best thing to do.

I had to wait a minute at the bottom of the companion-way while a bulky individual, evidently the skipper, came below. When I reached the deck they were casting off ropes on the jetty. As I watched, the gap between the other ship and the wall slowly grew. Was it worth making a dash for? Obviously not. A pier-head jump would cause far too much attention. Even if there were no police or pilot aboard, some bystander would certainly report the occurrence and she would be stopped farther down the ten-mile river. No, I had missed her, and that by seconds.

I returned to my steward friend, who went on deck to see for himself. When he came back he had already made up his mind. 'It is no use your staying here,' he said. 'You will be in greater danger than if you are ashore. Have you money?'

'Yes.'

'Well, stay away till Monday. If you come back, I'll take you to Gothenburg. Till then, the best of luck to you.'

A moment's thought. There was obviously some force to his arguments, and anyway I could not well run him into trouble. It had been quite easy getting into the dockyard area; it should be no harder to get out. Yes, I had better go. My hopes were still high as I left the ship. I had got my passage arranged. I could spend Sunday taking a trip up to Rostock for a look around in case there were anything better.

My return route was at right angles to the sentry's beat. I tried to time it to pass the danger zone when his back was turned, but I was just too late. As I walked away down the road a voice shouted after me, 'Halt!' I turned, trying to look as innocent and indignant as I could.

'What were you doing in the dockyard?'

'Seeing off a friend; the mate of that ship that has just left.'

'Where are your papers and dockyard pass? What, you have no pass? Then you must come with me to the guardhouse.'

I was taken there, and an escort was provided to take me to Battalion Headquarters. The Duty Officer was impressed with my papers and with my protests at the indignity of arresting a distinguished allied officer. He explained to me that it was his duty to check up on me since I had no pass. Could he look in my case?

As there was nothing incriminating in it, I showed it to him readily enough. He went out for a few minutes and held a conversation next door. When he returned, it was to say that the Kommandant thought it would be best for me to go to the police station: 'Just to get everything regulated.' It was a suggestion admitting of no refusal, and as my only possible line I agreed with outward enthusiasm, but with a sinking feeling within. My chances of fooling the professional police were slim – and the stories one heard of the German police were not encouraging. ...

We arrived at a building on the water-front marked '*Wasserschutzpolizei*'. They were, I suppose, the German equivalent of our Thames river police. Thank God it was not the Gestapo, anyway!

A fat, red-faced man listened while my escort told his tale; then, turning to me, he asked for my identity card. I gave it to him, and made a vigorous protest against being arrested. Paying no attention, he went over to a cupboard and took out a magnifying glass. After scrutinizing the card for a minute, he looked up and said: 'Where did you escape from?' The game was obviously up, but I said stiffly: 'I am afraid I don't know what you mean.' He replied: 'Yes, you know perfectly well.'

I gave him my full name, rank and camp, and produced my identity disc in support. His first action was to call in a junior, and together they congratulated the man who had arrested me. He was naturally delighted, and stood looking on with a grin from ear to ear. He, too, probably had visions of being home for Christmas.

The red-faced man showed the other my pass, and then, turning to me, said scornfully: 'How did you expect to leave Germany on a rotten pass like that?'

Before I could reply, the other cut in and said: 'Not at all. When you think of what few facilities they possess in those camps it's a very fine bit of work.' Turning to me, he pointed at the stamp of the Chief of Police, Cologne, and said: 'Look, that is your one bad mistake. You've put "*Polizei Kommissar*". It should be "*Polizei Präsident*".'

I was searched for weapons and asked to make a statement. I had no intention of playing around with the German police, so I made one, substantially true, but lying on all key points. They cannot have known anything about camp life, for they wrote down quite happily that I had walked out of the main gate at dusk when the sentry was not looking!

I had a strong desire – presumably a sort of defence mechanism – to boast of my time at large, and I derived the greatest pleasure from telling them of my night in the

Wehrmachtsunterkunft at Neu-Brandenburg. The man with the red face grew yet redder, and there were broad grins on the faces of the rest. The news of my capture seemed to have spread, for quite a number of others had come in to see the specimen. Baiting Red-Face in front of such an appreciative audience was great fun. ...

I was asked how I had got into the prohibited zone. Not without a certain feeling of satisfaction, I turned and pointed at my captor. 'Past him, when his back was turned.' Broad grin quickly vanished.

'At what time?'

'About 3.10.'

To the sentry: 'Were you on duty then?'

Sentry: 'Yes.'

One of the police went over to the telephone and rang up the C.O. I should not be the only man in jail over Christmas!

The questions being finished, the nasty one left the room. The younger man immediately offered me a cigar-ette, and I in return shared the rest of my chocolate with him.

A few minutes later he was detailed off to escort me to the local military jail. On the way there he informed me that the camp had been told of my recapture and would fetch me in a couple of days. He added as a rider to this that he was sorry, personally, that I had had such bad luck.

Taking advantage of his friendliness, I said: 'I suppose, of course, that you knew I was at large?'

'Naturally,' he said. 'We had a full description of you in the office yesterday.'

It was a lie. Why, I had to write my name out for them and spell the address of the camp. It would be useful for future reference to know that the Baltic ports were not informed when we were at large. I'd have to try that route again some time.

It was dark when we arrived at the military jail. Again I was searched, and my name and rank were put in a large register, but I was allowed to keep my small case and all my gear. A jailer led me along a dark passage till we came to a massive door. It was opened for me, and I entered a small cell. Behind me the door clanged, and, worn out, I fell on to the hard bed and went to sleep. . . .

*   *   *

. . . David James was unlucky that time but he was not the man to give up. He took his punishment for attempting to escape and within a couple of months he was out again – by exactly the same method. This time he travelled as a merchant seaman and succeeded in stowing away on a ship bound for Sweden.

CHAPTER SIX

Escape from Colditz Castle

AIREY NEAVE was another amateur, this time a soldier. Captured in Calais in 1940, he escaped from his first prison camp in Poland but was recaptured and sent to the 'naughty boys' camp' in Colditz Castle. It was to this grim fortress that insubordinate prisoners and persistent escapers were sent by the Germans in order to keep them together and under the most strict supervision. Like their special camp for aircrew, Stalag-Luft III, Colditz Castle was considered by the Germans to be escape-proof.

At Colditz the problem was not the barbed wire, searchlights and machine guns of the normal prisoner-of-war camp but the moat and immensely thick high walls of a medieval castle. This was a matter for lock-picking, tunnelling and the discovery of secret passages – above all, for attempts to escape in disguise.

Airey Neave's first attempt to escape from Colditz ended in a far from dismal failure. He had faked a German uniform by daubing an ancient Polish tunic with paint from the camp theatre. Although passable in daylight, the camouflage glowed brilliant emerald in the light of the arc-lamps outside the camp, surrounding the escaper with an aura of green light and making him appear (as he says) 'like the demon king in a pantomime'. Even the most stupid sentry could not fail to see that something was wrong and Airey Neave was soon inside the Castle again.

On his way back from the punishment cells after this escape Airey Neave noticed the 'Bridge of Sighs' which led to the discovery of a secret passage. . . .

... The camp theatre was a great room on the second floor of the building adjoining the gates of the inner courtyard. In this building senior officers of the Allied Nations were quartered. Here lived a French general, a Polish admiral, and a Polish general with senior British officers. Connecting this building with the guard-house was the mysterious Bridge of Sighs. What lay behind those tiny dusty windows above the gateway? Was there a passageway leading to the attic on the upper floor of the guardhouse? At either end of the bridge the rooms which led to it were locked and barred and doors bricked up. Roaming like inquisitive children around some mysterious mansion in the hours of daylight, we came excitedly upon the secret. There was a passageway. *The way to it lay under the floor of the theatre where a rough dais was raised to form a stage.*

The prospectors in this new territory were led by Pat Reid and 'Hank' Wardle, M.C., a Canadian in the R.A.F., who first discovered the magic entrance. 'Hank' was a very tall man of immense physical strength. He was of quiet disposition but immensely shrewd and, though he spoke little, his judgement in matters of escaping was excellent. He had already made one attempt to escape from Spangenburg. Pat Reid and he reached Switzerland in October 1942. Neither 'Hank' nor I could have foreseen at this time that eighteen months later I should be his Best Man at his wedding in England!

Beneath the stage the searchers found space enough to crawl and slowly sawed away the floorboards with stolen implements, making a square hole in the ceiling of the passage below. To disguise this hole Reid made an ingenious mask known as 'Shovewood'. Then, with the usual rope of mattress-covers tied to one of the supports of the stage, he climbed down into the sealed passage. Facing him was a locked door leading to the gate-bridge. He picked the lock and, walking softly in slippered feet through the musty air, he came to a further door on the far side of the bridge. It opened without difficulty, revealing steps into an attic above the guard-house. On the floor beneath was the German Officers' Mess and up the stairs into this gloomy place came the hoarse laughter of Hauptmann Priem and the tinkle of glasses.

Pat Reid proposed that teams of two, one British and one Dutch officer, should attempt to escape disguised as German officers. He selected John Hyde-Thomson and myself, and we both set to work to make the uniforms. My friends were not enthusiastic. The failure of other attempts had disheartened them. They did not believe that even in a German uniform would it be possible to get past the guard-room, and there were disheartening though friendly comments.

'It will only alert the Goons.'

'You are being rather selfish.'

'I can't think why they allow you to go.'

'My dear chap, I knew about the wicket gate months ago.'

I learned at Colditz that the escaper must have absolute confidence in his success. He must never be discouraged by the gloom of his companions or he is lost. He must above all calmly choose the right moment to attack. It seemed to me that if two men in German officers' uniforms were to descend the stairs from the attic and emerge from the guard-house door through the passage which the door of the actual guard-room opened, their appearance would not be questioned by the sentry outside. What more natural than that two officers, after visiting the mess above, should appear from the guard-room walking towards the *Kommandantur*? From the moment that the passage was discovered, I concentrated every thought on how to fool the sentry who was posted outside the guard-room. If the man were cold and bored with duty on a winter's night, would his numbed brain suspect two officers coming from his own guard-house?

As the weeks passed in rehearsal, I searched for a new and more authentic German uniform. My first and most valuable acquisition was a long, green uniform overcoat of an officer of the Netherlands Home Army. There were in the camp upwards of sixty officers of the Dutch Forces, who, rather than take an oath of allegiance to Hitler, had resolved to spend the war in captivity. All of them were men of high character who spoke good English and German. Most of the officers were of the Netherlands East Indies Army, whose uniform was a shade of jungle green and unsuitable for my purpose. The pre-war Home Army, however, had blue-green uniforms, whose colour could easily pass at night for field grey.

The Dutch and the British had early come to an agreement upon escape matters. Since the Dutch officers spoke German they were allowed to take part in British schemes and share the store of aids to escape. They also volunteered to hand over pieces of their uniform for the escape from the guard-house. The final plan agreed on envisaged the escape of two parties of bogus German officers at an interval of twenty-four hours. The first party would consist of Lieutenant Toni Luteyn of the Netherlands East Indies Army and myself. The second would consist of John Hyde-Thomson and Lieutenant Donkers of the Netherlands East Indies Army.

A bogus German uniform had to be most carefully hidden, for the enemy made constant searches of the room where I slept and of all my belongings. I was obliged to keep the precious Dutch overcoat rolled in some sacking under the floorboards beneath a 'mask'. If this hiding-place were suspected another would have to be found.

Such was the talent in the camp that I had no difficulty in discovering officers who could convert the Dutch material into a very passable German officer's overcoat. The epaulettes, normally of woven silver braid, were made from thick linoleum cut from the floor of the bath-room, painted silver and sewn to the shoulders.

I had decided to promote myself to the rank of *Ober-leutnant* and to take on the identity of an infantry officer named Schwartz. It was therefore necessary to provide small gold stars to denote that rank. These were fashioned from wood, cut with a penknife by Scarlet O'Hara and painted gold. Although the Germans, after several discoveries of imitation uniforms, stopped supplies of silver and gold paint to the canteen, a quantity had been saved and carefully stored. The epaulettes were finished with a gold numeral to denote an infantry regiment. There remained only the collar of the overcoat and the buttons. A dark-green collar was cut from green baize material. The buttons were of lead from lavatory piping poured into skilful moulds made by the Dutch. My belt on this occasion was of cardboard painted brown from a box of watercolours, and with a fine imitation revolver holster of cardboard filled with newspaper. My disguise was nearly complete.

Much of this faithful work was done for me by Squadron Leader Brian Paddon, D.S.O., D.F.C. Paddon was the most ingenious mind among escapers of my experience. He eclipsed even Scarlet O'Hara in the picking of locks and making of keys. Obsessed by such technicalities, he amassed a vast hoard of implements, many of which he absent-mindedly carried in his pockets. At nightfall he could be seen making the rounds of his private hiding-places or testing the strength of ancient locks. His long face bore an expression of morose determination as he haunted the more mysterious corners of the castle. His persevering nature was rewarded by a brilliantly successful exploit. He was returned to Stalag XXa to stand his court martial for insulting the German *Feldwebel* who had thrown Forbes and myself into the dungeons at the end of our escape in Poland. As the court was due to assemble, Paddon broke out of his cell and after many adventures reached the safety of neutral Sweden in 1942.

Among the many gadgets and contrivances provided by the fanatical Paddon was a German officer's uniform cap. In the army of the Third Reich an officer's cap had a black shiny peak resembling that of a chauffeur. Towards the beginning of December, I made a remarkable discovery concerning my own service-dress uniform cap which had been sent to me by my parents in a parcel. I stripped it of khaki material and discovered to my aston-ishment that, underneath, it had a bright black shiny peak. Paddon bent the brim and sides of the cap so that it stood high above the peak, and covered the whole with Dutch uniform material. The principal badge, a design of leaves in silver with a roundel in white and red in the centre, he cut from a piece of linoleum. The familiar eagle's wings and swastika design, also in linoleum, were sewn above. He finished this masterpiece by sewing white piping on the edge of the brim. With such a uni-form I could face the arc-lights once more with confid-ence.

Through that icy December, I rehearsed the part of Dr Calomel by day and collected the parts of my uniform by night. On several occasions precious pieces met with dis-aster. Epaulettes of linoleum and badges carelessly left about were found and confiscated. Often tragedies came thick and fast. John Hyde-Thomson sat on his German hat, crushing the carefully poised brim; there was a short-age of lead piping from the lavatories; the prisoners were banned from the theatre for several days for stealing a workman's coat.

Undeterred, we hastened our preparations in a running fight with the searching guards.

Toni Luteyn, my Dutch companion, was playing the drums in the camp orchestra. Since we were both occu-pied in the theatre we were able to transfer our disguises in Red Cross boxes underneath the stage.

*

On the morning of 5 January 1942 Luteyn and I were ready to escape. We held a conference with Pat Reid and 'Hank' Wardle and decided to try immediately after the nine o'clock *Appell* that evening. Our compasses, maps and a small bundle of notes were ready for hiding inside our bodies. The uniforms were now intact beneath the stage and our civilian clothes had so far escaped detection in

their 'hide'. In a moment of supreme confidence, I collected the addresses of relatives of my companions. Then
flushed and excited, I lay down to sleep throughout the
afternoon and early evening.

A few minutes before nine I went down to the courtyard, when the snow was falling lightly. The turrets cast
long shadows in the light of the moon and the steep walls
enfolded me for what I believed to be the last time. There
was once more the eternal sound of hundreds of men taking their meagre exercise in clogs. I stood waiting for the
Appell, eyeing the Dutch contingent where Luteyn was
waiting ready to join me. We wore cardboard leggings
painted with black polish. I wore my usual combination
of battledress and sweater, and my Army boots, being
brown, were also darkened with black polish. Underneath
I had my 'civilian clothes' with a pair of R.A.F. trousers.
I had an overpowering sense that this was my last evening
in the castle. The certainty grew with every minute, making me composed and determined.

There was a sharp order of dismissal and, mingling with
the dispersing prisoners, Pat Reid, 'Hank' Wardle, Luteyn
and I hurried quickly into the senior officers' quarters. In
the darkness of the theatre we felt our way beneath the
stage, then carefully prised up the loose floor-boards. Pat
Reid lifted the trap called 'Shovewood', which on its underside was whitewashed, disguising the hole in the ceiling of the passage below. I could see the strong, determined lines on his face as he worked in the glow of a
cigarette-lighter. The trap removed, the mattress-cover
rope was let down through the hole in the ceiling.
Cautiously we climbed down, holding the boxes of uniforms, and landed with soft bumps on the floor of the
passage.

The bright lights from the courtyard shone through the
cobwebbed windows in the outer wall of the passage.
Treading softly in our socks, we reached the door of the
gate-bridge. Pat Reid, shining his lighter on the lock,
swiftly picked it. It opened without a sound, for he had

oiled the hinges earlier in the week. We were in the half-light of a narrow corridor. We walked quietly across it and stopped at the door that led to the guard-house.

The German uniform overcoats were unpacked in silence and we put them over our workmen's clothes, leaving our battledress in the boxes. As we pulled on our boots there was no sound except the grating of Pat Reid's wire searching in the lock. A minute passed, and suddenly came fear and exasperation. The door would not open. Beneath our feet we could hear the creaking of the gates and the voices of sentries changing guard. We stood motionless, fully dressed as German officers, and waited with pounding hearts. Pat Reid spoke in a hoarse whisper:

'I'm afraid I can't get it open!'

He continued turning the wire in the lock. I could hear the wire rasping against the rusty metal as he tried again and again to open it. Ten minutes passed in terrible suspense. Through the cobwebbed window I could see the snow falling. I folded my arms and waited. Suddenly there was the noise of old hinges creaking. A quick snap and the door swung open, showing us the dim interior of the attic.

'Good luck,' said Pat Reid, and shook hands.

We waited till the door was locked behind us and we could no longer hear his muffled steps. Then we crept carefully to the top of stone spiral stairs at an open door on the other side of the attic. A wireless in the guard-room on the ground floor was playing organ music. It was the moment to go down, for the music was loud. We walked quickly down the first flight of stairs, past the door of the officers' mess on the first floor where a light showed beneath. We waited, then stepped confidently down through darkness, into the passage beside the guard-room. The guard-room door was half open, and I caught a glimpse of German uniforms inside, as we marched smartly into the blinding whiteness of the snow under the arc-lights.

The testing time had come. I strode through the snow trying to look like a Prussian. There stood the sentry, the fallen snow covering his cap and shoulders, stamping his feet, just as I had pictured him. He saluted promptly, but he stared at us, and as our backs were turned I felt him watching. We walked on beneath the first archway and passed the second sentry without incident. Then, between the first and second archways, two under-officers talking loudly came from the *Kommandantur*. They began to march behind us. I felt Luteyn grow tense beside me. I clasped my hands behind my back with an air of uncon- cern. I might have been casually pacing an English parade ground. In a moment of excitement I had forgotten my part. 'March with your hands at your sides, you fool,' came a fierce sharp whisper from my companion.

Again I saw the bicycles near the clock tower. Could they be ridden fast in this thick snow? We passed be- neath the tower, saluted by the sentry, and came to the fateful wicket-gate. As Luteyn opened it I watched the under-officers, their heads bowed to the driving snow, march on across the moat bridge. Down we went into the moat, stumbling and slipping, until we reached its bed. A soldier came towards us from the married quarters. He reached us, stopped and stared deliberately. I hesitated for a moment ready to run, but Luteyn turned on him quickly and in faultless German said crossly, 'Why do you not salute?'

The soldier gaped. He saluted, still looking doubtful, and began to walk up the side of the moat towards the wicket-gate. We did not look back but hastened up to the path on the far side, and, passing the married quarters, came to the high oak paling which bordered the pathway above the park. We were still within the faint glare of searchlights. Every moment that we stayed on the path- way was dangerous. Lifting ourselves quickly over the paling, we landed in thick snow among the tangle of trees. My cardboard belt was torn and broken and with it into the darkness vanished the holster.

Groping among the trees we struggled through frozen leaves down the steep bank and made for the outer stone wall. It was five minutes before we were at the bottom of the slope. Helped by Luteyn, I found a foothold in the stones of the wall and sat astride the coping. The wall, descending steeply with the tree-covered slope, was shrouded in snow and ice. Each time that I tried to pull Luteyn on top, I lost my foothold and slid backwards through the steep angle of the wall. Then, with numbed hands, I caught him beneath the armpits and, after great efforts, hoisted him up beside me. For a minute we sat breathless in the cold air clinging to the coping, and then jumped a distance of twelve feet. We fell heavily on the hard ground in the woods outside the castle grounds. I was bruised and shaken and frightened. I stood leaning against a tree looking at Luteyn. Another minute passed in the falling snow.

'Let's go,' I said, and we began to climb towards the east, seeking the direction of Leisnig, a small town six miles away.

*

At ten o'clock the snow was falling less thickly and the moon showed us a way through the trees as we continued to climb towards the road to Leisnig. Beyond the trees we stumbled over frozen fields with hearts uplifted. The headlights of a car, yellow in the bright moonlight, turned in our direction. We lay flat in the snowdrifts till the lights swung towards the east. As we felt the hard surface of the road, I turned up the collar of my dark-blue jacket against the cold. I had left the warm green overcoat behind me buried with the rest of the uniform beneath a pile of leaves and snow. The blue jacket was made from an officer's uniform of the Chasseurs Alpins. Shorn of silver galons and badges it became a rough workman's coat of serviceable cloth. I was given it by a Jewish officer, Capitaine Boris, who sacrificed his smart uniform for my escape. Boris was an elderly business man, a reserve officer in the Chasseurs Alpins and a great patriot. Such was the splendid comradeship of Colditz.

On my head I wore a ski-cap made of blanket and my

Royal Air Force trousers were now turned down over my Army boots. From this moment Luteyn and I were Dutch electrical workers with papers permitting us to change our place of occupation from Leipzig to Ulm in south-western Germany. Leipzig was twenty-two miles from the castle. We planned to reach it by walking the six miles to Leisnig, and there to take an early workman's train. Foreign workers, it was said, were numerous in Leipzig and some were to be transferred to the south.

We had no papers for the journey to Leipzig. Success depended on our safe arrival at the main station for the south. Pausing a while beside the road, we recovered money, maps and papers from the containers concealed in our bodies and then trudged smartly along the road. After two hours we passed a row of cottages close to Leisnig and came to what appeared to be a barracks. A faint light shone from the entrance-gate and in the moonlight we saw a sentry. We stopped, turned from the road, and floundered through deep snow towards a belt of trees on higher ground. We stood there, sheltering among the trees against the sharp winds of the night. The ingenious Dutch officers in Colditz had acquired by bribery a time-table of the trains from Leisnig to Leipzig. We therefore knew that the first workmen's train was due to start at five o'clock. Three hours passed. It was too cold to talk. We waited silently for the train, looking towards the town and listening to the sound of shunting on the railway.

There was not a stir in all that crystal stillness as we climbed down the slope, broke through a hedge, and came back to the road. The road descended into a valley and, walking boldly down the main street to the station, we passed an early-morning traveller and exchanged greetings. There was peace in the little town with its spires and snow-covered roof-tops. I thought of an illustration to the children's tale *The Tailor of Gloucester*, where a lone figure walks through the sleeping city. We had half an hour to wait. There was no one at the station so we walked away to the outskirts of the town unnoticed.

When the train was due we came slowly back to the entrance of the station where a small group of German working people had collected at the gate. As is the custom, the travellers were not allowed on the platform until the train was due to start. We stood silently aside from the others, sheltering from the cold beside a wooden hut. When it was nearly five o'clock the doors opened, and the crowd surged forward to the ticket-office. We followed in their wake and Luteyn, who spoke the best German, stopped at the *guichet* and bought two workmen's tickets to Leipzig. I followed him on to the platform, where we stood apart from the others, men and women carrying small baskets or bags of tools.

The orange front light of an engine appeared. It was a scene of true romance. Here were we, escaped enemy prisoners-of-war, standing on the platform of the little station, mingling with ordinary people travelling to their daily work. The train, puffing with determination through the snow, halted and we climbed into a wooden carriage.

We were herded together in the semi-darkness of air-raid precautions. The warmth inside the carriage covered the windows with moisture so that I could hardly see the dawn. I bowed my head and dozed beside an old and evil-smelling market-woman. Suddenly I was awakened by a sharp kick on my shins and looked up in fear. I met the half-smiling eyes of Luteyn. He sat hunched in a short tight overcoat, his ski-cap on one side. Then I realized that I must have been talking English in my sleep. No one had noticed or even listened to my murmurs. I watched the thin, strained faces of the working-men as they dozed shoulder to shoulder, and saw the dawn slowly appear through the sweaty windows.

I felt ashamed that Luteyn was more alert and awake. He was strongly built with humorous grey eyes and long dark hair. He was a strong and buoyant character whose life was spent in laughter and good fellowship. Yet he had a Dutch quality of thoroughness which made him a great escaper. He had staying-power and resourcefulness, and his great advantage lay in his superior knowledge of Germany and its language, so that he could take each fence with boldness and aplomb. He had a gay, attractive manner of speaking which disarmed the enemy and saved us both in the many dangerous situations which were to follow. For my part, rebellious by temperament though I was, I found him easy to work with and we seldom argued with each other.

At six o'clock we drew into the great station of Leipzig. The travellers, woken by shrill whistles, began to yawn and swear in low exhausted voices. We looked around us and followed the crowd towards a barrier, where we gave up our tickets. There came upon me a sense of alarm and bewilderment. It was twenty months since I had seen the outside world, except for my adventures in the wild, desolate country of Poland. Here, among the silent crowds of people moving in the dim light of the station, I was aghast at my helplessness. I felt like a peasant come for the first time to a city, unable to comprehend the paraphernalia of civilization.

We wandered timidly round the station watching the indicators for a train to Ulm and found that no train left until 10.30 in the evening. It slowly dawned on us that we must stay in Leipzig with nowhere to shelter or sleep for many hours. We tried to find refreshment. Entering a tea-room we ordered coffee, supplied with a small envelope of saccharine. This was all we could obtain, for every other article of food required coupons. The coffee warmed us as we looked shyly at each other, smiling a little, and not daring to speak in any language. After paying for our coffee, we wandered to a waiting-room crowded with travellers, mostly poor, who sat among their luggage and children, silent and obedient. I looked at these victims of Hitler's war and felt a great pity. The hopelessness in their faces brought a stark realization of suffering. We had heard rumours of their plight in the camp; they were now confirmed beyond our belief. Musing, I took from my pocket a huge bar of Red Cross chocolate and began to eat.

A young woman with fierce hysterical eyes gazed at the chocolate as if she had seen a ghost. I stared back at her uncomprehending. She spoke to an old woman beside her and they looked at me in anger. Immediately the crowd near us began to talk in threatening whispers. I heard the word *Schokolade* many times. Luteyn turned to me and frowned angrily. Slowly realizing the danger of my position, I put the chocolate back in my pocket. I had committed a terrible blunder. Chocolate had been unknown to working Germans for many months. Goering himself may well have tasted little. We British prisoners were well supplied. To sit eating this forbidden delicacy in the waiting-room of a great station made one an object not only of envy but of deep suspicion. We rose awkwardly and walked out of the waiting-room into the town.

Leipzig at nine in the morning on 6 January 1942. The snow was cleared from the streets and there was a distant hum of traffic in the sunshine. Military vehicles sped by us filled with hard-looking men in steel helmets who ignored the civilians. The sidewalks were a mass of field-grey and the mauve-blue of the Luftwaffe. We stared into the shop-windows, gazing like children at expensive dresses and furs. Around us, stiff, bourgeois young men in uniform tapped their smart black boots on the pavement, as they stood before the shops. Blonde girls, in short skirts, looked up at the soldiers with fiercely possessive eyes and clutched them tightly.

We entered a big emporium and moved among the bright lights and dance music and tinsel finery. We watched the people strolling by the counters. The Germans were young, confident and hopeful, and we, mere beggars with a few bars of precious chocolate, had only our own high courage between us and the enemy on every side. Only a few sad civilians of an older generation, shabby and worn, crept among the counters like wraiths. The Nazi Revolution of Destruction was at hand.

We were bitterly disappointed to see no sign of bombing, yet the civilians looked hungry and unhappy. We
threaded our way through the crowd and came to a
square of gardens where a few old men and women
walked in the sunshine with their dachshunds. I could
read memories in their worn faces and their hatred of
Hitler's New Order. I sat beside Luteyn on a seat watching their slow, hopeless perambulation among the snow-
bound flowerbeds and shrubs. For me the months of
imprisonment were gone and past. I was a detached spec-
tator watching Life go by. New sights and sounds, fresh
and clear, came to me after the darkness of prison. Elderly
business men and lawyers with brief-cases under their
arms marched past muttering sombrely to each other. A
girl left the procession of Life and sat beside me.

She was young and blonde and plainly of the working
class. She looked at me sharply as she sat on the wooden
seat. She wore a torn old overcoat and her short tight skirt
was above her bare knees. She looked down at her shoes
with *ersatz* wooden heels and kicked at a heap of snow.
Her mouth was set in a hard determined line. I struggled
to look at her calmly but with an inwardly beating heart.
Her prominent blue eyes had ruthlessness.

'Good morning,' she said.

I dared not answer or risk conversation. She pouted.

'You are unsociable, my friend.'

I turned to see Luteyn had already risen from the seat
and was walking slowly away. I followed him in dismay
and embarrassment and, for a moment, turned towards
the girl. She was looking hard at us. I felt her blue eyes
watching, deep with suspicion and annoyance. We hurried away and wandered among the side streets of Leipzig
till it was noon.

A cinema in enemy territory is a fine hiding-place for
the fugitive. After a lunch of *ersatz* coffee we came to a
cheap stuffy cinema at the bottom of an arcade. Luteyn
bought the tickets. Our small stock of German marks was
enough for only the cheapest seats. We stood, obediently,

waiting for the performance, regimented by a commis-
sionaire. In a few minutes, we took our seats among German soldiers and sailors and their girls and waited for the
curtain, and, as the lights went out, a tall young German
officer came in alone and sat next to me.

We saw first on the programme a news-film of events in
Libya. Rommel, standing beside a staff car in the desert,
talking decisively; then excellent shots of panzers in
action and a British plane being shot down. Close-ups followed of a British pilot taken prisoner by the Germans
and waving encouragement to his friends still fighting in
the air. In my excitement I clutched the seat in front of
me and was rewarded by the occupant turning round with
a harsh whisper of protest.

The feelings of a prisoner who for many months has
been shut out from the war and accustomed only to the
crudest enemy propaganda are hard to describe. I could
have wept from joy. At least the war was not yet lost. In
the next part of the news-film there came a most shatter-
ing revelation. The scene was set in a Russian winter. Up
a long snow-bound hill German soldiers struggled against
the blizzard, dragging guns and vehicles. There were
photographs of frozen bodies and men's limbs swollen to
unrecognizable size with frost-bite. If Goebbels wanted to
impress the Germans with the sufferings of their troops
to inspire them to greater sacrifices at home, he hid no
detail of their hardships.

There was a shocked silence when the news-film came
to an end. The lights went up in the shabby hall while
martial music played from a cracked loud-speaker. Young
men and girls chanted Nazi songs and around us their
clear voices sounded in perfect harmony. Only the old
people were glum and quiet. The music changed to: 'We
are marching against England!'

For a moment, I caught my companion's eye and, with
a faint grin on our faces, Luteyn and I sang loudly with
the rest.

The remainder of the programme was a film set in early

nineteenth-century Germany. The heroine, a hard-faced
simpering creature, was surrounded by heavy Prussian
admirers. The scene which won the most applause was
that in which the witty girl took refuge in an earth closet
at the bottom of the garden to repel their advances. It was
a hut with two heart-shaped holes cut in the door to which
she pointed knowingly as she entered. The Germans
roared without restraint and we, unimpressed by their
lavatory humour, were constrained to do the same for fear
of detection.

In the early afternoon the snow began to fall again and
the streets of Leipzig seemed full of foreboding for us.
A policeman watched us, and followed stealthily until we
evaded him among dark alleyways. Working our way back
towards the big shops and the crowds, we came to another
cinema where there was an atmosphere of plush warmth,
antiseptic, and wurlitzer music. We saw the same news-
film again as we sat high in the gallery among more
German troops on leave. Then came a royal fanfare of
trumpets and Hermann Goering appeared on the screen
appealing for higher output for the war. He wore the grey
uniform in which I was later to see him in his cell at
Nuremberg, but with a lavish display of decorations. His
throaty voice rasped out propaganda to an audience
which remained quiet if respectful. When his vulgar
performance had lasted ten minutes there came shots of
goose-stepping battalions of Nazis and someone struck up
the *Horst Wessel Lied*. But the singing was cheerless and
half-hearted.

From the cinema we walked again into the blackout of
the city. The moon had not yet risen and only the soft
whiteness of the snow guided us through public gardens
to the main station. Often at corners of the streets we
caught the faint reflection of a policeman's polished helmet and edged away among the crowds or dodged the
trams to cross the street.

We came again to the station waiting-room and sat

there, tired and cold and anxious. The numerous passengers in the waiting-room, many poor and infirm, assembled for the night trains. Then came the men in uniform, elbowing all the civilians aside. I watched them closely. The bullying S.S. men, the clod-like infantry-men, and the pale and spectacled administrative clerks. All in uniform, they tramped over the gloomy station like locusts, demanding refreshment or newspapers or anything they wanted. Such is total war.

Luteyn bought the tickets to Ulm. We had decided to change there and, if all went well, to take tickets to the Swiss frontier. At the barrier of the platform for the train to the south, military police stood to check the soldiers but there seemed no control of civilians. We waited beside the train before it started, preferring to find standing room than risk conversation in a compartment. As it began to move we climbed the steps of a carriage and stood in the corridor.

The compartment opposite was occupied by a single figure in the uniform of the S.S. I could see the man as we stood outside, a great ape-like person with a heavy jaw. His uniform was new and spotless and he crossed his legs which were in fine black boots as he read a newspaper with screaming red and black headlines. I caught only the word 'Rommel'. So that he should not watch us, we moved into the shadow at the end of the corridor and looked into the darkness where only a few pin-points of light showed the effective blackout of the city. The train jolted over the points and gathered speed with piercing whistles. Above its rattle I heard the door of the compartment open, and turning my head saw the big S.S. man standing in the dorway. His hands were on each side of the entrance door and he spoke to us in a soft voice.

'Are you Jews?'

'Certainly not. We are Dutch,' replied Luteyn.

'Good. Come in and sit here. This compartment was reserved, but my friends are not coming.'

We took our seats beside the big man who spoke very slowly to us, using simple phrases. His friendliness alarmed me.

'Where are you travelling?'

'To Ulm.'

'Why?'

'We are Dutch electrical workers transferred there from Leipzig.'

Luteyn was doing the talking. He had his genuine Dutch passport ready to produce in an emergency. Then the man turned to me and his stupid eyes examined my face, searching for something he did not understand.

'You are Dutch, too?'

'Yes.'

'How are things in Holland?'

'We have not been there for some months. We have been in Leipzig since the summer.'

It was Luteyn who spoke. The S.S. man turned to me.

'I am going to Munich,' he said unexpectedly. 'Then I go to Vienna for a conference.'

We nodded politely and the conversation stopped. Men and women passengers were walking up and down the corridor and were soon invited into the reserved compartment. They bowed respectfully to the high S.S. officer, took their seats and gave our shabby clothes a scornful stare.

There was no further conversation about Holland. I was glad of this. My sole visit to that country had been the journey in the barge up the River Waal to Germany as a prisoner in 1940. As soon as the passengers began to snore, Luteyn stayed awake according to our arrangement and I slept for a few hours until his turn came to sleep. I was awakened by a loud tapping on the glass of the door and two military policemen looked in. They checked the passes of the soldiers and even scrutinized the documents of the S.S. officer. They stopped for a moment to stare at our queerly tailored clothes. I wondered for a moment whether they would recognize the colour of R.A.F.

trousers, but the S.S. officer intervened importantly.

'These are foreign workers (*Fremdarbeiter*). Dutch,' he said with conviction.

The military police hesitated, then turned away as if suspicious civilians were nothing to do with their department. Now it was Luteyn's turn to sleep and I listened to the endless rattle of the express as we passed through Plauen and Hof and sped southwards into Bavaria. Lifting the blind, I glimpsed the snow outside or studied the sleeping faces in the dim light of the compartment. Towards four in the morning the train began to slow and came to a halt amid the sounds of a large station. I woke Luteyn, rose and stretched my limbs, and walked over to the doorway. In the gloom there was shouting and the bustle of passengers. I leant out of the window and saw on a sign before me the word 'Regensburg'.

It was here that we were due to change for the train to Ulm and we stepped on to the platform in the sharp cold.

'Good-bye, Dutchmen,' said the S.S. man pompously from inside the compartment.

We went into a waiting-room and sat down at a table. Passengers with their luggage came with us, and promptly fell asleep with their heads resting on the tables. Opposite, a man in railway police uniform stared at us in unfriendly fashion. We did not wait for him to speak but walked out again on to the platform and entered the booking-hall. We sat on the floor with other travellers leaning against a wooden partition. A man and a girl smelling of spiced sausages and garlic lay near us in a close embrace.

When the train to Ulm had filled with passengers it left the station in a cloud of steam and we found seats in a compartment, again taking turns to keep awake. When dawn came I saw that we were travelling through the wintry countryside of Bavaria. The snow, collecting along the edges of the windows, framed a picture of white roofs and towers set in the hollows of the hills. Sometimes beside the track an *Autobahn* stretched like a tape threading through the forests and long convoys of military vehicles moved into the mist.

At nine on the second morning of the escape the train drew into Ulm and we left it, making our way towards the booking office. Luteyn calmly asked the girl for two tickets to Singen on the Swiss frontier. She frowned and my heart began to sink. She asked for papers and we showed our papers to her.

'I must fetch the railway police. Stay here.'

We did not wish to run away, hoping that our papers would satisfy them. A fat, red-faced railway policeman in his dark-blue uniform asked us why we wished to go to the frontier zone. Luteyn explained that we were due to begin work in Ulm on the morrow and wished to spend a short vacation. The policeman, looking baffled, released us and we started to leave the station, walking across the big square in front. There was a shout behind us.

'Come back, gentlemen! I want to speak to you again.'

The policeman took us to an office in the goods-yard where a thin, tight-lipped German railway police lieutenant sat at a desk. He examined our false papers with bewilderment. It appeared to me that the writing on it did not make sense to him. I could hardly stop myself from laughing as he lifted them to the light, looking, no doubt, for water marks. He was, however, impressed by Luteyn's Dutch passport and there seemed no inkling in his mind that we were escaped prisoners-of-war.

'I don't understand these men at all,' he said helplessly. 'Take them to the Labour Office. I wish someone would control these foreign workers more efficiently.'

We walked across the square outside the station escorted by another policeman with a revolver. We chatted gaily in German, complimenting the man on the beauties of the town of Ulm. He was flattered and asked about our own country of Holland. So much did we win his confidence that when we reached the State Labour Office, where men in brown uniforms with spades stood guard at the entrance, he bade us walk up the steps on our own,

saying he would wait for us. His parting words were:
'You speak good German. Go and report to the office on
the first floor and I shall wait for you here.'

Smiling to ourselves and hardly able to believe our good
fortune, we climbed to the top floor of the building and it
was not long before we discovered some stairs on the far
side from the entrance. Hurrying down them we left by
another door. Avoiding the policeman and the guards with
spades, we made for the back streets of Ulm, and Luteyn
bought a map of the surrounding country in a small shop.

The cold had now become intense and, walking beyond
the suburbs of Ulm, we left the snow-capped roofs of the
university town behind us and hurried towards the town
of Laupheim. It was nearly dusk when we reached the
market-square and, asking the way to the station, we took
tickets to Stockach, a village as near to the Swiss frontier
as we dared to go. The country folk on the platform
watched us in silence as we sat upon a bench sleepily waiting for the train. When it arrived we entered a wooden
compartment too tired to be able to take turns to stay
awake. The train jolted on into the night. We wakened
only at the sound of a halt, and after passing the village of
Pfullendorf we reached Stockach about nine in the evening.

Of Stockach I only remember white cottages in the
moonlight and a doubtful station-master watching us as
we walked into the hills hoping to reach the frontier town
of Singen when the moon went down and the frontier was
in darkness. The road began to rise steeply through the
forests and great banks of snow were on either side of
us. Even by two o'clock in the morning we still had
many miles to go, struggling along the icy road as the
moon began to wane. The road slowly descended towards
Singen.

It seemed hopeless to try to cross the frontier that night
and we determined to look for somewhere to hide until
the following evening. At five o'clock on the morning of 8
January, we were still moving towards Singen. Lights

showed ahead of us in the roadway and to our tired eyes
they seemed welcoming and kind. Then the figures of four
men appeared. They were woodcutters walking to work
from Singen. They hailed us and we wished them good
morning. Something about us surprised them.

'Are you Poles?' said one of them.

'Yes,' replied Luteyn.

'I don't believe it,' said another. 'Poles are not allowed
out of their camp at five in the morning.'

Evidently there was a Polish labour camp in the neighbourhood. The four woodcutters looked startled and un-
decided. As for me, I was near to surrender. My feet
seemed to be frozen in my boots as if in blocks of ice. I
hardly cared that we had come so far only to be recaptured. I could only think of warm fires and beds.

'Go, Hans, fetch the police,' said the oldest woodcutter.
The man called Hans, who wheeled a bicycle, mounted it
and rode off towards Singen. The remainder confronted
us uncertainly. They did not try to detain us but stood
irresolute and dumb. We suddenly realized that they were
frightened of us. Without a word we dashed to the side of
the road and into the forest, running in the snow until we
sank exhausted. My breath came painfully and my head
began to swim. I could not look at the whiteness around
me without pain. We rose to our feet after a minute and
began to move across a clearing. There was no sign of the
woodcutters. As I walked there came over me a kind of
delirium between sleep and waking. I thought that I was
on some parade ground in England. I felt a figure beside
me and turned to see my old Colonel marching in the
snow in his uniform and field boots. I spoke to him and
addressed him respectfully.

'What the hell?' said Luteyn.

'It's all right,' I said ashamed.

Luteyn grunted impatiently, and a few paces across the
clearing we came to a large wooden hut surrounded by a
fence. There was the outline of a pathway, shrubs and
flower beds in the snow, and beside the hut were beehives.

We walked up to the hut and tried the doors which were all locked, but a small window in the wall was open. We lifted ourselves in and staggered crazily around the hut in the faint light of dawn. There was no sound of life. We found a kitchen and two rooms in one of which there was a bed. Tired and faint, we lay together on the bed in the intense cold and with an old blanket over us fell into a deep sleep, not waking until the afternoon.

When we awoke there had been another heavy fall of snow which luckily concealed our footsteps leading to the hut. From outside it seemed that we could hear the far-off sound of dogs and we got ready to escape into the woods. But as the hours passed no one came in sight and the sound of barking grew faint. Searching the hut, we found, in one corner of the kitchen, spades and shovels, and hanging behind the door, two long white coats evidently used by the bee-keeper.

According to our map, we were in the middle of a forest, two or three miles from Singen. We planned, therefore, to leave the hut at dusk and walk along the road to the town. West of the town and to the south lay woods through which ran the road and railway line to Schaffhausen in Switzerland. At some points the road formed the frontier between Switzerland and Germany.

Shortly before five o'clock on this afternoon of the eighth of January, we shouldered spades, and carrying the two white coats under our arms we cut through the forest to the road to Singen. For more than a mile we saw no one on the road, then the lights of bicycles came towards us and a voice called 'Halt'. in the glow of the bicycle lamps I could see two boys in the uniform of the Hitler Youth, each armed with truncheons. I felt no fear of them. Refreshed by sleep, I was determined they should not stop us. The boys spoke in a hectoring fashion.

'What are your names and where are you going?'

'We are Westphalians working in the neighbourhood and we are going back to our lodgings in Singen,' said the resourceful Luteyn. This was a good choice of disguise for the Dutch accent resembles that of the Westphalians. The boys seemed doubtful.

'What is wrong?' I said, trying to imitate Luteyn's accent.

'We have been told to look for two British prisoners who have escaped and are thought to be trying to cross the frontier tonight.'

We both laughed.

'They won't get far,' said Luteyn, 'it is much too cold for prisoners of war!'

The boys laughed uncertainly and rode off towards Singen and as we reached the town they turned again and came towards us. One said to the other:

'There are the Westphalians.'

As this conversation was taking place in the road I reflected that these boys alone stood between us and freedom. Afterwards I asked Luteyn what was in his mind.

'For me to kill one with my spade and you the other,' he said, 'what did you intend to do?'

'Exactly the same.'

We passed through Singen in the black-out, without incident, and skirting a great dark mound which seemed to be a slag heap we set off southwards through the wood, marching upon a compass bearing to the frontier. At two o'clock in the morning on the ninth of January we crossed the railway to Schaffhausen about two miles north of a point where the road forms the frontier. It was a fine, cold night and the moon was full. Wrapping ourselves in the white bee-keeper's coats for camouflage, we slowly advanced until we could see a gap in the trees and lights of cars passing along the road ahead. Not far to the east were voices and lanterns and what appeared to be a frontier post.

For an hour we crouched in a ditch beside the road and watched a sentry pacing up and down only forty yards away. Here we ate the remainder of our chocolate and swallowed a few mouthfuls of snow. Black clouds began to hide the moon and the cold increased with a rising wind. I watched the German buttoning the collar of his overcoat and saw him move towards the sentry-box beside the frontier barrier.

Before us across the roadway was a smooth plain of snow surrounded by distant trees. Beyond this few hundred yards of open No Man's Land was freedom. At half past four in the morning the sentry turned away from us. I could no longer hear his footsteps against the wind.

'Do you agree to cross now?' said Luteyn.

'This is the moment,' I whispered.

We crawled from the ditch and across the road still dressed in our white coats. We continued crawling across the field in front of us, ploughing on hands and knees through the deep snow. After what seemed an eternity we rose to our feet, and surged forward into Switzerland. ...

* * *

... Yes, they had reached Switzerland, a neutral country surrounded by the Germans. They were safe, but a soldier cannot fight in a neutral country. How Airey Neave escaped again from Switzerland and crossed Vichy France to Spain and from there to England is another story.

CHAPTER SEVEN

Crossing the Border

GEORGE MILLAR is the author of two exciting books about life among French Resistance workers in the last war. He was captured by the Germans in the Western Desert in 1942 and handed over to the Italians who took him to a prison camp in Italy. Later he was transferred to a monastery camp at Padula from which he made several attempts to escape. As a punishment he, like Airey Neave, was sent to a 'naughty boys' camp' – Campo V at Gavi, which like Colditz was an ancient fortress.

George Millar had not long been in Campo V before Italy capitulated and the Germans took over the Allied prisoners. With the new guards who did not know the fort, escape attempts were redoubled and when the Germans gave the order to leave for Germany in half an hour Millar hid in the hope of being left behind. But the Germans were very thorough in their search and he was discovered and sent to Germany with the others.

On the journey to a permanent camp in Germany George Millar and another prisoner, Wally Binns, jumped from the train and made contact with a party of French prisoners from a working camp. These Frenchmen, who were employed on the railway in Munich, fed and clothed the two escapers and stowed them away in a train destined for Strasbourg on the French border. In Strasbourg Binns became separated from Millar who was befriended by a group of anti-German Italians. They fitted him out with clothes and false papers and passed him on to Paris.

After more adventures and many narrow escapes George Millar made contact with a British agent working with the Resistance and was passed along an escape line to Perpignan on the Spanish border. He made two false starts (one with a guide named Pedro who was later

killed) before setting out with a band of American evaders
to cross the Pyrenees into Spain. It was January, the worst
time for such a mountain crossing, and the American airmen were out of training through lying hidden for so
long. ...

* * *

... Eight o'clock the following night found us once more
at the corner of the ploughed field outside Perpignan
where we had met Pedro.

The guide this time was a small, wizened man with a
very high voice that had a hollow, conch-like tone. He
spoke only the Catalan tongue, with a sprinkling of
French, but thanks to my sketchy knowledge of Italian I
clearly understood him. There was another man with him,
a tall husky fellow who smelled strongly of wine. This
man carried an enormous rucksack which clinked when
he covered rough ground, and which probably contained
contraband in the shape of bottles of alcohol or perfume.

Our little guide gave no melodramatic instructions with
regard to dogs. He only asked me to advise the Americans
to relax as much as possible while they walked and to
forget that they were covering the ground, because from
then until dawn they would be walking all the time.

'How can we forget? – ask him that,' said Charlie.

'Think of God, or a woman,' replied the old man.

'Ask him how we cross the River Tech.'

'We will cross nearer the sea than you did on your
attempt with the ill-fated Pedro, and you will see that it
is not difficult. Only I shall demand absolute silence,
especially on the far bank, which is apt to be closely
guarded.'

He set off, padding smoothly in *espadrilles* down paths
which we had followed with Pedro. If anything, this man
was more cautious than Pedro, and we reached the first
river in good time without causing a dog to bark. The
Americans were thoroughly broken in by this time, and

they were walking well, although I knew that their feet must hurt. Mine did.

The guide took off his shoes at the river, and waded in barefoot. I was glad, because I had earlier decided to do that in order to preserve my boots and make the walking more comfortable between streams. Also the level of this stream was much lower than it had been with Pedro.

He would not let us sit down for more than two or three minutes at a time.

'When you rest too much your legs get stiff. Just sit long enough to relax all the muscles. Then walk on. That is the way.'

He himself seemed to flow across the ground with tiny, smooth steps. Like Pedro, he carried a long stick. He said that he was fifty-five, but the assistant whispered: 'The old one is vain, very vain, and likes to think that he is still young. He is sixty-five.'

This time we reached the north bank of the Tech before midnight. The river looked wider and shallower at this point. The guide asked us to follow him at thirty-yard intervals in case the enemy saw us and began shooting. The water was terribly cold and the stones cut our feet. I counted 290 steps on the way across.

We sat down in dense undergrowth on the south bank and were drying ourselves and putting on trousers and boots and socks when a terrible shouting broke out. After a moment we realized what had happened. The old man had crossed first and had arrived farther down-stream. His assistant had followed him and all of us had followed the assistant. Now the old man (who had demanded absolute silence) could not find us, and was screaming insults at the assistant, who answered in kind.

When we linked up with him ten minutes later three of the Americans had got lost. There was more shouting until they arrived.

We walked on into the forbidden zone. We had not gone far when the old guide stopped so suddenly that we all cannoned into him. Three figures were crossing a field

towards us. In a flurry the guide turned, barged his way
through the Americans, and dashed back along the path
we had been following. We all followed him in a mad rush
for some 300 yards, when he cut off to the left down another track. He made a big circle, and soon we were on
our original path.

By this time the Pyrenees were coming closer. But the
closeness was deceptive. To get to the mountains it was
necessary for us to act as counters in some diabolical game
of 'Snakes and Ladders'. The rungs in our ladder were
rivers which had to be waded or roads which had to be
stalked and then crawled across. The guide was most careful with the roads. At one of them he turned to me and
whispered : 'I once lost a bottle of Napoleon brandy here.
A German bicycle patrol came round that corner just as I
was crossing. I ran so fast that I left the bottle behind.'

'Was it real Napoleon brandy?'

'Of course not. It never is. But it was marked clearly on
the bottle, and it would have fetched a Napoleon price in
Spain. I won it at bowls : the bottle I mean. The brandy I
had put in from something a little newer and more shape-
ly in the way of bottles.'

We began climbing when we came to the olive-groves.
It was hard work on the terraced ground. Then we left the
olives and climbed up woodland paths. At one of our short
halts I took off Pedro's oiled silk coat, which I had carried
in a roll over one shoulder. I took it off to make a seat on
the damp ground. And when we went on I forgot it. That
forgetfulness might have cost me my life.

At 5 a.m. we cleared the woods, and the bare mountains
were above us. The guide told us to sleep in some bushes
while he and his assistant went to a cottage farther up the
hill. We had been walking for nine hours. All of us went
to sleep among the sparse bushes and were awakened by
strange noises like the barking of a small lap-dog. They
were made by the guide.

'More climbing now,' he said. 'Fill your water bottles
passing the cottage. I apologize for leaving you outside.

But there are often German patrols here. If they found us they would take us for visiting shepherds. If they found you they would kill everybody, burn the cottage, torture my friend's wife and eat his sheep.'

At the back door of the cottage a thin woman wearing a jacket of sheepskin and trousers of some soft leather filled our bottles with earthy-tasting water. Then we went on climbing up a narrow path over and through big rocks. Often tough thorn-bushes closed behind the man in front, lashing those who followed with tearing branches. It was bitterly cold, although we could see a strong-looking sun beginning to rise over the sea horizon. We were tired, but would have liked to go on climbing to keep warm. At eight o'clock, however, the guide said that it was getting dangerously light.

He shepherded us into the thorn-scrub below the mountain path.

'You will enjoy several hours of sunshine here today,' he said. 'Tell your friends that if they get a good sleep and eat solidly in the evening, they should be in Spain tomorrow morning. Warn them not to drink too much water, because that is bad for crossing the mountains, and this crossing is never easy in winter. My friend and I are going back to sleep the day away in the cottage below. Au revoir, and don't move about. That big house down there is the headquarters of the German frontier guards. They occasionally send patrols over the hills during the daytime, and some of them have dogs.'

I faithfully transmitted his instructions to the Americans. They had borne up bravely all through the night. Now they seemed to have an enormous thirst. Before the end of the morning all our water had been drunk. I attributed their thirst to their unfit condition. The one we had called Clark Gable looked quite ill. He lay near me, heavily asleep, his face a greenish-grey against his mossy pillow.

The air at that height was cold and crisp, even when the sun was on our hill-face. A heavy coastal battery of German guns had firing practice during the afternoon. The shells fell a long way out to sea. The guns themselves were sited nearly a mile inland.

From our high resting-place we could see all our little mile-stones of the past three weeks stretched out below us in a huge relief map. We could see Perpignan, the first river, the Tech, and the subsequent rivers. There were the two roads making a wishbone forking towards us from Perpignan. And down below us, where the hills ran into the sea, lay Port Vendres, such a dramatic little port in the Spanish Civil War. Pale wisps of wood smoke rose from its distant chimneys against the pale winter blue of the Mediterranean.

Although I could not sleep, I ate all that I carried and lay as relaxed as possible on the slope. At the beginning of this attempt I had not had enough money to buy provisions. I had left Perpignan with two tins of French Army meat, two small loaves and one of the cakes that Serge and I had bought for the second attempt. The Americans wondered to see me finish my provisions, but I told them that it was better to have a full stomach before we set off on the worst part of the journey than to save up for a meal when we were across.

Within myself I felt an immense exultation, for I was convinced that in twenty-four hours I should be safe from the Germans.

The guides arrived promptly at five, but we had to wait until six before the old man considered it dark enough for us to begin climbing. The early going was good on a bare, rocky path.

We stopped at a spring to fill all our water-bottles. While we were there, three of the Americans got down on their knees and lapped at the water like dogs. When he saw this the guide stood on a rock above them and jabbered at them in his high voice.

'Bad, bad, bad. Water is bad on the hills. Much better drink wine.' He offered his wine-skin, but nobody felt like drinking wine.

The guide now wore a kind of fluffy woollen helmet,

which covered all but his sharp nose and his restless eyes. He led us up small paths made perhaps by goats, perhaps by men. Sometimes he left the paths to slither across steep hill-faces. He explained that he did this to avoid German posts which were often placed on the high ground.

A bitter north wind cut into our backs. I deeply regretted the loss of Pedro's coat, for even with the climbing I could not keep warm.

'This wind is the *tramontane*,' said the guide. 'It will get much worse and it will bring snow.'

'Tonight?'

'When else?'

We had been walking and climbing for two hours and a half when we stopped to rest in a small dark pine-wood. All of the Americans were extremely tired and were feeling their feet.

'Of what do they speak?' asked the guide.

'They speak of the possibilities of victory next year,' I lied.

'I know that they are talking about their tired limbs. That is because they have drunk too much water. Tell them they drink no more water. Let them ask for wine. Eh, *amigo*, pass your skin.'

His companion passed the wine with some grumbling, and this time we all drank, including the guide himself.

'Tell your comrades to have courage, for with courage man conquers all,' he continued with a chuckle. 'Tell them I lost my brother here one year ago.'

My translation of his morbid injunction was met by hollow groans from the Americans, for their extreme fatigue could not yet prevent them from laughing at everything, including themselves.

After this rest we slithered down a hill so steep that it just failed to be a precipice. At the bottom was a raging torrent which had to be crossed by leaping from boulder to boulder. Two of the Americans, the Chauve Souris and Gable, fell heavily but followed on. The Chauve Souris had been lagging for some time.

We had not, it appeared, traversed the main block of the mountains, and we turned west, paralleling what the guide said was the last ridge before the Spanish frontier. This paralleling was the most arduous work of all, for there were continual high ridges running across our path so that we were like some infinitely small animals climbing in and out of the squares of a giant honeycomb. Now, too, we were walking in snow, although it was not deep enough to present much of a handicap.

I explained to the Americans that we were working along the high ridge on our left, keeping well below the summit because there were German frontier posts and patrols there, and that the guide would turn up it at a place where he knew it would be safe to cross. But an exhausted man finds it difficult to reason and easy to complain. Our line grew more and more strung out. The guide frequently had to halt to allow the Chauve Souris, Charlie and Gable to catch up. I would have liked to push on much faster, for it was the cold, not fatigue, that worried me. My back was freezing in the *tramontane*.

Charlie told me at one point that he had seen cows and I thought he must be going mad.

'Can't you tell a cow from a goat?'

But a little later I saw them myself, a large half-wild herd of small cows. And I suddenly remembered Laurence talking with Alpine scorn of the Pyrenees as '*Montagnes des vaches*'.

The blizzard became so bad and so heavy with wet snow that the guide led us into a small cave in the hillside. Here there was just room for all of us to rest, squeezed together and dripping water from our soaking clothes. The others smoked. Some shepherd had left a crude oil-lamp there. The guide lit it and I was able to look at my companions.

My heart would have bled for them had I been less intent on surmounting this final obstacle. Except for Fritz, who seemed to thrive on the work, they were plainly in the last stages of exhaustion.

Gable, the biggest and toughest-looking of us all, told me that he could not go much farther.

'Why not?'

'My legs are passing out on me.'

The Chauve Souris and Charlie seemed to be equally miserable. The Trapper was little better, although he complained less since he came from tougher, less citified stock.

They begged me to ask the guide if we could either stop there for the night or if he could take us by a quick, direct route to the frontier.

'If we wait here we shall die from the cold,' he answered. 'I must take you by the proper route. Tell them it is only one hour from here to the frontier if this blizzard dies down, as I think it will very soon.'

The going was more difficult when we started out again, and the Americans, excepting Fritz, were slower than ever. At one short halt, when the guide left us for a moment to look at the crest of the ridge, Gable lay down on a patch of snow and shouted: 'I can't go on, I can't go on.'

Fritz and I went back to him.

'My legs have given out,' he said. 'Ask the old man if he can give us five minutes' rest.'

'Certainly not,' said the guide indignantly. 'Tell him to be a man.'

He noticed that some of them were stuffing lumps of snow into their mouths. For although it was deathly cold and eerie and wet on the mountain-top, we were parched with thirst. 'If you drink like that you will die,' shrieked the guide.

So we moved on slowly to what he said was the last slope. It was very steep, and the snow was deeper and softer. The four weak Americans were in grave difficulties. Fritz and I had to divide all that they carried between us. They struggled bravely at the slope. But there were times when they all lay down in the bitter cold, and we despaired of ever getting them over.

The guide and his assistant did nothing to help. They only got angry, screaming at us and jabbering in fast, incomprehensible Catalan. I have never given so many encouraging discourses in such a short time. They sounded false to me, up there in the whistling wind, and they had little effect on Gable, who, poor soul, was now almost unconscious with pain from his powerful legs. The others somehow, little by little, managed to drag themselves up. The Trapper and Charlie hung together and kept going inch by inch with a rest every few yards. The Chauve Souris, brave spirit, negotiated the whole slope on hands and knees. This left the two of us to deal with Gable.

At first he lay on the snow saying: 'I can't, I tell you.'

Fritz gave him a 'You're doing fine, boy,' piece of nonsense.

He responded by walking with our help for twenty yards, then he sank down again. While he lay there Fritz talked to him and the Chauve Souris passed us, crawling. I was reminded of the hare and the tortoise and burst out laughing. The old guide chose this moment to come back and scream that this was the most dangerous part of the whole trip.

'Kick him into activity. Does he want to kill us all?'

'Ask him to let me rest here for a half-hour, just a half-hour,' moaned Gable, his voice trailing away slowly in a sleepy drawl.

'Rest?' yelled the guide (I had not dared to translate the 'half-hour' request). 'Rest, I'll give him rest, the pig.'

He danced down the slope and slapped Gable sharply several times on the face. This roused the poor man, and, supported by Fritz and me, he did another fifty yards.

Then he collapsed finally. Fritz and I tried everything we could think of, praise, vilification, encouragement, massage, wine from the Spaniard's skin, alcohol from Fritz's little bottle. The big man would not move. Tears oozed from his eyes.

'Leave me here to die, you fellows. I can't go on.'

The Chauve Souris passed us again, going bravely on hands and knees. I pointed him out to Gable.

The only comment this drew was: 'Just give me a half-hour and I think I'll be O.K.'

Charlie and the Trapper were nearly over the ridge. The guide and his assistant were ahead of them. The Chauve Souris was nearing the top.

Fritz and I managed to raise big Gable. He sagged. We each got a shoulder under him, twining his heavy thick arms like dead pythons round our straining necks. We gathered ourselves together and managed to stagger up to the top and over the ridge. He kept saying maddening things like: 'Let me be, fellows. Just let me rest.'

The summit of the ridge was narrow and smooth: below it lay a few yards of scrub, then stunted pine-trees. The three of us fell in a heap. I lay there with the blood pounding in my ears.

When I picked myself up Gable again was asking for 'a half-hour's rest'.

Fritz and I worked on him. We ran the full gamut at first-aid, we talked to him lovingly, angrily. Nothing happened. The other three lay around us in the scrub, offering advice. The two Spaniards stood sourly under a tree, watching us. Occasionally the guide hurled piping invective at us. At last he came over to look at the prostrate giant.

'The Spanish frontier is thirty minutes' easy walking from here,' he said. 'We go down to the burn below us, over it, up on the other side, and then across the plateau. At the far edge of the plateau is the frontier, and you can see the lights of the Spanish town of Figueras from there.'

'Why don't you leave me, then?' said Gable. 'I'll make it when my legs get some strength back in them.'

'We won't leave you. You must come with us now. It's too cold to lie here.'

'I'll cover myself with leaves. See,' he began to scrabble leaves over his legs. 'After an hour or two I'll go on down to Spain. Now I got to get some rest. . . .'

'Enough of this foolery,' screamed the guide. 'I have been taking men across all this winter and I never saw such women. This is the worst part. Sooner or later Germans will pass here. Are you all going to throw your chance away for one weakling?'

He sudenly darted on Gable.

'I will *make* you go on,' he shouted. Before we could stop him he seized two handfuls of Gable's black hair and began to bash his big head against a tree-trunk. Gable only moaned gently.

'I don't care what you do to me. I can't go on.'

When I had translated the guide's remarks about German patrols to him he only replied: 'What do I care about Germans? My legs hurt so badly. Please go on without me. I'll be O.K. I see the way. You none of you'll make it if you take me along. It's the only hope, to leave me. When I've rested I'll go down into Spain. . . .'

After all the ground that had been covered I could practically see the Spanish frontier. After the help of Wally Binns, the French prisoners, the Strasbourg café plotters, Ramon and Alban, Greta, Scherb, Dolores, Pascal, La Pepette, Xavier, Elizabeth, Clément, Laurence, Serge, Estève, Cartelet – after all that I was stuck here, almost within jumping distance of the frontier. Stuck, stuck, stuck! Because one American had been too lazy to do three deep knee bends each day that he was hidden up in Paris. Was my duty to this man, or to all that lay behind me and all that lay ahead?

I could not decide. I asked Fritz.

'I reckon we should leave him, as he asks. He may make it in the morning. If we stop here it may mean all of us get lost.'

I asked the Trapper, Charlie, and the Chauve Souris. They were all of the same opinion as Fritz. By this time the guide, who did not understand what this talk was about, was screaming: 'To perdition with you all, you bunch of women! I am going on. I will not throw myself away for you. . . .'

We covered Gable's body with leaves and left him what food and wine remained. We showed him the road to the frontier again.

The others moved off. He had relaxed, and looked much better now that he knew he was to be allowed to rest. When I was hurrying after the others, I bumped into a man in the darkness.

'Who is it?'

'It's me,' said the Chauve Souris. 'Listen, Lieutenant. I was in the same house with him for six months in Paris. I'm going to stay with him. Furthermore, my legs are just about all in too, and I would be a drag on the rest of the party. I could never make the frontier tonight. We'll go on down together in the daylight. See you in Spain. . . .'

'Keep each other awake,' I told him. 'It's too cold, dangerously cold, to go to sleep. If you go to sleep you may never wake. Drink all the wine and eat the food. Rub each other's legs and get on down as soon as you feel you can move. I'm glad you're staying with him. It's a good thing to do. A decent thing. . . .' But already we had separated in the wood, and I was running down towards the burn, after the others.

The Trapper and Charlie were both in a bad way, and the effort of carrying Gable had taken a lot out of Fritz and me. We worked our way slowly up the wooded slope beyond the burn. There seemed to be a numbness in my legs. The guide was nervous and ill at ease. He repeatedly hissed at us to be silent or to hurry.

At last we came out on the plateau. It looked unnatural, like the face of the moon. The bitter wind swept across it, bludgeoning us forward, stabbing us forward. The guide nudged me and pointed to a kind of hillock at the far edge of the plateau.

'Keep that on your left hand,' he said. 'It marks the Spanish frontier. But you must make them run across here. We are in full view. It's not far. Look. Only 300 metres.'

He and the other Spaniard began to run away in front of us.

'Run,' I shouted. 'That's the frontier. Run. Run.'

The Trapper and Fritz ran on. Charlie was too tired. He stumbled after them. A wild exaltation gripped me, filled me, maddened me.

'Just 300 yards now, Charlie boy,' I shouted at him. 'Run with me.'

'I can't.'

'Run. Run. Run.'

I took him by the hand and pulled him as you might an unwilling child. The pair of us broke into a shambling trot. I pulled and the wind pushed. Charlie responded nobly. Our speed increased. We crossed the plateau; and suddenly we were running away with ourselves as we dropped over the edge of the plateau – into Spain.

*

But were we in Spain?

It was true that far below us, beyond the slope of the hills, stretched a great plain with splashes of light on it from towns and villages, startling splashes to eyes accustomed to war-time darkness. Louis had warned me, however, that we could not be certain that we were in Spain until we had actually descended to the plain itself. He had also hinted that the Spanish frontier guards might hand over to the Germans anybody whom they captured actually on the frontier.

When we stopped at a spring to fill our water-bottles I realized for the first time that I had seriously twisted my left knee, possibly when we had fallen with Gable. It was difficult to stand up again.

The spring was high up in the hills. I had doubts about my ability to walk far.

'How far to the farm?' I asked.

'A good fifteen kilometres [nine miles],' replied the guide.

'Is it certain that we are in Spain?'

'Certain. This is your first trip. I have been crossing these mountains for twenty-six years. But we must walk on, and fast, because here in Spain I am in more danger than in France. And you are all in danger too, at any rate in danger of going to Miranda jail and having your heads shaved and catching a dose of the pox.'

'I'd a hell of a lot rather catch that than keep on walking,' said Charlie when I had translated. But they did keep on, he and the Trapper, although their feet were raw and they were nearly dropping. Crossing the frontier seemed to have given them a second wind, whereas for me there was emptiness and pain. True, every fifty yards I told myself that I was FREE, but my whole body seemed to be sagging, and the pain in my knee made me gasp for rest. After a time the guide noticed how lame I was, and he bound the knee up tightly with a crêpe bandage.

Descending the hills on a good, wide, stony track, the *tramontane* came whistling down into our backs again, cutting into my kidneys. Despite the labour of walking, I was desperately cold and shivery. I imagined that I was sickening for some illness. Through the short temper and unreasonableness of fatigue we became very angry with the guide and his companion.

At one point, just before leaving the hills for the plain, the two of them dumped us in a small wood and went off 'To see if there were any of the Guardia Civil in the neighbourhood.' They came back when we had shivered for a miserable hour, and we were positive that although they said that they had found no sign of the Guardia Civil they had certainly found some good fellowship and much liquor, for of the latter they both smelled strongly.

The provident Spaniards had refuelled their large wine-skins, and the farther we progressed the better-tempered they became. They were generous with their skins and I drank freely of the wine, which had a tart, resinous tang that murdered thirst.

When we were on the plain the little man drove straight on for a time and then turned east towards the sea.

Usually we were on tracks or small roads, but he avoided villages, and there were more icy streams to ford. The walk seemed endless.

It was 5 a.m. when we arrived in a large village and the Spaniards pushed us into an old cow-shed.

'Wait here, please,' the guide said. 'There is a sale of wine in this village and I can assure you that it is a village famous for its wine.'

'But you cannot ask us to wait here. The floor is one metre deep in dung.'

'Dung does not bite. And we go to buy wine not only for ourselves but also for you.'

'Let us accompany you.'

'My friend, you would have me hanged. But listen. Here I will meet my son, who will take the message to have you met by your friends from the British Consulate in Barcelona.'

To pass the two hours that we waited in the dung we ate a tin of sardines which Charlie carried in his pocket, and the remnants of the bread the three of them had brought from Perpignan. The Americans were all three in good spirits, though we speculated grimly on the fate of Gable and the Chauve Souris, still up there in the cold wind.

Our Spaniards arrived, singing, and arm in arm. The guide began by hanging a large, full wine-skin round my neck.

'This is my son,' he said, presenting a dark young man in white shoes. 'He has been in touch with your people and tonight you will meet at ten o'clock a representative of the British Consulate. He has also arranged for you to have a splendid dinner today. Now we will continue our promenade, but ask your friends to be quiet, for there is much police vigilance about here.'

We walked south-east for another two hours, and day was breaking when the guide stopped in a lane, pointed to a thicket of bushes and young trees on the left and said: 'You will be very comfortable in there.'

'For how long?'

'Only a short while. Do not fret now.'

Obediently we climbed through a fence and disposed ourselves about the thicket. The three Americans lay down to sleep. But my leg hurt me too much and the cold had bitten too deeply into the small of my back. I stamped to and fro in the thicket, working myself into a really bad temper. The guide's companion had remained in the lane, as though he were keeping guard on us. My movements evidently worried him.

'For the love of God, keep still,' he hissed into the bushes.

'I refuse to keep still. I am too cold. How long are we to remain here?'

'All day.'

'All day! I refuse to remain here all day. Are we not going to a farm-house?'

'Yes, tonight. What is the matter?'

'I am freezing, and I think I am sick. If we must remain here I will light a fire.'

The Spaniard stood up and peered in at me. Finally he shrugged his shoulders.

'It is your own suggestion, so why not? And I will gladly help you,' he said.

Fritz and I built shelter walls by hammering in long uprights and weaving brushwood, while the other three gathered wood. In this way we soon had a small enclosure, well sheltered from the piercing wind, and with an enormous fire in the middle.

I lay beside the fire and let the blessed heat soak into my back and my knee. All that remained in the way of food was French tinned meat, *singe*. We divided this into four portions, toasted it on long sticks, and ate it without bread. Then, having banked our fire, all four of us went to sleep. That was a life-saving fire.

Soon after 4 p.m. I awoke. The others were sitting up, complaining of hunger. My leg was very stiff. Otherwise I

was stronger. We recalled the guide's promise to give us
a fine meal that day. We laughed at his promise.

But at 4.30 he arrived with two more wine-skins and a
large basket which he handed to us, saying: 'We bought
these few things for you on the black market.'

The things were fried sausages, the English type of
sausage, bananas, tangerines, and long loaves of white
bread. We toasted the sausages until they were burning
hot and tasted faintly of wood smoke, and I do not think
that I have ever eaten a more delicious meal by way of
contrast to what had gone before. He also produced for
the Americans long black cigarettes.

At 6 p.m. the guide led us out of the thicket and headed
south-west, tearing across fields and on the beaten tracks
around vineyards with his now familiar dancing, quick
little steps, and heading for the silver line of a big river in
the distance.

'How far are we going?' I asked.

'We shall be there in four hours at this pace.'

Four hours! All of us had thought that we were going
perhaps one mile, perhaps two.

'Ask him if there are many rivers to cross,' said Charlie,
for that was now our chief dread.

'Only two, but they are big ones.'

The four hours slowly passed and we stopped in a hollow beside another stream, but this time we were not going to wade it. The guide's companion was going to his
home by another route. Before he left he embraced us
warmly, insisted that we finish all the wine that remained
in his skin, and then embraced us once again.

A few miles farther on, the guide tapped with a long
stick on a farm-house window. A light went on inside and
then vanished. He tiptoed round to the front of the house,
motioning to us that we must follow at his heels. When he
had waited there for a few minutes to make sure that we
were unobserved, he led us quickly through the front yard
into a byre where there were two cows and a bull, through

the byre to a stable occupied by a pony, a mule and a draught horse, through the stable to a cellar filled with wine-casks and demijohns, and thence up a spiralling stone staircase to a long living-room where several people were gathered around an open fireplace.

A thin, nondescript Spaniard came forward, said in French that he was from the British Consulate in Barcelona, and asked us to fill in our particulars, rank, regiment, etcetera, on a paper he carried.

The Catalan women took charge of us. They gave us warm water to wash with and cooked us a copious meal on the open fire.

The firelight sparkled in a decanter of red wine, a decanter with a narrow glass jet sticking out of its normal neck.

'All black market – a fine place this,' the Spaniard from Barcelona remarked to me.

'Fine, fine,' agreed our old guide testily. 'But not so fine as my home, Englishman. Only I am outlawed. Here I am twelve kilometres from my home, and not allowed by the Government to sleep with my own buxom wife – I am an old man, but I believe in young wives, none of your scraggy old hens for me.'

'Where are you going now, then?' For he had eaten a little, had drunk considerably, and was now dressing for the road.

'Where am I going? Why, home, of course. Nobody can prevent me from climbing in at my own bedroom window. And tomorrow I cross the mountains again. Au revoir.'

'An astonishing man,' I said to the Spaniard from Barcelona.

'There are many astonishing men in Spain, but not many like him.'

'He was divinely made,' said one of the women. 'He forgets that he is old, so he is as young as his grandsons.'

They led us off to sleep in the hay. One of the sons forked down a lot of it; they spread blankets over this when we had flattened it out to make a big bed. All four of us lay down together; they put more blankets on top of us and more hay on top of that.

'You will sleep more comfortably tomorrow night, if all goes well,' the Spaniard told us. 'Try to sleep most of tomorrow. I shall return in the evening and we shall journey on together. We have to be very careful. I should warn you that the Spanish police are more clever than the Germans.'

We slept until midday, when one of the squarely built farm women brought us a splendid golden-brown stew with mutton, beans, garlic, onion, and pimento in it. There were beakers of a strange pinkish wine, strong and sweet.

Our new guide returned at five o'clock. He led us into the country for a few miles and then made us crouch beside him in a wood not far from what appeared to be a mixture between a level-crossing and a station. Perhaps in England it would have been called a 'halt'.

'That town is Figueras,' he said, pointing to a glow of lights in the distance. 'We are not going to board the train there. But if the police search the train and arrest you, then you must say that you boarded it at Figueras, and your tickets, which I now give to you, will bear out that statement. Is that understood?'

He waited while I translated.

'Next thing. We must not be seen by anybody outside the train while we board it at this station. We shall therefore leave this hiding-place just before the train arrives. It will slow down well before the station and we shall jump in while it is moving. You will follow me into a long carriage like a Pullman car. You will separate, and will sit singly in opposite corners of the carriage. You will speak to nobody. I shall leave you in that carriage and sit in the carriage nearer the engine. The trip will take about two hours. When it is time to alight I will walk back through the carriage. I will say nothing. I will not even look at you, but you must all individually get up and follow me. Is that understood?

'Now listen carefully. We must not be seen alighting

from this train. You will follow me out on to the rear platform of the carriage. The last of you will shut the door
behind him, and we shall all jump off while the train is
moving. Be careful how you do this. We will drop off the
right side of the train. Let your right foot gently down
until it touches the ground, then run. We have no time
for accidents. Is that understood?

'We will then find ourselves in a town. You will follow
me at one-hundred-metre intervals, but staggered. That is
to say that the man who follows me will be on the opposite
pavement, and so on. When we pass the main hospital of
the town we shall find a car waiting for us, a large black
car. The car will allow us to pass, then will follow us to a
piece of waste ground, where we shall all jump in. Is that
clearly understood?'

'Oh, boy,' said Charlie, when I had translated the last
bit. 'Does that car sound good!'

Although his plans had sounded a little fantastic to tired
men, everything went exactly as he had predicted – until
the bit about the car.

We passed the main hospital, we turned up a side street,
we arrived at the piece of waste ground. But not a car was
to be seen. Our guide was so angry that he could scarcely
speak intelligible French.

'There has been some accident. Wait here while I telephone for instructions. Remain standing against the wall,
motionless and in absolute silence."

It was so cold out there in the moonlight that it was impossible to remain motionless without demanding frost-
bite. He had placed us against the wall because the moon
was casting dark shadows. We stood there doing the cab-
man's exercise, and stamping our feet on the iron-hard
ground.

Our position was made the more uncomfortable by
contrast in that there was a large block of wide-win-
dowed flats at the edge of our waste ground. Through
the plate-glass windows we could see men and women
sitting around, talking or reading or sewing or warm-

ing their buttocks by the dancing flames of large wood fires.

The guide's bad temper had not abated with his telephone conversation. All he would say was: 'That creature has trains on the brain.'

At length he calmed down sufficiently to tell me that our plans had been changed; we now had to jump a freight train.

'This is no easy matter. How many of you have jumped freight trains before? Have *you*?'

'No,' I said.

'No,' said Fritz.

'No,' said Charlie.

'Yup,' said the Trapper.

'Ah, one at least. That one must mount last of all. You, Englishman, since you have a bad leg, will mount first. Now, follow me.'

He led us to the dark shade of a shelter in a cluster of miserable allotments. We were a few hundred yards outside a large marshalling yard and our shelter was fifty yards from the line. This guide was certainly an expert on trains. We waited for over an hour, and whenever a train pulled out of the marshalling yard he would peer at it in the moonlight.

'Confound it, not that one,' he exclaimed. 'These Spanish railways are really damnable. Always late, never on time, I earnestly assure you.'

At last he shouted: 'This is ours. Follow me closely.'

He darted down to the railway, scaled the fence, and soon we were running with him alongside the train, which was picking up speed. I was carrying Charlie's parcel, and my first jump for the little iron ladder at the back of a truck failed because the weight of the parcels swung me round. At the second attempt all went well. The others followed me. The guide hung on to the ladder for a minute.

'Count the stations,' he shrieked at us above the roar of the train. 'Just before the *sixth* station, jump off. I shall remain on the truck behind this one.' He vanished, climbing over the buffers.

Those Spanish freight trucks had tiny brake cabins stuck at the back, the roof of the cabin being raised some three feet above the roof of the truck. There was just room for the four of us to stand upright beside the heavy iron brake-wheel. Any movement was out of the question. The top of the truck, stretching in front of us, was covered with a five-inch layer of gleaming white frost. There were no windows on the cab. As we stood squeezed there, like tinned asparagus in a refrigerator, little icicles formed on our hair and our eyelashes. The language in our cabin was terrible. When the train stopped at small stations, railway-men would walk or run past us tapping at the wheels, un-hooking a wagon behind, or shouting at somebody in the distance.

We saw the guide leap from the train like an elongated monkey, and scuttle off the track. We all did our best to emulate him, and followed him along a path that circled the sixth station and then rejoined the railway.

'We have a walk of three hours in front of us, going fast,' the guide told us. 'Most of it will be easy walking along the railway line.'

By this time my leg appeared to have got accustomed to walking, but otherwise I knew that I had a chill and no amount of fast walking could warm me.

We arrived in the early hours of the morning at a hand-some farm-house with shuttered windows and beautiful wrought-ironwork on balconies and gates. The guide found a key in the garden and opened the door of a garage containing, of all things, an Austin 7. From there he led us through a hall which held a lot of shining old furniture and a suit of armour, and then into a large kitchen.

A middle-aged couple came out in woolly dressing-gowns to meet us. They lit a huge fire of brushwood and gave us coffee and white, home-baked bread with a lot of butter. The wife was pleased with me because she was French and I spoke her language.

'You have the red lights of fever in your cheeks and you must go to bed,' she told me. She explained to the Americans in English with a powerful French accent: 'The Englishman must have the single bed tonight because he is sick. You three will have to sleep in the double bed, but it is a very beeg one.'

On the upstairs landing there was a portrait of General de Gaulle with the British, American and French flags hanging above it. The bedroom was airy. French windows opened to a balcony with a view of moonlit hills and vineyards. There were linen sheets on my bed and coloured blankets edged with silk.

The following morning they gave me some kind of draught, but nothing to eat. I slept most of the day, half-conscious only that my American friends were being spirited away from me.

I was alone when I awoke at three o'clock and Madame gave me a treble brandy with warm milk.

'You will be well enough to eat dinner,' Madame said. 'Many of our young men arrive in your state. Sometimes we get the doctor and he says that it is a physical state, but I do not agree. He says it is a plain chill caught in the mountains and exaggerated by physical exhaustion. That is why it always passes quickly, he says, when the sick man has time to rest and sleep in a good bed.

'But I look at the young men who arrive like that, and I believe that the thing he calls a chill is a symptom of mental strain, nothing physical. It is because the young man has been wanting so much to cross the mountains, and for so long. He crosses them and something that was taut inside him suddenly sags. The doctor says it is a chill. But doctors are still groping in the dark. Now you are all right. I will bandage your bad leg (the doctor must see it in Barcelona), then you will put on your new clothes which you see laid out there, and you will come down and eat a solid meal with us. Just me and my son. My husband has gone to Barcelona with your friends. We like eating, my son and I.'

While I memorized a plan of the route from Barcelona
station to the British Consulate, Madame made a few
quick alterations in my clothes. They were new clothes,
Spanish ones, so that I should not arouse suspicions on the
way to Barcelona. Then we ate.

We ate first a risotto with mussels and oysters. Then for
the three of us she brought in a platter with twelve large
steaks upon it. Each of us ate four steaks, underdone,
rubbed with garlic and pepper and salt, and cooked in
butter. Then we had salad with dressing made from olive-
oil grown and pressed on the farm itself. I was surprised
to find that I still wanted to sleep.

It was a small village station, and the passengers waiting on the unsheltered platform when I arrived early next
morning were going to Barcelona for the day's work. It
was still dark. Now I was respectably dressed (according
to the standards prevailing locally) and they had given me
a second-class ticket, since those were the least crowded
carriages on that train.

The only thing that worried Madame about my appearance was my long, straw-coloured hair, which stuck out
in a kind of ruff over the back of my collar. I had not been
able to have it cut properly since *le cocu* had taken me to
the barber's shop near the cathedral in Strasbourg, three
months earlier. It had been cut once at Les Daines by the
tall railway policeman who had helped us to leave Annecy
station. He had been a barber in civil life, and he claimed
a barber's altitude record, for he had cut the hair of
maquisards high up on Mont Blanc. But he had asked
me: 'I suppose you want *la coupe anglaise*?' And when I
replied in the affirmative he shaped the hair around my
ears but left the back uncut.

Long before my train arrived in Barcelona my carriage
was filled with suburbanites. Once again I was obliged to
feign sleep in order to avoid being drawn into conversation.

I hurried through the station, well-lit and imposing, and
crossed the town by memory from the plan Madame had

made me memorize at the farm. They had told me that I should have no help on this walk unless I lost my way, but that I should be watched. And half-way to the Consulate I saw our train-jumping expert on the other side of the street. He stopped to light a cigarette, and cast one glint from his black eyes at me.

I found the Consulate without difficulty and, as instructed, walked quickly past the Spanish policeman who sat in the hall and up the staircase. At the top there was a man behind a desk, and rows of well-dressed townspeople waiting to make inquiries or to see people.

I gave my name to the man behind the desk.

'Just step along to that door marked "Waiting-room", Mr Millar.'

A young Englishwoman came into the waiting-room to find me.

'You are George Millar. We have been waiting for you for a long time.'

I was almost home. ...

* * *

... In Madrid George Millar learned that the two Americans, Clark Gable and the Chauve Souris, had reached Spain and were in Miranda prison. Soon he himself was sent to Gibraltar and so to England where he heard that Wally Binns had been recaptured but had again escaped and was now in Switzerland.

Once home George Millar volunteered for special service and after intensive training was parachuted back into France to work with the *Maquis*. For his war-time exploits he was decorated with the D.S.O. and M.C. and made Chevalier de la Légion d'Honneur with the Croix de Guerre avec Palmes.

CHAPTER EIGHT

Escape from Hospital

LIEUTENANT-COLONEL ANTHONY DEANE-DRUM-
MOND, M.C., is a professional soldier. In 1941 as a Lieutenant he was one of a picked team of paratroopers who
were dropped in southern Italy to blow up an aqueduct.
Their mission completed, they made for a rendezvous on
the coast where they were to be picked up by a British
submarine. They were captured and sent to the prison
camp at Sulmona.

Deane-Drummond made two attempts to escape from
Sulmona and on the second managed to get via Milan as
far as the Swiss border but was recaptured there. After
serving thirty-five days in the cells as a punishment for this
attempt he was sent to an escape-proof camp near Pisa.

Realizing the difficulty in escaping from this special
camp he faked illness and managed to get transferred to
the military hospital in Florence. He took with him into
hospital a navy-blue roll-neck pullover, battledress trousers with the outside pockets removed, brown shoes and
an Italian field service hat dyed chocolate-brown. Although
his room was on the top storey of the hospital building he
determined to escape through the window....

* * *

... When I was in my room a *carabiniere* guard was on
watch outside my door continuously, being relieved every
eight hours. The door was kept locked. Every time I
wanted to go to the lavatory I had to bang on it, when it
was unlocked, and the *carabiniere* would walk with me to
the lavatory just down the passage. When I sat on the
veranda he came too, and the prospects of getting away
did not seem very bright. Luckily the prison camp had

not warned the hospital that I had escaped before and was considered 'dangerous' or otherwise they would have taken rather more stringent precautions. Six months later in England I heard that the wretched commandant of the prison camp was sent to the Russian Front for not having warned the hospital! The dread the average Italian has for fighting for his country always amused me. He would be prepared to go to any lengths for a job at home, and being posted to an active front was always regarded as punishment. No wonder they were never much use as soldiers.

Outside my window was a seventy-foot drop to the courtyard below and no handy drain pipes to slide down. The old device of knotted sheets for a rope could not be used because of their rottenness and the fact that the number I would require was many more than I could raise. However there was a decorative moulding about four feet below my window, which ran all the way round the outside of the building. The top of the moulding was in the form of a slightly sloping ledge about five inches wide, and I thought it might be just wide enough to use.

Gradually my plan evolved. I would get out of my window and move along the ledge, past the Italian officer's bedroom window, round the corner of the building and then in at one of the lavatory windows. I could easily make sure it was open by going to the lavatory about midnight. I would then go through the lavatory door, which I would also leave open, and then down the stairs which were in a well of their own and separated by doors from all landings. The snag was that I could not very well open the door leading down the stairs when I went to the lavatory, but I hoped that over a course of days I would be lucky one night and find that it had been left open. The *carabiniere* always sat in his chair facing my door and he would be most unlikely to hear me flit in stockinged feet between the already-opened lavatory and the stairway doors. Having reached the ground floor I would jump out through a window into the courtyard, and circling round the building to the right I could quite easily get on to the main road leading down into Florence.

I had been in the hospital a fortnight when my plan had crystallized. About then a Flight-Sergeant Cox came into my room for three days with tonsillitis. He was working as a batman at the Generals' Prison Camp at Fiesole, just outside Florence, having been captured when Air Vice-Marshal Boyd was landed by mistake in Sicily instead of Malta. He gave me all their news. He told me how Air Marshal Boyd spent his whole time doing carpentry, how General Gambier-Parry was a very able sketcher and artist, and how General Younghusband was a most successful gardener within the limited area which was available. General Carton de Wiart was the only one he could not understand, but 'he has only one arm, one eye, and a v.c., so that must explain a lot'. I agreed.

At the time I thought it was just possible that he was a stooge and so I did not tell him of my intentions. It was a welcome respite, however, to be able to talk in English again.

As soon as Cox had gone back to Campo 12 at Fiesole, I started my midnight visits to the lavatory, but it wasn't until ten days later, on the evening of 13 June 1942, that the door leading down the stairway was left open. 13 June was St Anthony's Day, which I felt was a good omen for my adventure.

I decided to start about 3 a.m. and aimed at being on the main road by 4 a.m. This would give me two hours to walk into Florence and get an early train to Milan. In planning for our escape from Campo 27 I had remembered that an express train for Milan was due to leave at 6 a.m. and that was the one I hoped to catch.

I dressed as silently as possible putting one shoe in each trouser pocket where they would not be in my way, and at 3 a.m., in my stockinged feet, I swung my legs over into the darkness and found the ledge with my toes. Holding on to the shutter outside the window with one hand I started to move sideways to the left, flattening myself against the wall as much as possible. I had not gone more than a few steps when an attack of giddiness seized me, and I quickly went back just managing to clutch on to my shutter again. My knees were shaking and teeth chattering with excitement as I climbed back into my bedroom.

Ten minutes went by while I recovered my breath and my nerve. An occasional grunt came through the door from the *carabiniere* or a squeak from his chair as he shifted his seat, but otherwise the night was silent. My imagination kept telling me that I might slip off the ledge, or it might crumble under my weight. But I knew I must do it. This was my chance; I might never get another one.

Once again I tiptoed to the window and without looking downwards levered myself out and slowly slithered my feet down the wall on to the ledge. This time I was not going to get back into the room, and to make sure of it I swung the outside shutters across the window, and I heard a click from the latch on the inside.

I had always meant to do this to keep the Italians guessing how I had got out, but on my first try I had forgotten all about it in my excitement. I had bought some particularly obnoxious and sticky hair oil whilst in the hospital, and I had used this to lubricate all the hinges and catches on the shutters and on the lavatory door, to stop any squeaks.

There was no going back now. I held on to the closed shutter with my right hand and slid as far as I could along the ledge. My left hand could not reach the shutter over the next window but I forced myself on and inch by inch moved along the ledge. I wanted to press against the rough wall as tightly as possible, but if I did this it made a scraping noise which might alarm some wakeful patient.

After six feet with nothing to hang on to, I reached the next lot of shutters and using them as hand holds, quickly passed under the window. I then came to the worst part of the ledge, where it went round the corner of the building out of reach of all shutters. Again I had to leave go with my right hand and move spreadeagled to the corner.

Here the fingertips of my left hand were able to follow the wall around and give slightly more security. At the same moment the ledge under my left foot suddenly felt loose, and I had visions of the whole corner of the building breaking away. All at once my giddiness returned and I felt sweat slowly trickling down the side of my nose. My knees shook, but I held them still by pressing against the wall, while I gingerly transferred my weight to my other foot and felt around with my left toe to see what was loose. Something was very wobbly right on the corner and looking down I could just see that the cement surface was quite free and, if dislodged, a three-foot length would crash into the courtyard below. The moulding underneath the surface felt solid enough. It made a gritting noise as it wobbled and felt very insecure, but I slowly worked my way round the corner and then along a short length of wall to another corner, which was an inside one and much easier. A few more yards and I was under the lavatory window.

I heaved myself up and dropped on to the lavatory floor, where I stood for a minute or two to get my breath. Never have I felt so relieved as I did when I had finished that awful traverse along the face of the building in pitch darkness. Never do I want to do anything like it again. It might have been child's play to an expert mountaineer, but I was not one.

Cautiously peering round the corner of the lavatory door I saw the *carabiniere* awake and looking disconsolately at the ground in front of his chair. I saw that, if I crossed the passage to the other side before moving along opposite the doorway to the stairs, he could not see me if he looked up. All went well and soon I was standing opposite to the doorway leading down the stairs. There was not enough room for me to get through and I prayed and hoped that it would not squeak when I opened it a further few inches. The door opened without a murmur and, like a flash, I passed down the stairs without the *carabiniere* knowing what was happening. I would have a clear five hours' start till about 8 a.m. when I was called, and by that time I hoped to be well on the way to Milan. In case the *carabiniere* put his head inside my room during the remainder of the night, I had rolled up a greatcoat to look like me in bed, and I was confident it would pass all right for any casual look.

Creeping down the stairs I arrived at the bottom, and dropped into the courtyard through an open window on the ground floor. I rather misjudged the height because I landed on the paving stones on all fours and severely strained my wrist in the process. I crept round the outside of the hospital and then through an allotment and so came to the wall bordering the main road where I put on my shoes. I also pulled out a brown paper parcel from my trouser seat, which I planned to carry instead of a bag to give me the necessary *raison d'être*. It was five minutes to four, and at four o'clock precisely I swung over the wall and started to walk down the main road towards Florence.

*

This time I had decided to wear no outer insignia to suggest that I was a German. I did not in fact have any papers with me as it would have been too risky to bring them into hospital. Only if I was challenged would I say I was a German, and then only if I had to say more than a word or two in Italian. By 5 a.m. I had reached the centre of Florence and had to ask my way to the station, which I reached about twenty minutes later. To my relief I found that there was a 6 a.m. to Milan, but decided to wander round the station till about ten minutes to six before buying my ticket. By that time there would be a good-sized queue and this would give the booking-clerk less time to look at me closely.

Florence station is modern, and puts ours to shame by its cleanliness and neat layout. I looked round for a bench where I feigned sleep to avoid complications in talking. When the time came I pulled out my money and rose to join the queue for tickets. Unfortunately my 500 *lire* note was slightly mutilated because it had been hidden up the tubular leg of an iron bedstead at Campo 27 and little holes had been torn in it. Eventually my turn came and I said my usual *'Terzo Milano'*, at the same time pushing over the note. To my horror the official started turning the note over and over, examining it against the light, and, after what seemed hours, asked me if I had another. I replied with a shake of the head and a monosyllabic mumbled 'no'. However, with a shrug of his shoulders he pushed the ticket and change towards me. Cold sweat had started on my brow and the palms of my hands were decidedly damp as I walked away.

The express from Rome came in ten minutes late, and was very full. As soon as it came to a halt the crowd surged forward, myself included, and we fought for places on the steps leading up to the carriages. Putting my head down I got aboard after giving a kick on the shins to a man on my left who had tried to pull me back to get in himself. At last we all crammed into the corridor, where I stood in the corner near the lavatory, chin on chest, pretending to doze. I kept my ticket in my hand and whenever the collector passed up and down the train, which happened frequently, he just took the ticket out of my hand, punched it and put it back without apparently waking me up.

A lot of people got out at Bologna and I was glad to find a seat to myself in a compartment, as I would need all my energy when I reached the frontier. Unfortunately no *'cestina'* lunches were being sold on the stations, rations in Italy being much shorter now than when I had travelled to Milan six months earlier.

On one occasion when the ticket collector came round he had two railway police behind him, and they took a good look at me when punching the ticket. He took the ticket out into the corridor and started examining it closely with his back to me. After a minute or two he returned it and passed on to the next person. Scare over! Apparently they had a special key which fitted the ticket exactly for detecting forgeries. In all my travels on the railway I always saw hundreds of *carabinieri*, railway policemen and ordinary railway officials but they were always more concerned with the traveller who had no ticket. As long as you had a bona fide ticket they did not seem to worry.

I managed to avoid all conversation by pretending to sleep in my corner, and at 11 a.m. we pulled into Milan Central Station. My plan was to hang about the station till about 4.30 p.m. and then take a train to Varese, as I thought Como might be watched by now. The frontier was only thirteen kilometres from Varese at Porto Ceresio on the edge of Lake Lugano. If I arrived at Varese about dusk I would then walk to within two kilometres of Porto Ceresio and then strike up the hill and with a bit of luck might be in Switzerland within twenty-four hours of getting away from Florence.

The waiting-room was much emptier this time and I killed time by wandering round the station. I bought my ticket, just in case anybody asked me what I was doing and got a return this time to make my travelling to a frontier town more plausible. '*Terzo Varese andata e ritorno*', accompanied by a 50 *lire* note produced my ticket without any questions being asked. I was always a little self-conscious about my dress, but it never seemed to excite any suspicions. Luckily it was fairly cool at that date and the roll-neck pullover did not look too out of place.

I had a cup of *caffè al latte* for my lunch, and buying a few papers took them to the waiting-room for a four-hour wait till my train, which left at 4.37. I saw in the paper that a German ship had been sunk in the Mediterranean and the survivors landed at Genoa. This might be a useful story if ever I was stopped, and my navy-blue sweater would help. I could always pretend I was taking a short holiday before going on to Germany.

The journey to Varese by electric train was without incident and I arrived at about 6.15 p.m., just when it was beginning to get dark. My half ticket was taken without any questions being asked and I went out into the town. My plan was to strike off along the road which led roughly in the right direction and hope it brought me to a signpost which would put me on my way. I walked right through the centre of the town and past groups of men and women gossiping on the pavements and sitting at open-air cafés; but they seemed to be far more interested in their own conversations than in me so I passed through unmolested.

A crossroad on the north side of the town put me on the right road and told me I had twelve kilometres to Porto Ceresio. By this time it was dark and the sky was overcast, but a moon shone behind the clouds for the first half of the night. The road twisted and turned in all directions but always seemed to be flanked by small fields, high walls or precipitous mountainsides. It was no country to choose one's own route until much closer to the frontier. The road seemed to be interminable. My month in hospital without exercise had not helped and my muscles were very soft. I passed through one or two tiny villages and eventually came to the three-kilometre stone from Porto Ceresio, where I could see Lago Lugano with its searchlights playing on the water. By this time it was 10 p.m. and I struck up the hillside through a wood which flanked the road at this point. Thorn bushes seemed to reach out and grab me with every step I took and made progress very slow and painful. It was dark in the wood and I was forced to move so slowly that, having gone about two hundred yards, I decided to wait until morning when I would be able to avoid some of the worst hazards. Feeling thirsty, tired and cold, I curled myself up in some dead leaves and went to sleep. The cold woke me up about an hour before dawn, and after rubbing my stiff muscles back to life I crawled up the hill trying to avoid the demon thorn bushes. After half an hour, I saw I was coming to the top of the ridge. Suddenly, outlined against the morning sky, I saw a sentry-box with a tall row of barbed wire behind it. I immediately dropped to the ground and saw that the sentry-boxes were spaced about fifty yards apart all along the top of the hill. Just round the corner, and lower down, I could see what looked like a cemetery. This was really too much! My map did not show the frontier in any great detail but I had never expected to find it so close to the main road and so well guarded. In a minor panic I slithered back down the hill up which I had just crawled, and wondered what to do next. I was really flabbergasted, having hoped that this piece of the frontier would not have been more difficult than the part near Chiasso that I had seen six months before. Rightly or wrongly I decided to lie up where I was for the rest of that day, and then to walk back to Varese and on to Como that night. I would then try to get over a piece of frontier that I knew.

Later on, in Switzerland, I found a large-scale map of where I had been, and the frontier could not have been there at all and was at least another two kilometres farther on. To this day I do not know what I had stumbled into, and can only suppose that it was some kind of military dump that was being extra well guarded. I had not bargained for that sort of bad luck. To make matters worse it rained cats and dogs all that day, and I was soaked to the skin. I had to remain perfectly still so as not to attract attention and I don't think I have ever been so cold in all my life. My teeth kept up a permanent chatter and the feeling went out of my hands and feet after an hour or two. Slowly the time went by and at last it was dark enough to allow me to walk down to the main road and get my circulation going once more. It was about twenty miles to Como and I thought I could arrive in its vicinity by midnight.

It was lovely to be warm again and my clothes soon dried out, but I was certainly not out of the wood yet. I passed through Varese for the second time about 9 p.m., and found the Como road without difficulty. I began to feel extraordinarily tired and my brown Italian shoes were working up beautiful blisters on my heels which did not help progress. To my left I could see the outline of hills and over them I knew lay Switzerland, my dream country for over a year past. The road seemed never ending and I began to curse myself for having decided to walk all the way round to Como before trying again. If I had had a more accurate map of the frontier I would have gone across country but it was too risky on my own and would have been more guesswork than map reading.

I don't know what possessed me but I went on walking after midnight, always a dangerous thing to do. At about 1 a.m., while passing through the little village of Ogliate, I was challenged. My spirits fell as I went up to the man who proved to be a Maresciallo of Bersaglieri (equivalent of R.S.M.). He asked me for my papers. I went into a long explanation of who I was and brought out my newspaper to prove it, but all I could get out of him was that I would have to go in 'dentro' (inside) for the night. The last card I had to play was to knock him on the head, seize his bicycle and make a run for it, but before this I tried my last piece of bluff. I told him that if the German Consular authorities in Como did not see me by 8 a.m. in the morning there would be trouble for any one who had held me. I said this with much gusto and repeated myself several times. With much head-shaking and more muttering of 'dentro' he said I could go on this time, but it was most irregular and I must not do it again. My luck was holding out, but that scare had brought me to my senses and I did not make such a stupid mistake again. I went on through the village and slept in a ditch about one kilometre along the road till about 4.30, when I started to walk again. I passed through another village and had a dirty look from a carabiniere on duty, but soon after this I discovered a little wood near the road that would do as shelter for the day. Creeping in under some undergrowth, I curled up and went to sleep, mentally and physically exhausted but thankful that I was still a free man.

I woke up at 11 a.m. to the sound of woodcutting and children playing about a hundred and fifty yards away in my wood. Children and dogs were my worst enemies that day, but luckily none came near enough to find me, though it had the effect of keeping me mentally alert and awake all the time. I was now getting very hungry and thirsty and my blistered feet did not help my physical condition. However, I knew that I was now within a few miles of freedom and that, given a bit of luck and provided I did not make a fool of myself, I would have a good chance of succeeding. It was my gamble against at least another six months in prison, if not for the whole war. I was playing for uncomfortably high stakes. I suppose the chances of getting out of a prison camp are at least a hundred-to-one against. In Italy at this time, one's chances of getting to the frontier area having got out of camp were about twenty-to-one against – provided one did not do anything too stupid. Having got to within five miles of the frontier the chances of getting over would be about evens. I had now, for the second time in six months, arrived within five miles of the frontier, so I considered my chances were really good but did not mean to take any risks.

That day, thank goodness, was dry; for I don't think I could have stood another soaking. When dusk came I started on what I hoped would be my last lap. The road began to climb and, in a series of gentle turns, I went on upwards for the first three hours. The country was getting very hilly and the mountains to the north seemed to tower to endless heights above me. An occasional car swept by and I would shield my face from the lights and try and keep in the shadows on the sides of the road. Houses were built on either side and became more frequent. They were obviously summer villas for rich business men from Milan, and must have been delightful with an endless view stretching out over the Lombardy plain.

A few men passed me going the other way and once two or three soldiers went by, but they had no eyes for me and I certainly had none for them. At last my road started to wend its way down the hillside and, far below, I could see some lights with a lake beyond. At the time I assumed they must be Como, but I discovered later that it was the goods yard at Chiasso, on the frontier, at which I was now looking.

Eventually at about 11 p.m. I came to a road junction and turned left towards the lights thinking that it would lead me to Como through which I should have to pass before reaching the frontier area at Chiasso. In fact, of course, my road had by-passed Como, and I had just joined the Como-Chiasso road where I had been caught before. I suppose I should have recognized it, but it looked very different by night and distances were deceptive.

I walked on down the hill to Chiasso and did not realize my mistake until suddenly I saw the frontier barrier right across the road and not two hundreds yards away from me. I nearly had a fit on the spot. Trying not to hurry myself, I retraced my steps to the outskirts of Chiasso, and, not wishing to be caught on the roads again after hours, I decided to sleep in a culvert under the road until about 4.30 a.m., when I would go back towards Como for about a mile and then strike up the hill. My culvert could not have been more than a few hundred yards from the frontier, but it was a case of safety first at this stage. Unfortunately it was not entirely dry and an evil-smelling stream of dirty black water trickled down the middle. I had an uncomfortable, worrying five hours perched on some flat stones which remained dry at one side of the stream.

At last 4.30 a.m. crept round on my watch and, making sure that nobody saw me coming out of the culvert, I started walking back down the road. In ten minutes I found a convenient turning off and soon I was following a small footpath that led up the hillside and in approximately the right general direction. I would be much too early for any woodcutters going to work, and my only worry was the possibility of frontier guards coming back from duty along my track. However, I reasoned to myself that the relief guard would surely have to use my track to go out, and I could not imagine a changeover much before 6.30

a.m. With any luck my path would be all right for at least an hour, and after that I must keep well clear of all tracks. My progress along the path was five times as quick as it would have been across country, as by now I was climbing nearly vertical slopes with thick thorny undergrowth on either side.

At 6 a.m. I decided to leave the track and started climbing straight up the hill. I was now about 2,000 feet above the valley. I could see Chiasso quite plainly with its long goods sidings, and an obvious fence at right angles through the middle which was the frontier.

I decided to climb for about another hour and then to start moving very slowly along the hillside till I sighted the frontier. I would then lie up all day watching the sentries, and try to get over that night.

I thrust my way up the mountainside and swept aside the bushes that tried to hold me back; what did a few scratches matter now? Soon I came to a belt of pine trees, and walking through them was a great relief after the thorn scrub lower down. I came out of the pine trees and went on upwards through hazel plantations and every sort of mountain shrub, which all grew in profusion everywhere. At last I thought I was high enough and I started to move cautiously along the hillside in the direction where I knew the frontier to be. I had not been going more than half an hour, when, just across a little valley and not more than four hundred yards away, I saw a sentry-box amongst the trees. I dropped down on one knee and could pick out one or two more and the line of fence poles behind. The little valley between me and the frontier was quite bare and open and the fence and sentry-boxes were a few yards inside the wood beyond. I found a comfortable hole full of dead leaves in which I could sleep and from which I could watch the frontier. I had a very welcome meal of blueberries, which grew all around, and after watching the frontier for an hour or two fell asleep.

About half a mile up on my left hand, and just about

where the frontier ought to be, I could see a red roof. I assumed this to be one of the posts which housed the relief sentries, and occasionally I could see one wandering along the wire. They changed over every even hour. The sentry-boxes were about two hundred yards apart, which was not too bad, and I carefully marked down the route I should take that night in order to bring me out exactly between two boxes.

At last darkness fell and, although I felt like going bald-headed at it, I had decided to play safe and try to cross at 11 p.m. I would allow an hour to crawl the four hundred yards and that would give me at least another hour before there was any more large movement of sentries to and fro. The sentries on that frontier were not over-keen on wandering about by day, so with any luck they would be even less alert at night. A light rain started to fall about 10 p.m. and I cheered inwardly to myself. No Italian sentry would wander about in the rain unless given a direct order by an officer!

I crawled slowly through the undergrowth and across the open patch at the bottom of the valley. I did not make much noise, but to my ears I sounded like a bull charging around. The rain pattering on the leaves made all the difference as it blanketed my sounds from the sentries. I could just hear one singing away to himself in his box, little suspecting that a British officer was at that very moment within a hundred yards of his post.

By 11 p.m. I had reached the path used by the sentries and just over the other side the frontier wire was stretched. I saw that it was a fairly formidable obstacle. It was made of diamond mesh wire of fairly heavy gauge and was constructed all in one piece and at least twelve feet high. Poles in the form of an inverted V suspended the wire from its apex, and all along the top bells were hung. The slightest touch on the wire would start them clanging. The problem was how to get over, through or under. No branches overhung the wire anywhere near and as I had no pliers my only alternative was to try to burrow a way underneath. I could have risked the bells and climbed over the top but it might have gone wrong and was not worth it if I could find another way.

The bottom of the fence was pegged every six inches with eighteen-inch wooden stakes, but luckily the soil in the wood was mostly leaf mould and the stakes pulled up easily without shaking the fence. I had soon freed about a three-feet length, pausing between each stake to listen for any footsteps on the path.

All was quiet. The sentry on my left was still crooning away to himself about 'Mamma mia', but I could hear nothing from the one on my right. The rain came down a little harder now, and a damp moist smell came up from the disturbed earth when I started to scrape it away with my hands. It reminded me of sheltering from the rain in an English wood in autumn after a dry summer. It was a musty clean smell quite different from the usual pungent Italian aromas.

I slowly scraped away, using one of the stakes to loosen the earth, and then removing it with my hands.

After I had been going about ten minutes there was quite a respectable hole and I tried to squeeze underneath the wire but there was too small a gap and I became stuck with one shoulder and one arm in Switzerland and the rest of me in Italy.

Several things then happened at once. The bell above me gave a very small tinkle, a branch crashed down near-by, the sentry stopped singing and the noise of shunting goods wagons in Chiasso suddenly became very loud owing to a change in the wind.

I prayed that the sentries would stay where they were, whilst I slowly pushed myself back into Italy. The hole would have to be bigger.

After a few very long seconds I was clear and I crawled back over the track and lay in a bush for a few minutes. If the sentry had heard anything he would surely come along and inspect the wire at once.

My luck was in and after five minutes' complete silence

except for the rain on the leaves, and the noise of the shunting, I crawled back across the track once more. On this occasion I was not going to be stuck under the wire, and worked away for ten minutes before the gap was big enough. My hands reached through to Switzerland, this time much farther, and I was able to grasp a tree root and draw myself through without shaking the fence above me. ...

*   *   *

... Anthony Deane-Drummond reached the British Embassy in Berne and arrangements were made for him to be passed along an escape line through France to the Mediterranean. He was picked up by the Royal Navy at a spot some fifty miles west of Marseilles and landed in Gibraltar. Ten days later he was in Scotland.

This was not Deane-Drummond's last escape. He was dropped by parachute into the famous Battle of Arnhem, and made prisoner again. He escaped after hiding for thirteen days standing upright in a cupboard in a German guard-room. With the help of Dutch patriots he regained the British lines.

CHAPTER NINE

The Land of You-Never-Know

LIEUTENANT W. B. THOMAS, a New Zealander, was badly wounded and captured by the Germans in their invasion of Crete. His captors flew him to the mainland of Greece, where he was taken to a military hospital.

Although there was a gaping wound in his thigh Lieutenant Thomas dreamed of escape; but it was nearly four months before he could get out of bed.

His first escape from the hospital, with his leg still not healed, was a gallant wire-cutting attempt under fire from the guard. Both he and his companion got away but were soon recaptured.

Thomas's next idea was to feign death and be carried out of the hospital in his coffin. This plan might well have succeeded but the German doctor with whom Thomas had become friendly came to take one last look at his prisoner-patient. When the sheet covering his face was reverently drawn down the 'dead' man giggled – and the game was up.

The final attempt to escape from the hospital was the signal for his guards to send him to a permanent prisoner-of-war camp in Germany. It was from the transit camp in the port of Salonika that the following successful escape was made. ...

* * *

... Soon after midday on 30 October, with snow-capped Olympus on our left, we steamed up the Gulf of Salonika to tie up in that historic port.

Above the harbour the old stone city walls, the towers and the fortresses standing out on the hill gave a medieval atmosphere, but around the docks things were modern enough. There was a small amount of German and Italian shipping about, with here and there a cruiser or a destroyer from Mussolini's fleet. German Marines, none of whom seemed more than eighteen years old, paraded on the wharves, constantly saluting their smart-looking officers. Everybody seemed busy, but all were very interested in the Englanders as we were off-loaded and shepherded into Red Cross vans. We were driven along the water-front, past the great circular tower of Salonika, and in a few minutes were at the gates of the prison camp.

My heart sank at the sight. Here was no hospital wire. This was a real prison camp. High mazes of barbed wire ran at all angles. Throughout the camp were great towers on which sentries could be seen fondling their machine-guns. From behind the wire near the gate a crowd of un-kempt and undernourished prisoners gathered to gape for-lornly as we were formed into ranks and our luggage checked.

It was almost dark by the time all our personal belong-ings had been strewn on the gravel and the Guard Officer satisfied that we carried no implements for escape. The great gates opened and we poured in, to be ushered into various buildings.

In a large dormitory I met again quite a few of the offi-cers who had come up from Athens in the hospital ship. We all fell to exchanging experiences, and I felt quite at home amongst them. Two in particular I came to respect immensely. Lieutenant-Colonel Le Soeuf, tall, dark, and quietly spoken, had been captured with his unit, the 7th Australian Field Ambulance, when they were overrun at Heraklion in Crete; Major Richard Burnett, a regular officer, had been C.O. of his unit on Crete and had been captured while making a reconnaissance in the dark.

Salonika was a bad camp in every way. In the past many shocking atrocities had been committed by guards who had been former members of the Nazi Youth Move-ment. Burnett was even then investigating a horrible case – a German sentry had thrown a grenade into a latrine packed with dysentery cases and the carnage had been frightful. The only explanation given on Burnett's protest was that the men were whispering in a suspicious manner. The authorities supported the sentry's action.

In a recent unsuccessful attempt at escape, three men had been shot out of hand and their bodies left for days in the hot sun, while for other escapes soldiers had been bound with barbed wire and whipped as a warning to all. Drunken guards had been known to walk into the compound and cruelly maul unarmed prisoners, while it was said that the officer in charge of the young Nazis would ask daily of his guard how many English swine they had killed and congratulate the murderer effusively.

It was an alarming picture, quite different from the treatment I had experienced in Athens. Listening to it all I regretted very much that I had ever left the hospital.

The camp had been an old Greek Artillery barracks, but the Germans had allowed it to deteriorate badly, so that now it was in a terrible state of sanitation, with practically no drainage at all. Millions of flies swarmed around the latrines and cookhouses and formed ugly black heaps where refuse was dropped. Scores of mangy cats slunk among the barrack-rooms.

The prisoners in the compound were the stragglers of the large army which had already passed through to Germany. There were thirty officers and some two hundred men, one hundred and fifty of whom were maimed in some way.

About fifteen were men who had lately been caught in and around Salonika. These were a grand crowd of fellows, and I made a point of talking to them and gaining much valuable information.

Some had been out and recaptured four or five times; indeed, the greatest joke amongst them was the case of the Australian who was picked up as a matter of course by a German patrol each Friday at a house of ill fame. Others with higher motives for escape had been free for long periods, only to be recaptured either on the very borders of Turkey or at sea moving south to freedom.

One, a tall New Zealand sergeant with a sense of humour, had seen his chance on a day of pouring rain, when a German officer had visited the camp hospital. The officer had walked into the lobby, and hung up his dripping coat and hat before entering the German guard-room. The sergeant had donned these quickly and marched out into the rain. The sentries had all, one by one, frozen into a salute. Thereafter, he walked down into the streets of Salonika. It was truly an escape to fire the imagination.

A long-haired lad from Sussex had clung to the bottom of one of the contractor's drays and had been carried out of the camp. A very young Cockney told us of his adventure in going out in a bag of rubbish.

The prisoners were even then working on a mass escape plan. But they had the shrewdness of experienced escapists. It was some days before I was to be allowed into their confidence.

Meanwhile, the atmosphere in the officers' mess was unpleasantly strained. There were bickerings over food all round, and quarrels between the Medical Corps and the combatants over such futile things as seniority and the post of Senior British Officer in Captivity. On one occasion feeling ran so high that one side actually asked a German N.C.O. to consider and settle the dispute.

It was not a pleasant place. Consequently I was pleased when Dick Burnett asked me to share a room accorded him because of his rank.

Burnett was keen on escape. He had been free on more than one occasion in Crete and in spite of his forty years was determined to risk all the hazards to get back to his regiment. For as long as he was to be a prisoner he was firmly resolved to cause as much trouble for his captors as possible.

For the first three or four days, I think, he was weighing me up as a possible partner for the months we might have to spend together before reaching British lines.

Then we began to lay our plans.

The section of the camp we were concerned with was only a small part, a sub-section, of the main Salonika Prison Camp. Most of the other sub-sections were now empty and unguarded, with the exception of the one immediately to the west of ours. This held political prisoners from Greece and Yugoslavia. In there one day we had seen an old lady awaiting execution for aiding British escapers.

The sub-section was an oblong, some three hundred yards by two hundred, containing seven large barrack huts, a cookhouse and a large new building. The only exit was the gate at the north-west corner, and apart from the roving sentries within the compound, the Germans relied mainly on the guard posts immediately outside it. At the southern end these consisted of two twenty-foot towers, each with two sentries, a machine-gun and a movable searchlight. At the northern end there were the sentries on the gate, those on a tower by the gate, and two sentries with machine-gun and searchlight on the roof of a small shed used for storing horse fodder. The south and west sides were bounded by other sub-sections, the north by an open space and the Salonika road, and the east side had a wide gravel road which separated the compound from rubbish and salvage and which led along to the stables.

A whole morning spent watching guards, drawing innumerable diagrams and getting annoyed with one another disposed of the front, the west and rear sides as quite impossible. Only the east side was left, and we had little hope that it would produce the answer. In common with the others it had some three hundred yards of wire tangle, ten feet high, ten feet wide, but there was one difference. There were two buildings which broke the obstacle, that is, the wire tangle ran in between them, and rambled up and over them. It did not run along the back.

One of these was the cookhouse. It had a thick cement wall for a back and, furthermore, was less than a stone's throw from the southern sentry tower. We mooched around it for half an hour after lunch and rejected it as impracticable.

The second building was a fairly new three-storeyed building. A preliminary examination revealed no possibilities; all the windows facing out were heavily barred with steel and barbed wire, while even if work could free them it would be too dangerous to be lowered to the road below in full view of the searchlights at either end.

But just as we were deciding dejectedly that a tunnel was the only solution, we espied a staircase winding down from the ground floor to hide what must be a back doorway on to the gravel road below. The passage down was blocked by large empty crates. The door was of itself unimportant. There were still the searchlights and machine-guns covering the road outside. But Dick had an idea and we climbed again on to the first floor to discuss it.

The two searchlights which concerned us covered the road very efficiently. The one at the south end from the tower had an unobstructed view, while the one on the roof of the hay shed was only limited by its position from seeing the actual back of the building in question. But, and on this our plan depended, these posts had the additional task of covering the south and north wire respectively: their searchlights were on swivels and they would swing from one task to the other every few seconds. For the most part one or other of the posts would have its light focused on the gravel road, occasionally both would play together along it for minutes on end. But with an understandable human error, often for a few seconds, both crews would switch simultaneously on to their secondary task. This would leave the road in darkness until either of them realized the position and swung his searchlight back. Burnett and I considered that, given luck, this erratic few seconds would give us a chance to make the initial dash across the road and use the scant cover of a shallow culvert before the searchlights swung back.

And so we examined the door.

The crates barring the steps down from the first floor were really no obstacle and would afford good cover for any work we should do. The steps ran down in two short flights on to a very small landing, and the door-frame was set firmly in stone. There were steel and wooden bars across it, both bolted and nailed, and the whole was covered with barbed wire on staples. Formidable certainly, but, provided we were not hurried, we thought it could be done.

One remarkable thing about our work on this project was the complete absence of the adventure spirit and the elation of imaginary success. Every step we took in this venture was coldly methodical. We took very few into our confidence.

Amazingly enough, the tools for the work were no trouble at all. I bought a pair of excellent pliers from a Greek electrician working in the barracks; Burnett made some useful crowbars from sections of our beds; and Fred Moodie, a camp doctor, provided a pair of strong plaster cutters. Fred also arranged for me a good supply of the German cod liver oil salve which had proved very soothing and beneficial to my wound.

We started work that night. Immediately after the evening check we made our way to the building with innocent unconcern and talked to various orderlies until curfew, when we slipped behind the crates under the first flight of stairs until all was quiet.

The work was necessarily slow, and not a little nerve-racking. Each nail, each bolt had to be worked out slowly and with great caution; a loud squeak would leave us perspiring and fearful for long minutes. Every now and then the crunch of heavy feet on the gravel outside would hold us up, and on three occasions during the first night two of the guards talked for a long time just outside the door.

By four o'clock we had removed all the wooden bars and two of the six more formidable steel bars. We tacked the bars back loosely into their old positions and generally

tidied up the evidence before setting off on the quite
hazardous trip back to our barracks. The two sentries
detailed to prowl round inside the compound had orders
to shoot on sight after curfew, and though the twenty
minutes they took on their regular rounds provided ample
time for us there were the searchlights to pin us down
occasionally and always the chance that the sentries might
vary their tactics.

We reached our room without incident and were sound
asleep for the six o'clock room check. Having previously
convinced the Germans that it was less trouble not to
order us out to stand by our beds each morning (as laid
down), we were left to slumber on until almost lunch time.

Our progress on the second night did not compare with
the first night. There were too many interruptions – stable-
hands coming home late from leave and arguing out on
the road, restless sentries and irregular changing of
guards. And we were discovered at work by a group of
Australian and British medical orderlies, and it took us
some little time to impress on them the need for absolute
secrecy. However, we worked out two more steel bars and
managed to loosen a third before an early rooster, crowing
beyond the stables, warned us of approaching day.

On the third night we made very good progress indeed;
by eleven o'clock the last of the steel bars was disposed of.
We had brought a rough chisel and a screwdriver to remove the lock, but, to our amazement, we found that it
was not, in fact, locked. A few nails had been hammered
at random around the edges, however, and just after midnight the last was worked out and we were able to move
the door.

It opened two or three inches and then stuck. We
realized that there was an apron of barbed wire stapled
on to the outside. With some difficulty it would be possible to worm a wrist with pliers through the opening.
After a short consultation we decided to leave it as it was
until the night of the break, knowing that it would only
take a few minutes to open it.

We made our way carefully back to our room, secreted our tools under our mattresses and in the stove, and undressed in the dark. It was only about one o'clock and, tired as we were, the prospect of a few extra hours' sleep was very pleasing.

No sooner had we said good night, however, than we were suddenly startled by the tread of heavy feet in the passageway outside. There was a guttural order, our door burst open, and three soldiers rushed in. Torches flashed in our faces, our blankets were pulled off roughly, and the room quickly but not thoroughly searched. Then, as if satisfied, the officer barked an order and the party clattered out and away, leaving two very shaken men behind.

Now that visit was unfortunate. The explanation was quite beyond us, particularly as ours was the only room searched. Perhaps someone had discovered and reported that we had not been sleeping in our beds at night; or perhaps it was merely a check on me as a known 'bad lad'. But the effect was this: Burnett decided not to come. Three nights' work had taxed his nerves badly and now he thought our whole plan was discovered. Even when daylight proved that no attempt was made to re-fix the door, Burnett saw the possibility of a trap – a machine-gun covering the exit to make an example of anyone who attempted to escape. He was still as determined as ever, but with the caution of forty years he weighed the chances as too dangerous, and started straight away on a new plan to throw ourselves from the train on the way through Yugoslavia.

His pessimism shook me not a little. I spent the morning watching the area near the cookhouse, and after lunch sat down and tried to come to some decision. His arguments were very sound; the plan had been hazardous enough without the new threat. Yet at the back of my mind was a conviction, however unfounded, that the plan was still secret.

Finally I took out a piece of paper, and ruling a line

down the centre, wrote in two columns all the pros and
cons I could think of.

That was a poignant half-hour. I knew well that the
wrong decision might cost me my life. Yet I felt very
strongly that it was a case of 'now or never'; that, if I let
this opportunity pass, I might never be presented with another.

As the page filled up, Burnett sat quietly watching me.
I knew that he was apprehensive, but, having stated his
arguments once, he made no attempt to dissuade me further.

Before I could make up my mind we were besieged by
some five or six of the more hardened card players and I
was quite willing to procrastinate an hour for a game of
pontoon. Perhaps it was my abstraction, but within half an
hour, without effort, I had taken every *drachma* off the
whole school. After a drink of cocoa from my Red Cross
parcel they all departed very disgruntled, threatening that
they would come back on the morrow to get it all back. As
soon as they had gone, at Burnett's suggestion, I entered
under the 'Pros' the fact that I now had 8,000 *drachmae*
for escape purposes.

At six o'clock I made my decision. It was, I am sure, the
decision of my life. Our original plan had been to get
some greatly needed rest that night, Saturday, and escape on Sunday about nine when the guards not on duty
were on leave. But now, as things appeared to be
moving rapidly and because my nerves were so tense
that I could not sleep, I decided to go on my own that
night.

When Burnett saw that I was determined, he gave me
everything he had; all his bread, condensed Red Cross
food, a civilian coat, and all his savings, including some
English money. He cooked me up a wonderful farewell
meal and set himself to do a thousand and one little things
to help me to get ready.

It was now after curfew. It was therefore necessary to
move with great care over to the building. Soon after

eight-thirty, I said good-bye to Burnett. He was terribly apprehensive of the risk I was taking and heartily miserable that he was not coming with me. I realized I was going to miss his company very much.

It took me almost an hour to go the two hundred yards from our barracks. The searchlights seemed particularly restless and the roving patrol sat down and talked for nearly half an hour while I lay in what shade a wirenetting fence afforded. When finally they moved off I ran quickly up the steps and through the door into the hall of the medical building. As soon as I latched the door behind me a startled voice greeted me.

'Are you *mad*? Surely you know that it's dangerous to be out at curfew?'

It was an Australian medical orderly. When I told him of my plans he immediately offered his help.

We moved on to the first landing, from where we could look through the barred window down on to the road. Everything seemed quite normal. We watched for half an hour, but, with the exception of a team of horses being taken out from the stables, only the usual movement was apparent.

The orderly and a friend appointed themselves to keep watch while I worked. We arranged a code of signals whereby, should they wish to warn me, they would throw something small down the steps leading to the escape door. The 'all clear' would be one or the other whistling from *Rigoletto*.

The door was as we had left it. I removed all the loosely held bars and convinced myself that no one had tampered with them. The door opened noiselessly some three inches and even with great caution it only took me twenty minutes to cut the eight or nine restraining wires on the outside.

As I cut the last one and felt the door suddenly swing easily towards me, the first alarm signal in the form of a leather slipper clattered down the stairs behind me. I closed the door quickly, my heart in my mouth. Outside I

could hear heavy feet crunching slowly down the road. As
they approached the door I held my breath in apprehension. With the searchlights full on I felt that no one could
miss the tell-tale loose ends of wire. But, although I could
have sworn there was a slight pause just level with the
door, the danger passed and in a few seconds I heard a
soft but unmusical attempt to whistle the arranged all
clear.

I opened the door a few inches and studied the ground.
The road was only some fifteen feet across, but I realized
that unless the searchlights settled down I would never
get over without being seen. The sentry in the tower on
the south end was unusually restless; his light was flickering to and fro every few seconds. I decided, as it was then
nine-thirty, to wait until the ten o'clock change of sentries
with the hope of getting someone more placid. During the
wait I worked out each step across the road, and the point
where I should get over the low wall into the rubbish on
the other side.

Just before ten the team of horses, which had gone out
earlier, returned noisily up the road, and, although I did
not look, I imagined they were towing some vehicle.
When they had passed up towards the German stables I
stole a look out. I thought for a moment that the opportunity was ideal, for one of the searchlights was playing
on the stable yard, probably to help the unhitching of the
horses. I had just made the decision to go and was in the
act of opening the door when some object clattered down
the stairs behind me. A second later came the sharp order
of the Corporal of the guard as he turned his ten o'clock
relief up the road – I shivered as I realized how very
nearly I had run right into them.

For fifteen minutes after the old guard had clattered
past the door on their way to the guard-room, the searchlights on both ends were seldom still for more than a few
seconds, but soon after that the new sentries began to tire
of their vigilance. Sitting back on the stairs I could count
up to four seconds while no light shone through the key-

hole or under the door. So I opened the door cautiously and looked out.

Looking across the road, I realized that although the tower at the south end shone direct on to the exit, it would be the light from the roof of the hay shed which would be most dangerous, as it shone over the rubbish. I started counting the irregular breaks of darkness. Sometimes there would be one or other searchlight shining on the road for over ten minutes, then for an erratic five minutes it would be in darkness every few seconds.

'One – two – three,' I counted, 'one – two – three – four getting better now, one – two – three – four – my word, I could have made it that time, one – two – three – phew, just as well I didn't then . . .' and then there would be another period of light. The most unnerving thing about it all was the fact that there was no way of knowing how long any particular period of darkness was going to be. I knew that whenever I made the decision it would be final. The success or failure of the whole plan depended on nothing more than luck.

I think perhaps I must have been poised there for half an hour. But it seemed years to me. I alternated between self-reproach for having missed a good chance and a chill of horror when a period of darkness lasted only one second.

And then I went. Not running, but carefully over the road, my stocking-covered shoes making little noise on the gravel. But as I prepared to throw myself over the low wall on the other side of the road, I sensed the return of one of the lights and involuntarily dropped to the ground, realizing instantly that I must present an ideal target to either sentry post.

First the light from the hay shed played idly up and down the road, and so brilliant was it that it shone right into the gravel where my face was buried. Then I sensed the other one flashing over my shoulder. My body tingled with terror and for the first time in my life I felt the hairs on the nape of my neck pricking and rising.

I could hear two of the sentries talking quite clearly. They did not sound at all excited and yet surely they must have seen me. My body began to flinch and cringe as I imagined a bullet striking home. My mind went numb, and I had no idea how long I lay there, but at last, one after the other, the lights swung away.

I sprang up. Instead of vaulting the low wall I passed along it, turned into the courtyard of an M.T. garage. I dropped behind a large oil drum as the first light swung back. Here I was not so frightened, for the low wall now shielded me completely from the one searchlight and the drum from the other. I must have been pinned there for all of ten minutes. It was uncomfortably cramped, and I was apprehensive lest some driver or later-returning guard should discover me.

But when darkness came I was able to slip over the wall, and worm through the rubbish towards the outer ring of wire. There was no need to stop even when both lights were playing down the road, for there was sufficient shadow amongst the rubbish and small scrub to mask cautious movement. There was thirty yards of this cover stretching over to the outer ring of double apron barbed wire. This presented no problem with my wire-cutters. But I was surprised when I was through it to run into a wire-netting fence. Following it along, I came to a break covered by a sheet of iron, which I crawled through to find myself in a small cleared space littered with large boxes. I was just passing one of the latter when a movement somewhere near stopped me. I hugged the ground, my heart in my mouth. All was quiet for a few minutes, then just as I prepared to continue, again came the small movement, much closer this time. I placed it as just behind the box. I was becoming really scared when from inside the box came the unmistakable clucking of a disturbed hen. I was inside the guards' chicken run.

I crossed the run to the rear corner of the garage and cut a small square to let myself out. I found myself in a grass enclosure, bounded by two very high stone walls, which ran into a corner some two hundred yards away. Very clearly I could hear the rumbling of the trams on the main Salonika road.

The wall bounding the road was about ten feet high and I could see glass glistening along its length. But it didn't present any great obstacle – the Germans had attempted to make it more formidable by giving it an apron of barbed wire – thus making an ideal ladder.

I climbed up it carefully. The road was still very busy for that time of night. In addition to the trams and army vehicles there was a steady stream of civilians and soldiers on both sides of the street. I waited ten minutes and was thinking of retiring for a few hours to let things settle down when I fancied I heard a single shot from back in camp. I listened for a full minute. Although I heard nothing further and was almost convinced that it was my over-taxed mind playing tricks, I decided to push on and take the chance of discovery.

With the glare from the lights of the prison camp there was quite a shadow on the road side of the wall, and as soon as there was a perceptible break in the traffic below I lowered myself so far as the lowest strand of barbed wire would allow me and dropped the remaining four feet, falling in a heap on the footpath.

My first reaction was one of acute pain. The jar was considerable. But almost immediately I became aware of two figures standing some fifteen paces away arguing volubly. They were both soldiers and I saw by the rifle he had slung over his shoulder that one of them was on duty. But as I picked myself up I knew I had not been seen. The second soldier was obviously very drunk and was abusing the sentry roundly.

I moved quickly up the street for two or three hundred yards, stopped and removed the spare pair of socks which I had worn over my shoes, and walked very quietly into Salonika.

The whole of the venture up to this stage had been cool and methodical. A desperate fear of the risks had numbed my mind against any anticipation of success. But now at every step I felt welling within me a glorious exhilaration, an ecstasy so sweet that my eyes pricked with tears of gratitude. All the oppression, all the worry and boredom, which had so weighed me down, seemed to disappear as though they were taken like a heavy cloak off my shoulders. The air was pure and free.

For perhaps an hour I let my exuberance lead me drunkenly up and down strange streets. Every unsuspecting soldier I passed was a boost to my confidence. As each approached, I weighed up his size, darted a glance right and left for possible flight and then, as we drew level, either made a great play of blowing my nose or whistled the one Greek tune I knew in what I hoped was a nonchalant manner. But soon I realized there was no need to regard each as a suspicious enemy – each was going about his own business whether leave or duty; probably the last thought anyone had was that the stream of pedestrians might include an English officer.

Although there was some attempt at a black-out the streets were full of gaiety. From every restaurant and wine-shop came the laughter and music of the conquerors. Happy, and here and there inebriated, couples thronged the alleyways. At one street corner a lone violinist was playing old music rather sweetly. I felt wonderfully at ease, confident and vastly superior to all those in field-grey uniforms who had not the sense to recognize an enemy in their midst.

However, somewhere in the centre of Salonika, the exhilaration quietened and allowed reason to prevail. I turned reluctantly to follow my plan of being well clear of the city by dawn. With some difficulty I orientated myself. Striking south, I moved through a suburb full of cheerful chatter and houses that glowed with homely light until I came to the foot of the great Salonika Hill. I followed up the same zigzag path trod by many a conqueror, sitting down occasionally on the stone steps to rest and marvel at the beauty of the subdued lighting fringed by the sea below me. One by one the lights in the nearby houses went out as the city quietened down. By the time I reached the old Salonika wall with its massive gateways all was quiet.

I sat down fifty yards from the gateway and watched for a while. All the exits to Salonika were under guard. Occasionally every civilian would be forced to produce his identity card, but this particular gate divided the city from one of its more modern suburbs. From somewhere in the prison camp had come the information that, with the large numbers passing to and fro, the sentries had become very slack.

The sentry on duty moved out of the shadow of the archway and shifted his slung rifle from one shoulder to the other. A group of civilians, coming from a side street near the wall, passed through quietly, so I braced myself and slouched through after them, blowing my nose noisily; indeed, so interested was I in appearing nonchalant that I almost collided with a sentry who was moving across the archway. But he hardly glanced at me. And so I went through the last suburb and down to the outskirts of the town. I drew my coat close around me, for the wind was bitterly cold.

Soon there loomed ahead of me a massive grey building, and the path I was following took me quite close to it. Just as I passed from the moonlight into its shadow, without warning and so suddenly that it froze me to the spot, a harsh order rang out and there before me in the dark I could see the glint of a bayonet some five inches from my throat.

Slowly I raised my hands to my shoulders, and as my fear was replaced by an overwhelming disappointment, muttered miserably:

'English – *Engländer* – *Englezi.*'

What happened then was typical of any adventures in Greece, the land of 'you-never-know'. The rifle clattered to the ground, two hands reached up and grasped mine, and before my startled wits could register what was happening a bristly face had planted a kiss on both my cheeks. In the dark I could see my new friend was in uniform. Looking again at the silhouette of the imposing building, in whose shadow we stood, some memory of a conversation in the camp convinced me that I had run into a Greek policeman guarding the civilian jail. It was the first indication, and a surprise after my other experiences, to find that the Greek police were not necessarily pro-German.

But after the first emotional outburst had spent itself fear seized him and immediately he fell to gesticulating violently and whispering urgent instructions. I gathered he wanted me to make myself scarce and also not to continue along the track I had been following. When I shrugged my shoulders in an expression of hopelessness he seized my arms and pointed to some lights in the far distance with repeated whispers 'Bon, kala, goot, bon, kala, goot'.

Half an hour, over a bare and stony hillock, brought me to the lights, a group of perhaps thirty poor houses. Most of them were in darkness and quiet, but the lights I had followed indicated that someone was still afoot. I moved in to try my luck, and knocked at the door of the nearest house.

We say an Englishman's home is his castle; so it is with the Greek. He won't let the drawbridge down at night until he recognizes a friend. He peers furtively at you from the window on the left of the door, then from the one on the right, and finally decides through the keyhole and from your foreign jabber that you are no friend. And after that no amount of noise nor knocking, no entreaties nor threats will affect him. You will hear urgent whispers inside, and movement near the door, but you are lucky indeed if it opens.

I tried every house in the first group whether lights shone or not, but always with the same result. I felt desolate and cold, and the unusual exercise was causing my wound to tug uncomfortably at my thigh. To make things more desperate, suddenly from one of the dark alleyways between two houses bounded a large village dog, fiercely growling and snarling. Three or four of its kind joined it and I was forced to move warily along one of the walls with my boots ready and my heart in my mouth.

At first the brutes showed a certain caution, would move back a yard or two if I made as though I had something to throw, but gradually, as their numbers swelled, they took confidence and started snapping at the cuffs of my trousers. The situation was ugly. There seemed no possibility of help from the dark, aloof houses, and I knew that to run would only bring them upon me in a ferocity far beyond my strength to combat. But in the end that is just what I did. Panic seized me and I ran full pelt down the rough street with them all at my heels, until, seeing a flight of steps leading up to a small house I ran frantically up and hammered on the door. The first of the dogs came half-way up the steps and paused, the remainder stayed snarling and yapping below.

From inside some order was called, then repeated, then footsteps padded over and the door was flung open. The smallest of men, about five feet high, smiled up at me and spoke rapidly in Greek. With a gesture I said '*Englezi*' and indicated the bristling dark forms below. With that unique fluttering of the hand which is the Greek beckoning, I was waved into a tiny living-room.

In the centre of the room, huddled round a tin of ashes on the top of which were a few live coals, were two more small people – an old lady and a young fellow. On my entry they both stood up and looked over inquiringly. The first one said something, which I took to be an introduction of sorts, and the old lady, dear fragile thing that she was, reached up and patted my arm. She sighed deeply and suddenly I felt in that sigh all the sympathy I had been craving for so long. They indicated a chair, and as I collapsed into it, both body and mind relaxed into a relief that brought me almost to tears.

They fussed around me, talking excitedly to one another. A very stiff *ouzo* was followed by a meal they prepared from a cabbage out of their garden. They apologized in Greek, until even I understood that they had no bread in the house to give me. We all sat round the small tin of ashes, occasionally blowing on the four or five coals, and I tried to explain with my hands the adventures that led me to their door.

Finally they decided it was time for me to get some rest and ushered me into another equally small room. The smallness of the whole house was unbelievable. There were only two rooms and neither was more than eight feet square. I was given the only bed in the house and the brothers spread rugs on the floor beside me. As I stretched comfortably in the short bed the old lady came round and patted my forehead, sighing deeply. She then murmured something over me, crossed herself reverently and departed into the other room where I could hear her preparing a bed on the couch. Even after the house became quiet, I could hear her deep sighs as I myself lay, sleep impossible, and tried to consider my position and convince myself that I had really succeeded. Occasionally a half-moon broke cloud and shone wanly through the tiny windows. Outside the last of the dogs ceased its baying and left a peaceful stillness, made homely by the steady breathing of the two brothers on the floor. . . .

*   *   *

. . . This was by no means the end of Lieutenant Thomas's escape. On foot he found his way to Mount Athos, that strange and lovely peninsula in the Aegean Sea, which has for twelve hundred years had no female, not even a female animal, among its population. Here he was hidden by the monks until with the help of another British escaper and a party of Greeks he stole a boat and set sail for Turkey. They were nearly shipwrecked on the voyage but finally reached Smyrna – and freedom.

Major W. B. Thomas, D.S.O., M.C. and bar, U.S.A. Silver Star, is now a regular officer in the British Army.

CHAPTER TEN

Jump for Freedom

PETER MEDD, like David James, was rescued by his enemies from the sea. This time the enemies were Italian. As a pilot in the Fleet Air Arm, Lieutenant Medd was flying from the deck of H.M.S. *Warspite*. In August 1940 he was shot down into the Mediterranean.

His first prison camp was near Sulmona, the monastery camp from which Anthony Deane-Drummond made his first two escapes. Medd was moved from camp to camp in Italy until he found himself with George Millar at Gavi. This story begins when the Italians capitulated on 8 September 1943. . . .

* * *

. . . Armistice! We heard the news at eight o'clock on the evening of 9 September. Down below, outside our small barred mess windows, there was an excited twittering from the Italian guards, cries of '*A casa!*', gestures of contempt for everything military. There were soberer feelings among the prisoners: feelings of relief that a long weary chapter had come to an end; feelings of expectancy, uncertainty, the realization that now we must think for ourselves again, and perhaps think quickly. There was no wild celebration – the *vino* had run out.

Our commandant, Giuseppe Moscatelli, known not the least bit affectionately to his charges as 'Joe Grapes', had lived up to his reputation and left the camp in this important hour. We were in the hands of that incompetent pair of old dugouts, de Cesare and Odino, who refused to take any action until their colonel returned.

At seven o'clock next morning we were startled by a burst of tommy-gun fire and the boom of a grenade –

Germans. Soon, a very demoralized Italian ration party returned to the camp bearing the corpse of one of their number. Jerry had done his job well, posting machine-guns to cover the fortress before dawn, and now, truly appreciating the Italian character, striking terror and demoralization by one quick act of brutality. The rest was easy. Joe Grapes handed over the entire camp, lock, stock and barrel, to a German N.C.O. and sixty men. Gavi Castle, true to its thousand-year-old tradition, had once more surrendered without a fight.

Followed four days of feverish thought and activity. We had been unable (except once) to find a way out; now one *must* be found in a hurry. A tunnel was started, to join a secret passage of which we had been told by a *cara-biniere*. The diggers worked long hours desperately and promised us success. The tension was appalling: would it be finished before they took us away?

The diggers forecast success for Monday night, 13 September. Our hopes ran high; we began to think of 'out-side' instead of 'how to get outside'. Then came the bomb-shell. At ten o'clock on Monday morning it was announced that all officers would leave the camp in an hour's time. This possibility had, of course, been foreseen, and hiding-places had been arranged for a certain number of us, in the hope that after we had left the Germans would evacuate the camp themselves. I had been allocated a bunk-hole, but at the last moment it seemed to me that this was merely walking into a trap: there was no other exit, and the Germans, being in no hurry, would be quite prepared to wait and starve us out; but about fifty others hid up – too many, for Jerry was bound to notice the absence of that number.

And so the forlorn remnant left Gavi for ever, more miserable even than when we had arrived at this gloomy fortress, struggling down the hill with the fraction of our accumulated possessions that it was possible or permissible to take. Past the great sun-flowers, whose heads seemed turned in shame, past the Italian officers' mess, where a little group of quislings gazed at us dispassionately, down the dusty winding road to a line of commandeered buses and trucks heading, strangely, towards France.

Now, for the first time, our captors realized that we were not all there, for the special seat reserved for the brigadier remained empty. A storm burst, which, for volume of noise and confusion, rivalled anything produced by Italians. It was four hours before the convoy left for Acqui, each lorry guarded by three tommy-gunners and loaded with prisoners keyed to hair-trigger readiness to escape at the slightest opportunity, with a desperation which overcame all fear.

The greatest bogey to spontaneous escape is apathy. A fleeting opportunity occurs; you say to yourself: 'No, a better opportunity is bound to occur soon.' Or you suddenly think of the danger to the others, and, thinking, the chance slips by, never to return. You know you are determined to escape, but the starting friction is terribly hard to overcome. The secret of spontaneous escape is: Don't think – go.

On this long, uncomfortable truck ride two successful breaks were made, simultaneously. The trucks were going slowly up a winding hill, with a wooded downslope on the left, when Frank Simms and Pitchford jumped. There was no shooting: the dusty tommy-guns had jammed. For minutes there was no panic – the guards were bewildered. Then, of course, hell was let loose.

At Acqui we entrained, but there was a wait in the station for four hours before we left. During this time we were allowed to stroll on the platform. Tommy MacPherson made a daring dash for the road, and a shooting match started in the centre of the town, ending with his recapture. Two months later I found Tommy had beaten me to England, having escaped in Germany and into Sweden. No prisoner more deserved success, for his mind was passionately concentrated on thoughts of escape.

By now I was getting more desperate than ever, saying

to myself that I *must* go, to justify my decision not to hide
up, thinking back on three monotonous years, and forward to an unknown number of even more monotonous
ones. But no opportunity seemed to come my way. Then,
just before the train left, twelve of us were moved to a
cattle truck near the back and locked in without guards.
This truck had a sort of sentry-box sticking up in the roof,
with a window for the guard to look along the top. It
seemed almost too good to be true.

We left Acqui at ten-thirty in the evening. Now we had
to move fast, for at Alessandria, in half an hour, we had
to change trains. Quickly Captain Liebenberg, u.d.f., and
I broke the sentry-box window, squeezed through and
climbed down on to the buffers, he on the left side, I on
the right. There we clung, waiting for the train to slow
down, with a thrilling warm wind in our faces, and a wide
moonlit countryside rushing by, and an overflowing feeling of freedom and happiness in our hearts. Then:
'Jump!' shouted Lieby, and I jumped.

I landed on hands and knees, and didn't even roll over
– didn't even hurt myself. In a flash all my inhibitions
about the risks of train-jumping dissolved. We were passing through a cutting, and the bank on my side was too
high to climb, so I lay alongside the rail, under the run-
ning-board, and prayed that no inquisitive sentry would
notice me as the last half of the train rumbled by. Then
suddenly I found myself alone in the moonlight, with the
train's red tail-light quickly receding, and not a sign of
Lieby. I climbed the other bank and set off rather aimlessly
across the fields, my one idea being to get away from the
railway. My sense of freedom was overlaid with a feeling
of loneliness and bewilderment. Here was I, alone in the
great open world for the first time in three years, dressed
only in check shirt, plus-fours, stockings and shoes, my
only possessions a tin of Ovaltine tablets and one hundred
lire, for in the last-minute excitement my well-prepared
escape outfit was forgotten. Here was no comforting routine, no certainty, no solid foundation of prison camp life

to drug my senses. Now I must think, and act, and make decisions. The responsibility seemed overpowering.

So I walked to a farm-house, told them how I had escaped, and asked for help. What a friendly welcome for a refugee! I was pressed into a chair, given bread and cheese and wine, surrounded by a crowd of inquisitive and excited people. Here was the *padrone* of the house and his family, and charming Mariuccia Pesca and her sister, evacuated from Genoa – the first girls I had been face to face with for three years – and one of their male admirers from a neighbouring house.

We talked of escape, and Germans, and Mussolini, and my plans. They were pathetically optimistic: the British would land at Genoa in a few days, and my best plan was to get into 'plainer' clothes and remain hidden in the district until rescued. I accepted, at least, the offer of plain clothes, and Mariuccia's boy friend took me to his house to get them.

There, his pretty young sister came down in her nightdress and found me more bread and cheese and wine, while I changed my too-English clothes for worn black coat and trousers, a blue shirt and Trilby hat. Then I left them: wished on my way by whispered *auguri* and bits of advice, touched and encouraged by such spontaneous generosity. Living in Italy as a refugee was not going to be so hard, after all.

I wandered up into the hills left of Acqui, revelling in the warm night, the full moon, the wide space and freedom. At last I made myself a bed in the bracken in a small coppice and fell asleep to the murmer of strange forgotten sounds – wind rustling through trees, an owl hooting, the distant bark of a watchdog. It was hard to distinguish where reality ended and dreams began. I half expected to see Titania appear.

*

The sun woke me, flickering through the leaves, casting long shadows across the bracken, stirring into life suspicious blackbirds and inquisitive lizards, and industrious spiders who seemed intent on binding me to my brackeny couch.

I climbed to the top of the hill, where the wood ended and vineyards began, with widely spaced farm-houses, still asleep. To the south-east the slope dropped steeply to the Alessandria-Acqui Valley, containing the main road, railways and river, with, beyond, a jumble of hills fading to the faint outline of the Gavi Mountains. To the south lay the main range of the Apennines, higher and more wild, stretching away to France. To the north the ground sloped down to the broad Po Valley, with, beyond, a suspicion of Alps, the great massif of Mont Blanc and Monte Rosa.

So I lay there till noon among the vines, feeding myself on fat red and white grapes, sweating slightly as the hot sun rose in a cloudless sky, watching the endless German convoys going south along the road, and trying to decide on a plan.

There were three choices. I might go to France. It was only fifty miles away, and the German guards had told us a landing had been made at Toulon. If not, one could probably get to Spain, but that would be a long way, and I couldn't be certain of help from the French. Or I might go to Switzerland. This was close, too – just eighty miles across the plain – but we had heard the Germans and Swiss were guarding the two sides of the frontier, and, anyway, once there, would one ever get out? Unlimited winter sports would be magnificent, but it wasn't war. Finally, there was the walk down through Italy to join our advancing army. With luck, they would do most of the walking. Little did I guess how wrong I was!

So I chose the third, but first I decided to go back to Gavi. The Germans might have evacuated it, and the boys hiding up might want the tip to come out. Then, David Stirling, one of the hidden, had selected a commando team, in which I was to practise guerrilla tactics in north-ern Italy. There might still be a chance of joining up and having our fun.

About noon I descended the hill, crossed the main road in a lull between convoys, and headed through the maize-fields for the river, sheathed in its coat of tall poplars and thick undergrowth. There I found a ford, where the swift knee-deep water rushed in foam over the tumbled rocks, and waded across, feeling rather ridiculous under the placid stare of a couple of sleek white oxen.

Soon I reached a road again, and here I got my first fright. A sinister little man in a black hat – the swarthy aquiline type of Italian – said to me: *'Dove andate?'* ('Where are you going?') in that unpleasant tone of voice I had already learnt to associate with Fascists and *cara-binieri*. I mumbled an unconvincing reply and hurried on as fast as I could with dignity, heading for the hills.

There on the hillside I found a white house, with a white-haired old man mending a wine-cask outside the front door. I told him I was an escaped British prisoner and asked for help. He looked up fiercely. 'How do you know I am not a Fascist?' Then his blue eyes twinkled.

He was a retired merchant skipper, evacuated here from Genoa, with his family. We went indoors and met his wife, thin and frail, and utterly worn out with years of too much work. This family – there was a daughter, too – was living on the starvation line. They had nothing, absolutely nothing. The neighbouring farmers charged them fantastic prices for food, or refused to sell, so they lived on the ration, which was inadequate and not always obtainable nowadays. Their Genoa home had been bombed, and here they lived in this empty house with a few salved bits of furniture and bedding. They suffered in silence. Her sympathy was all for me, a *poverino* who couldn't go home, and he never talked about hardships except to say gruffly that it was all their own fault for ever having put up with Mussolini. In this he was the most enlightened Italian I ever met.

The day faded. Mrs Valente set about preparing the supper, and we went out on to the flat roof and looked at the landscape through a pair of ancient binoculars, the

sort that every retired old sailor has, which shows two
images and is unadjustable. There we talked of the sea
dispassionately, for he showed no feelings of any sort. Yet
I think he was glad to be able to talk once more with another sailor. Then we went in to supper.

Polenta – the staple dish of the poor in northern Italy –
tomatoes and walnuts. This is what they lived on. She
apologized continually: he grunted and said nothing. After supper the daughter arrived, bringing a breath of fresh
air into this rather embarrassing atmosphere. She worked
in an office in Genoa: left home on foot at four-thirty
every morning on a two-hour walk to the station. (You
daren't bicycle these days: the thing would be stolen
within twenty-four hours.) Then a two-and-a-half-hour
ride in a cattle-truck, owing to the shortage of rolling-
stock, would get her to the office about nine. There she
worked until four-thirty in the afternoon, when the long
ride home began.

In spite of a sixteen-and-a-half-hour day, she had a
freshness and gaiety about her which was charming. As
she described her day, there was never a hint of hardship
or overwork. Her Italian accent would have penetrated an
air-raid shelter; her Genoese dialect was quite incomprehensible. She had brought back the week's ration of flour,
sugar and salt. Each pathetic little package was unwrap-
ped with the excitement of a child over a Christmas stock-
ing. We all went to bed early, for tomorrow morning we
must get up at four. I had a mattress on the floor of the
old man's bedroom and slept like a log.

The alarm-clock woke us punctually, and we breakfasted off hot milk and stale bread in the pungent light of
an acetylene lamp. Mrs Valente, her daughter and I left
the house at four-thirty for the long walk to the station. I
don't know whether the chaperoning was on account of
me: the old woman excused herself by saying she made
the trip every day.

My way lay eastwards towards Ovada, so I left them
short of the station and set off along the road in the pale

dawn light. For the first half-hour I met nobody, but then the countryside began to wake up. Sleepy bullock-carts rumbled by, the fields seemed imperceptibly to sprout with peasants engaged in the eternal task of hoeing. I was glad to find I raised no curiosity in them. But as the morning activity increased I decided to leave the road – it was the sight of a German ambulance parked by the kerb just ahead which finally decided me – and travelled eastwards across a country of steep hills and gullies, vineyards on the slopes and thick undergrowth in the hollows. My lunch was a handful of walnuts and some stolen grapes, eaten in the sunshine in the dry bed of a stream.

About noon I reached Ovada. Here, I remembered, was a German headquarters; the place had been stiff with troops when we came through three days before. I sneaked across the main road, and under the railway by a culvert, and so up into the wooded hills to the south. This was not the most direct way to Gavi, but I wanted to reach the main west–east ridge of the mountains, where going would be easier and safer than among the foothills, with their criss-cross systems of rivers, roads and railways.

By now the sun had vanished in a white haze, which darkened and condensed to torrential rain. Even this did not lessen my unaccustomed joy of freedom. There were more pleasures to be rediscovered among these woods: the intoxicating scent of damp pine-needles, the sight of bright-eyed little birds hopping silently through the undergrowth, the sudden explosion of disturbed partridges taking to the air, or of a startled hare zigzagging across the hillside. These were strange, exciting sensations for me, and I thought to myself, in the old familiar words: 'Ain't nature wonderful?' It was not until days later that I realized the absolute paucity of wild life in Italy. A similar countryside of woods and mountains in England would teem with life, yet here in Italy one sometimes walked a whole day without seeing flesh or fowl, save the vulgar crow wheeling overhead, and lizards and snakes

scuttling for cover. I never saw a rabbit in Italy, except a
tame one. There were a few hares and partridges, fewer
squirrels and pheasants. Even the small bird-life is practically non-existent. For every Italian countryman carries a
shotgun, and anything over the size of a sparrow is fair
game to him. There are laws, indeed – shooting begins
officially on 1 October – but all laws, the Italian believes,
are made to be broken. This year the German requisition-
ing of all firearms will probably give Italian wild-life such
a chance as it has never had before, though even this
order, carrying the death sentence as penalty for dis-
obedience, is only being partly carried out.

Up there, in the mist and woods, I lost my sense of
direction, so decided to go down and take shelter in a
farm-house. I found one in a fold of the hill, almost overgrown by the wood, attached to a tiny vegetable-garden
and vineyard, which seemed the only means of support
for the swarm of dirty children and old women who filled
the single ground-floor room. Here they gave me bread
and wine, and gazed at me in wonder, tremendously in-
trigued to meet an Englishman for the first time. Then,
the rain stopping, a small child guided me down to the
river and across the Ovada–Genoa railway, and left me to
climb into the oak woods on the other side, north-east-
wards towards Gavi.

A quarter of an hour later, passing a farm-house, an old
man came out and called : 'Come in, *giovanotto,* and have
a drink.' I refused, for it was getting late and I had far to
go, but he insisted. His son, he said, had just reached
home from France, where he and his fellow-soldiers had
been ordered to lay down their arms after the armistice.
When I admitted I was English, the soldier turned to me
and said earnestly : 'Never tell that to anyone. The country is full of Fascist spies. Say you are a soldier of the
Italian 4th Army, disbanded in Toulon, returning to your
home in Trieste. Your accent will pass for a Triestino in
this part of the country.'

This was interesting. I hadn't realized till then that Italy is such a honeycomb of self-contained cells, each having its own customs and speaking its own dialect, that country people are easily fooled by the accent of a 'foreigner' from a different part of the country.

Shortly afterwards, on the road to Gavi, I had an opportunity of trying this out. An old peasant attached himself to me, and we walked together for five miles, discussing every sort of subject, and to the end he believed me a good Triestino who had laid down his arms in the service of his country, and was now going to the only sensible place for an Italian – home.

This road led us along the crest of a tortuous range of hills, scarred by deep eroded gullies and cut by streams. Here and there in this desolate landscape were fantastic villages, perched on the very tops of rocky pinnacles, secure from the invader of olden days who ravaged their vineyards and fields on the lower slopes.

The rain had cleared and left a fine, steamy-blue evening. The old familiar Gavi landmarks drew slowly closer. The peasants were going home, many of them heading for their nearest village, taking their firearms to be handed in to the German command, or local *podestà*. One man passed us, almost hysterical with anger, waving a big ·45 revolver, and crying that he had tried to hide it, but had been denounced.

At last Gavi Monastery came in sight, winking like a lighthouse in the setting sun. I climbed its winding ramp in the dusk, considerably excited at seeking refuge so near to the lion's den.

After the armistice, our Italian chaplain had told us that, in the event of escape, we could safely ask for help at any monastery, and that he would warn Gavi Monastery to expect refugees. I didn't know who to ask for or where to go, and before I knew where I was, found myself face to face with a white-coifed nun. I asked for the priests' quarters and foolishly told her that I was an escaped British prisoner – so soon had I forgotten the soldier's advice. In a moment the news had reached all the

women, and even the children in the attached orphanage
heard about it and came to peer at me round corners.

Then I met the father. He led me to the ramparts and
looked at me a long time without saying a word. Then:
'Are you a Catholic?' he asked. 'No, a Protestant,' I con-
fessed, and felt for a moment that I was going to be turned
shamefully away, an infidel and outcast. 'Never mind,' he
said, 'we offer shelter to everybody.' We stood in silence
gazing across the valley to where Gavi Castle reared its
gloomy shadow out of the mist, the very embodiment of
all that is evil and sinister. The arc-lights glinted bale-
fully: so the Germans were still in occupation. I thought
miserably of those unfortunate fellows who lay hidden
there, walled up in cold, dank holes, unable to talk or light
a match, or move about, wondering whether Jerry was
still there or not, wondering whether the next moment
would bring a hand grenade bouncing down on them.
And I was very glad of my decision not to hide up.

The father was talking in a low, precise voice. It was
a reprimand to me for spreading the news that I was English. 'Those women cannot hold their tongues. Already
the news may be down in the village. The Church is always suspect, and we are closely watched here.'

I was beginning to be quite windy. But that was nothing to what was to come. I was told to hide in the garden
while he removed the watchdog from the side door. Then
we crept quickly in on tiptoe, up the stairs to his room,
and locked ourselves in. Soon there was a knock at the
door. 'Who is it?' asked the priest, and there was a
mumbled reply from outside. 'Well, you can't come in
now, I am busy,' said the priest in a tone of voice which
would have raised curiosity and excitement in the dumb-
est listener. If there were any who hadn't heard of my
arrival from the nun, they would soon learn now that
there were strange goings-on in Gavi Monastery that
night.

When the steps had died away, he led me on an inspec-
tion of the bolt-holes. 'You see,' he said, 'we have two

exits from this place. If they come by this door, you creep down the stairs, through the vestry and out the back. If they come by the back door, I'll keep them talking until you can get out the side door. And just to be quite certain, we'll hang this rope out of the pantry window, and you can climb down that.'

By this time I was thoroughly jittery, seeing a German round every corner. Then suddenly I realized that this good man was enjoying himself as never before. The traditional monastic spirit of intrigue flowed in his veins. This promised to be the best thing that had happened in Gavi since the days of the Borgia Pope. I laughed to myself and went up to enjoy my supper with a quiet heart.

I fed alone – steaming *minestra*, bread, cheese and wine – watched by the father and another priest. They told me the Germans showed no signs of leaving the castle, but so far had caught no prisoners. We talked little, for I was very tired.

The father's quarters consisted of a sitting-room, bedroom and pantry. The inside wall of the sitting-room had a window giving out into the chapel. In this room they made me up a bed on a couch; spring mattress and clean sheets, and two pillows. As I slipped into this heaven of softness, a boy started to play the organ, slow, quiet chords. The dangers of life seemed infinitely remote. I went to sleep with the peace of mind of the medieval refugee who sought sanctuary at the altar and knew he was safe. Even the rope in the pantry window couldn't keep me awake.

*

The good father woke me at four-thirty, and I think he was disappointed the night had been so uneventful. While I ate my bread-and-wine breakfast, he gave me his advice. He suggested I go and call on the parish priest of a near-by village, Alice. 'He is a well-informed man, who knows the country and always listens to the English broadcasts.'

I slipped down the hill in the half light, before the inquisitive nuns were awake, and took the road eastwards

to Alice. Away over on the left was the sombre fortress of
Gavi, brooding over its secrets. Neither hill nor wood
seemed to hide me from the baleful stare of those arc-
lights.

The sun was up when I reached Alice, and mass was
about to begin as I entered the vestry and introduced myself to the *parocco*. He was fat and genial, his face full of
an owlish wisdom, and his eyes twinkled as he heard my
story. He thought for a while, suggested a course of action
at great length, cancelled it, and thought again. From
time to time a black-veiled woman would come in and
urge him to begin the mass, but his mind was on more
worldly matters now. Then he began talking again. It was
his opinion, too, that I should stay round here and wait
for a nearby landing, and he suggested the name of a
family, who lived way up in the hills, who would look
after me or pass me on to their relations. I decided to go
there: perhaps it would be possible to get passed on from
house to house, right down to the British lines? I had no
faith at all in the theory of a British landing up this end
of the country.

So I left him to take his mass, and was pulled into the
kitchen by his niece (the rectory, in country Italy, is at-
tached to the church) and served with hot milk and bread.
She was also an evacuee from Genoa. Her enthusiasm for
Britain, and her desire to help me, were most reassuring.
I began to realize that I was in a friendly country.

On I went, then, across the tiny stream in its wide bed
of smooth white pebbles, where the village women were
already ranged on their knees, pounding their dirty linen,
and up the other bank through the vineyards to pleasant
oak woods. Here was a *riserva di caccia* – a game reserve
– which seemed to contain more game than the unres-
tricted areas, in spite of occasional shots in the distance.

At last I found my house – the 'Casa Brucciata' – a
neat, clean farmhouse sitting on a green, undulating
grassy alp. There was suddenly something rather Swiss
about the scene, a change from the nearby oak woods.

In the doorway sat an old woman peeling potatoes. I told her of my visit to the parson and introduced myself as an escaped British prisoner. 'How can you prove it?' she said suspiciously. This was a bit difficult, because I had no identity marks. The letter addressed to me at Gavi which I had saved for this very purpose was still in my coat on the way to Germany.

'Well, I can't prove it, but I certainly am English,' and my ingenuousness must have convinced her, for she softened a bit. Then I asked her if I could stay, as the priest had said, and she was again cautious in her reply. 'You must wait until the men return. You understand, I, too, am under orders here.'

So I went out on to the grassy mountainside and slept in the sun until lunch-time. I got back to the house just as the men were coming in from work. I and my story were received gravely, but with great politeness. I could see they weren't particularly taken with the idea of putting me up, or passing me on to friends, and I wondered what my next move should be.

Lunch was now ready, and we went into the kitchen. The *padrone* – the old woman's husband – took the end of the table, and motioned me to a place on his right. At the other end of the table sat his two sons and a youth of about fourteen. An immense bowl of steaming *minestra* was placed before him, and he filled my plate and his. Then the other men helped themselves. It is delicious filling stuff, this *minestra*, made of macaroni, potatoes, beans, herbs, sometimes bits of meat, all mixed into the consistency of Irish stew. We had three helpings each (second and third helpings are the rule in Italy; what a pity it is considered greedy at home!). We drank water, the *padrone* and I having a glass each, the remainder drinking from a huge ladle, which they dipped into a central bowl. When all the men had finished eating, the *minestra* was removed and the women got down to their share – not much, for there wasn't much left – which they ate sitting on stools in corners, or standing. Then all the men got up

and went upstairs for two hours' *siesta*, with never a word
to me.

This was my first introduction to Italian peasant society.
The feudal primitiveness of it is almost terrifying. Man is
a god, the head of the family a super-god. The women are
servants, never speaking in the presence of men unless
spoken to, never pushing themselves forward, working
ceaselessly from before dawn to dusk, uncomplainingly.
They know their position; it would never enter their
heads to try and alter it.

The woman had told me that many Italian soldiers
passed the Casa Brucciata on their way home, so I
decided to await the afternoon in the sun and attach myself to any party who would have me. Living in this
austere family would be impossible, I realized, and, anyway, it wouldn't help me to join with our army.

About three o'clock a party of five arrived at the farm,
singing and chattering like a covey of magpies. They
welcomed me enthusiastically. They were going to Rome
and, of course, I could come along with them.

We swapped stories in front of the farm-house, while
they munched the bread given them by the old woman.
Then suddenly, with no apparent word of command, they
were off again up the path to Rome, laughing and shouting, and I with them.

Carlo, Giuliano, Augusto, Giuseppe and Renzo. It was
Renzo Baccani who invited me to come along. He
attached himself to me almost as personal bodyguard,
taught me the peculiar ways of Italian soldiers, steered me
through many dangers, and shared everything he possessed with me. Carlo Bergamino was our leader. He
might have been the original Charlie Chaplin: the little
cane, the outsize trousers, the absurd moustache. He
walked in decrepit sandals. And on top of this music-hall
personality he had a superb power of command, which
enabled him more or less to control his irresponsible companions and to stifle at source the many embryo arguments.

We had only walked for ten minutes from the Casa Brucciata when the whole team suddenly stopped, unpacked their lunch, and settled down to a huge lunch of bread and cheese and tinned fish, in which I was compelled to join. But ten minutes later Carlo had us on the road again.

We climbed to the top of our particular mountain, from which we looked down into a deep valley, and beyond the imposing *massif* of the big mountain which used to dominate the Gavi landscape. Down to the right the valley led away to Voltaggio, and this was our direction.

Voltaggio presented a certain danger. We knew it to be full of Germans, yet there was no avoiding the town. But here again we were lucky. A charming Genoa evacuee attached herself to us and offered to guide us through the town by safe back streets.

On the far outskirts of the town we stopped again and said good-bye to our fair guide. An admiring crowd of spectators collected round us, and the whole story of the escape from France had to be retold.

These soldiers belonged to the 4th Italian Army, garrisoning Toulon. On the signing of the armistice the general ordered his men to lay down their arms and confined them to barracks. Followed a mass break-out by the troops, breaking down the doors with hand grenades. The fugitives took the train to Turin (still in Italian hands), where they broke up into small parties, changed into plain clothes, and started the long trek to their homes.

We were about to move on to find a lodging-place for the night farther from the town, when the *padrone* of the nearby farmhouse invited us to stay with him. We accepted. It was convenient, for here close to the farm flowed the river, and we were able to have a bathe and wash our clothes. Then we sat on the stoep in the twilight talking to our hosts, and two lovely evacuees brought us *vino*. They drew me aside and said : 'You are not Italian, are you? American or English?' Then one of them told me she was engaged to an Italian naval officer, Lieutenant

Casinaghi, and would I please call on him when we crossed the line, for he had gone to Malta with the Italian fleet, and she had had no news of him for a long time. I realized then it was no good trying to fool an educated Italian with my accent.

I fell in love with these girls from Zena; in fact all the Genoese girls I had met. Their soft accent is delicious. They know how to make themselves attractive in a not-too-sophisticated way, in spite of the rigours of war. There is a practical good sense about them, so different from the hothouse-plant type which one associates more with this Mediterranean climate. They reminded me of the English girls of Shanghai: vivacious, hard-working, with an immense appreciation for life.

Then we had supper – a hugely amusing supper. The *vino* flowed, the *minestra* came again and again in steaming platefuls, and Carlo and Augusto kept up a cross-talk – mostly in different dialects – which kept the company in fits of laughter. Augusto has one passion: catching chickens. He dreams and talks all day about catching chickens. And now he described, in brilliant fashion, his failures and successes in this line since leaving Turin.

Finally, we were shown to bed in the loft, all rather tipsy and hysterical. Life seemed good. We were free, we were going home. Soon – any day now – the British would land at Genoa, and there would be no more war, but instead unlimited food and luxuries and work for all. Poor, self-deceiving Italy! ...

*   *   *

... Peter Medd walked with his 'Crazy Gang' for several days until, in a small village, they met Major Frank Simms of the Royal Warwickshire Regiment, who had escaped earlier on the journey from Gavi. Together the two Englishmen walked seven hundred miles in forty days to meet the advancing Allies. It was indeed a 'long walk home'.

Lieutenant-Commander Peter Medd, M.B.E., Royal Navy, was killed in a flying accident in August 1944 before he had finished writing his book. The narrative was completed by his fellow-escaper, Major Simms.

CHAPTER ELEVEN

Through Enemy Lines

WINTON K. SEXTON dedicated his book to the courageous men and women of Italy who helped him in his
escape. It is the tribute of a brave man to equally brave
men and women of the other side. The people of Italy
had a Fascist Government which many of them hated and
war for the Italians was not the same thing as it was for
us or for our Allies. It is difficult for us, who have never
lived under a government imposed by force, to appreciate
the feelings of men and women who would hide and aid
an escaping enemy airman. The penalty of capture for
Lieutenant Sexton, U.S.A.A.F., was return to the prison
life from which he had escaped: for the Italians who had
helped him it was death.

Lieutenant Sexton was a pilot in an American Bomber
Squadron and was on his thirtieth mission when he was
shot down on a bombing raid over Sicily. Badly wounded,
he was picked up by the Germans and sent to a hospital
in Italy. When the Allies landed and Italy capitulated all
the prisoners who were patients in the hospital were removed by rail to Germany.

Winton Sexton (although he had a broken leg encased
in plaster and several other unhealed wounds) jumped
from his train before it reached the Brenner Pass, seven
hundred miles behind the enemy lines. During the next
nine months he made his way slowly down the length of
Italy towards the advancing Allied armies. This account
opens when he is within a few miles of his own troops
camped on the outskirts of Anzio. ...

*   *   *

... The next morning I got my hands on a pair of field-glasses. For the next two days I sat on a high rock, planning an approach to the lines. I would gaze over the area until I saw some activity and would put a dot on the map at that location. In two days I had a line of dots, and by drawing a line through them I had a fair battle-line to work with.

With the help of my battle-line I planned an approach. The Germans had flooded several thousand acres of land about five miles south of the lines, and because of this there was little fighting there – more of a holding action. I decided to work south between the water and the lines and find a hole to get through. If I were going to go in a straight line to the front I could walk the distance, if uninterrupted, within two hours; but to buck the line there would put me directly into Cisterna, the point of heaviest fighting.

The Italian with whom I was staying walked up one afternoon and asked what I planned to do. He looked for a while at the front, and then pointed to a pond out on the plain about a mile out on my course. 'See that pond,' he said. I noticed. 'You'll be caught before reaching it.' I was through arguing with all these people, so I said nothing. Since escaping from the Germans, I had walked over five hundred miles through 'Hell and high water', and I wasn't going to sit down now, just ten miles from freedom.

My plans for an approach to the lines were just as thorough as possible. I had to walk about ten miles in order to work into the position I had planned to crack the line. Considering the distance and the very slow speed I would make, I allowed myself four days to get this position. As provisions, I took one loaf of bread, two large links of sausage, a couple of ounces of sugar and a pint of alcohol distilled from wine. None of this was to be eaten unless I got pinned down and couldn't move. I knew there were a few Italians still living in the battle area, and they were to supply me with food whenever possible.

On the afternoon of 25 March 1944 I decided I was ready. That night I checked and oiled my automatic, wrote a note to be given to the American troops in case I wasn't successful, and went to bed.

At 4 a.m. the following morning, I set off down the mountain. The front was relatively quiet with sporadic firing.

By daybreak I was down on to the plain. It was unusual not to see a flock of Italians going into the fields at dawn. Most of the population had evacuated the area, leaving behind their empty homes and unplanted fields.

About midday I spotted an Italian family milling around a *capanna* along the path ahead. They were friendly, and I had my first meal out on the Pontine flats that Mussolini had converted from swampland into a fertile asset to the country. According to these people, there were Germans billeted in many of the vacant houses over the area. They were in the front lines one day and back resting the next. Evidently they were not being pushed too hard in this section of the front, which was my reason for picking the south line to cross.

Later in the afternoon I passed a house with three 'Jerries' sunning themselves in the yard; but they paid no attention to the peasant as he nonchalantly trudged down the path. They probably remarked how foolish anyone was to stay around risking death if he didn't have to. The peasant agreed with them!

By dusk the first night I had made remarkable progress. Long before noon I had even passed the pond I wasn't to reach at all, and also succeeded in finding another family with whom I stayed for the night.

With the break of dawn, I was off on my second day. I soon came to the Via Appia – this new road to Rome. To the north, the Allies had cut this highway and were holding about a mile of it. I had to walk about a half-mile south along it to cross a canal on the west side. This section of road had been under fire, for it was covered with splintered trees and shell holes. I didn't consider it wise to stay around there any longer than necessary. In a way it was nice to be so close to our troops but, on the other hand, it wasn't particularly safe.

By mid-afternoon I was lying on a clump of grass a few feet from the Mediterranean. I had hit the coast about three miles south of the town of Sabodia, which I decided was just about on the line. I stayed for a while just looking out into the sea. I closed my eyes and listened to the waves lap the shore. I could hardly realize that men were dying just three miles north of this peaceful spot. Why couldn't I find a small boat and after dark row three miles up into friendly waters? The wind was coming out of the west and that along with the waves would be a terrific fight. No, it was too risky, at least for now. Finally, I backtracked about one-fourth mile and then started slowly north towards the line. I spent the night in an evacuated house. It was equipped with blackout shutters so after dark I made a fire and was quite comfortable. That night for the first time I was able to hear sporadic small-arms fire. The artillery was not firing south but was fairly heavy all night. I estimated that I was within two miles of the line.

Then next morning I moved about a half-mile north and met an Italian. I was able to get some milk and a little bread from him. He advised me to get out of the area because the Germans had organized a battalion of Italian Fascists and were moving them in to defend that sector. They were taking billets in all the vacant houses and were questioning everyone they met. About noon I found a two-storey house that was still vacant, so I went upstairs and spent the afternoon looking over the country around me.

Sabodia was about a mile to the north-west, and I could see the town of Littoria about four miles to the east. I saw little activity in the area. It was evident that if there were many Germans around, they were all right in the front line. Just after dusk I walked another half-mile north and snooped around until I found another vacant house.

I was awakened several times during the night by trucks passing the house, but none stopped. Just before dawn an artillery duel started, and I moved to a room downstairs. Being unable to sleep for the noise, I walked outside to watch the show. To my amazement, I noticed that the German artillery was firing from quite a distance behind me, and the shells were arching overhead.

The German shells were landing about a mile north of me, so I judged the front lines to be between a half-mile and a mile away.

As dawn came I went back into the house, sat by an upstairs window, and looked the situation over. The town of Sabodia was just a half-mile west of me and was separated from the sea by a long lake. About noon I could hear mortar fire and noticed that the Germans were firing at a point on the sandbar separating the sea from Sabodia. Immediately, our troops put up a smoke screen which blanketed the area for the entire afternoon.

At dusk I set out for Lake Sabodia, our troops being on the other side. It took me about three hours to walk the half-mile to the lake shore. Every foot was dangerous for it was necessary to pass through the German mortar line, and I wasn't sure where it was located.

Just as I reached the water's edge, the Germans fired a flare over the lake. I covered my face and lay motionless until the flare was extinguished. The Germans were afraid our troops were sending patrols across in rubber boats, for about every fifteen minutes a flare went up. Somewhere along the shore there were 'Jerry' guards, and as far as I knew I might have been lying right next to one.

It was pitch black, and the call of an occasional night bird was the only sound audible. I lay for a time, not knowing what to do. By swimming fast I could cross the lake in five minutes; but the noise would bring another flare, followed by a stream of bullets – just like shooting fish in a barrel. It was March and the water was still ice cold to the touch, making slow swimming hazardous.

I decided after a time to try swimming dog fashion

across the lake. I took off my clothes and hid them, together with my automatic, under a bush. I then got the bottle of alcohol out of my knapsack and consumed the contents, hoping that the alcohol would help to limit the effects of the cold water.

The Germans fired another flare out over the water; and, in a few seconds, everything was black. I quietly let myself into the water and soon became so numb that I could hardly move. I started swimming out slowly, with just my head above the water. After only about a hundred feet the startling realization that I would never reach the opposite shore struck like a bolt of lightning! Because of making noise, I couldn't swim fast enough to keep my circulation up and I was beginning to cramp. I turned and, using every ounce of energy at my command, was barely able to make it back to shore. I groped around in the darkness until I had found my clothes and automatic. After dressing I fell on the ground, completely exhausted. I was stuck and I knew it! It would be suicide to attempt to crack the line there by land. The Germans, as well as my own troops, were well dug in, and the area between them was heavily mined. If there was a battle in progress with some movement in the line it would be somewhat easier to cross, but Anzio was quiet.

Suddenly I heard voices, and before I could move a 'Jerry' patrol passed within a few feet of me. I didn't know if the Germans were looking for me or not, and I didn't care much about it then. As soon as they were out of hearing distance I crawled inland a few hundred feet, and then walked back to the house I had stayed in last.

There was a canal running by the house, and a bridge crossed within a few feet of it. About noon the next day, our artillery started firing on this bridge. The first shell landed about one hundred feet short of the bridge, and for the next ten minutes I was busy getting away from the house. They finally succeeded in hitting the house, but they failed to damage the bridge.

That same afternoon I did some serious thinking. The

way things stood, it was just a matter of time before I would get caught playing around the front lines. If the 'Jerries' didn't catch me, I'd probably get hit by Allied fire.

I got my map out and studied the situation. I knew the Allies would try to break out of the Anzio beach-head. The question was: Where would they head for then? However, it wasn't hard to see that Rome was the greatest prize left in Italy.

According to my map I was about forty miles due south of Rome, but to get there I had to go back east at least ten miles in order to circle the main spear-head of the beach-head.

I wasn't too sure that I could get into Rome, but I decided to try. I certainly wasn't getting anywhere down there.

Two days later I was still sixteen miles from Rome. I was tired and hot, and my feet were a mass of blisters. I would walk a few hundred yards and then sit down, unable to go farther.

One of the times I was resting with my shoes off, a German soldier not over seventeen years old came walking over a hill with a gas can in his hand. Any attempt to put my shoes on and rush off would be obvious, so I just sat there studying him as he came up. I did manage to slip my automatic between the folds of a jacket I had in my lap.

'Signor,' he said and then asked a question in German. It was obvious he had run out of gas somewhere up the road and was asking me in German where a gasoline dump was along the road.

'Signor,' I said in my best and fastest Italian, 'I have come a long way and am not familiar with these parts. You might inquire at that house,' I said pointing down the road. He didn't seem to understand what I was saying, but did catch on about the house.

'Grazie,' he said with a smile and walked on down the road.

I just sat there rubbing my burning feet and watching him swing his gas can. 'What the hell,' I thought to myself, 'I don't give a damn any more.'

Finally, I came to one of the main highways leading into Rome. The dome of St Peter's was visible now to the west, but feeling as I did, I could never make it. I sat down on the shoulder of the highway and watched the steady stream of Italians coming and going, with an occasional German truck making a dash for it between Allied air patrols.

As I was sitting there, an elderly man and a boy on a bicycle stopped to rest. They immediately started a conversation which I took up, but of course they knew I was not an Italian. I told them I was going to Rome and asked how to get by a German road block that I knew was somewhere ahead. They told me where it was but also stated that the 'Jerries' checked the identification cards of everyone passing in and out of Rome. There was no chance of going around the block, at least until dark.

The boy asked if I had an identification card, and I answered, 'Yes'. However, I didn't exactly want to show it to the Germans. When I showed it to the boy and the old man, they understood.

The boy told me that just over the hill was a tram-line that ran into Rome. He said the Germans weren't in the habit of checking it and suggested I take it into Rome. I laughed at this idea, but the more I thought about it the better it sounded. I was feeling bad anyhow, and it had been a long time since I had been on a tram. Besides that, the old man was going to ride the bicycle into Rome and the boy would accompany me. What a nice deal this was going to be!

When we arrived at the station, there was a handful of people waiting. I instructed the boy that when the tram came he was to buy my ticket and then pay no attention to me, just in case something happened.

While we were sitting there a British Spitfire patrol flew over. I asked the boy if they ever strafed the tram, and he said that the car always stopped under a tree when they were flying over.

Finally we saw the car coming, and everyone started out to the track. I followed the boy into the car, he paid two fares, and we sat down together.

It was a wonderful feeling to see the miles click by and not have to walk each and every one of them!

Just as we came into the outskirts of Rome, the tram started slowing down. Before I could figure out what was happening, it had stopped and a German guard was at each landing. There was nothing to do but sweat it out. Two 'Jerries' came through the car, but instead of asking for identification cards they were checking bundles that people were carrying! I had nothing but a light jacket; and although they checked the bundle of food my friend was carrying, they just looked at me and went on to the next seat.

After they left I looked at my pale friend and let out a whistle. As soon as the tram started up again the boy asked the conductor what the idea was. He told him that they only checked bundles on every other trip – the other times, they checked identifications! I almost passed out when I heard that.

The tram took us right down-town. Rome is a beautiful city with a surprising number of ultra-modern shops and cafés.

War hadn't come to the heart of Rome as yet, and the people as they hurried here and there seemed strikingly similar to those of New York, Chicago, or Kansas City. I began to feel as if I were home and I wanted to drop a nickel in the nearest phone and ask the operator to give me Harrisonville, Missouri, and quick. Then I was going to shave, take a bath and find the biggest steak a cow ever wiggled at a farmer. Well, at least it didn't hurt to think about those things.

Finally we came to the end of the line, and the boy said we would transfer to another car which would take us to his home.

We passed by the famous Coliseum and over the river. The boy's parents were evidently well to do, for they lived in a very nice brick apartment house.

While waiting for the father to arrive on his bicycle, I bathed my feet and went to sleep. About 7 p.m. he arrived, and we had dinner. I couldn't eat much because of a headache and fever. After dinner I asked the father about several addresses in Rome that I had acquired. He had at one time been an employee of the city, so he knew about where each address was located. However, he thought I should try to get into Vatican City rather than take a chance on the leads that I had given him. I laughed when he mentioned the Vatican as a place to go. It was common knowledge that there were a number of American boys there, but they had all 'crashed' the gate and were just lucky. Anyway, I was so sick and my feet hurt so badly that I could have hardly walked in – much less run in!

Instead of discouraging me, he kept telling me ways he thought I could get into the 'free city'. The more he talked, the better the deal sounded. There was one dangerous drawback in any plan, however. The German Secret Service in plain clothes were constantly milling around the place, and any suspicious actions by anyone were immediately checked. With this in mind, any plan to get into the Vatican could be dangerous. Once put into operation, the plan had to 'click', for if there was any slip-up it would be all over very quickly.

I asked in detail about the duties of the famous Swiss guards that were constantly on duty at all the entrances and came to the conclusion that they were there to protect the Vatican. I had no intention of harming the Vatican – all I wanted was to gain entrance, and I wondered what their reaction to that would be.

For years the people with whom I was staying had attended mass at St Peter's. They were familiar with what went on at the main entrance to the left of their famous cathedral. Also, it was possible to telephone into the

Vatican from any place in Rome; but, of course, the S.S. probably were listening.

I knew that our government, as well as England and Germany, had an ambassador in the Vatican; and I began to wonder just how much fruit a few minutes of conversation with our ambassador would bear. Calling in from an outside station would be too dangerous, so this idea was shelved for the time being.

At 9 a.m. the following day, the boy and I were sitting at a table in a coffee shop across the street from an entrance to the Vatican – just about two hundred yards to the right of the main entrance. I was still sick with a terrific headache and fever and feared I had contracted malaria in the swamps near Anzio. I gave myself a full day before I would be flat on my back. I was desperate!

The boy's father knew an operator that worked on the Vatican radio station. He called him and asked him to come to the gate across from the coffee shop where we were. I wrote a note to be given to the American ambassador inside and gave it to the old man.

In a few minutes the operator appeared at the gate and my friend went to meet him, and in a few minutes was back, saying that the note would be delivered, and for us to wait.

The boy recognized two S.S. men who came in and sat down for a cup of coffee. We paid our check and leisurely walked out of the place, going south towards the columns that form a circle around St Peter's.

'I know both of the guards there at the main gate,' the boy said. 'Why don't I go see what they can do for you?'

'What if they tell the S.S.?' I asked.

'They wouldn't do that,' he said. 'I'll go up and talk to them, and if everything goes all right, I'll motion for you to come up.'

'Good luck,' I whispered as he started off.

I watched him as he went towards the huge fountain and on up the driveway to the left of St Peter's.

I noted the friendly greeting exchanged between the guards and my friend, and I knew he was getting down to business. After a time they walked to a door to the right of the main entrance and, as they went in, the boy motioned to me to come up.

I was shaking like a leaf now. I didn't know if I was walking into a trap or not. I sat there for a minute, afraid to go, but I had to, there was no question about it.

I stood up and started off towards the entrance. I suppose it was a quarter of a mile across the huge square and I fully expected to be nailed by the S.S. before reaching the gate. I made my approach just as casual as possible, looking at the columns, the fountain and acting the role of a tourist as much as possible. To me it seemed that the eyes of Rome were upon me, but that was a natural feeling.

I approached the small entrance and boldly walked in. Inside I found my friend talking to the guard, in fact we were in the Swiss guard-room. They both saw me come in but continued talking, so I sat down in a chair and rubbed my feet.

Soon the guard went to a telephone on the wall and my friend came over and told me he was calling the American ambassador.

'Signor, this is dangerous business,' I said. He smiled and said nothing.

Within a very few minutes a small man in a business suit came, followed by a priest.

'I am the secretary to the British Embassy, and this is Monsignor McGough,' the little man said. 'I understand you are an American.'

'Yes, sir,' I said.

'How did you get here?' asked the secretary, and then I related in detail the story of my being shot down and my walk through Italy. I gave him my identification card and other cards and things that I carried in my pocketbook.

Both men studied the cards very thoroughly, saying nothing for a time. I began to wonder what would happen next.

'How long ago did you say you escaped?' the secretary asked.

'It was 28 September last year,' I answered.

The secretary handed me back my pocket-book and he and the Monsignor went into a huddle in the corner. Shortly, the Monsignor left through a door in the rear of the guard-room, and the secretary approached me.

'In a few seconds,' he said, 'you will see the Monsignor pass by the door,' pointing to the door that I had just entered. 'Follow behind him and he will take you to a safe place.'

I thanked him, as well as my friend who had helped me, and as soon as I saw the Monsignor pass by the door I waited a few seconds then walked out of the door into the square.

The Monsignor was about a hundred yards ahead, and I decided that was about the proper distance. No one could observe any connexion between the two of us. I would stop now and then to glance into a shop window and then continue on, at no time allowing myself to pay any noticeable attention to the person I was following.

We were on the outside of the great wall around the Vatican, and were following it to the right. I began to wonder where we were going. I was so sick I could hardly keep moving, but I couldn't give up and stop to rest.

We had walked a good mile when we came to another gate in the great wall. Two Swiss guards were walking back and forth as the Monsignor approached. The guards came together just as the Monsignor reached the entrance and they saluted as he nodded and passed into Vatican City.

The sweat popped out on my face and I thought my knees would buckle under me. The guards had not moved since the Monsignor had passed through, but were still standing at attention facing each other. I had not slowed my pace and was within two hundred feet of them now.

The guards in their traditional striped uniforms and ancient helmets were holding fast, their long spears in a vertical position resting on the pavement.

I slipped my hand into my coat pocket and felt my automatic, but then I decided not to try to force my way in at gun point. I took my hand out of my pocket and kept walking.

Just as I approached the entrance, both guards did an about face and started marching in opposite directions. I walked into Vatican City.

I was inside Vatican City, shaking hands with others who had successfully escaped into this famous, free city. These boys took me in like a long lost brother; and, believe me, I needed a brother or two about that time!

Regardless of the number of attempts I make, there just aren't enough words in the English language to describe the feeling that came over me. To me, this place was heaven, after walking endless miles in the heat of the Lombardian Plain during the previous fall; stumbling over the snow-covered mountains of central Italy with nothing but a dim ray of hope that I might ever see our troops again; sleeping in stables, haylofts, and, occasionally, out in the open with an automatic pistol always cocked and ready; arousing suddenly at the slightest noise; listening breathlessly for footsteps meaning death or torture; awakening at dawn, still wet and cold, to start another endless journey; sweating out the German ambush, trapped like a rat and unable to move; and, through it all, waiting and praying that somehow I could be one lucky soldier that the 'Jerries' would overlook.

The memories of begging some poor family to give me a worn-out pair of shoes in exchange for my pair with no soles so that I could keep going; seeing the look of despair on the children's faces around the table as I devoured a share of food that they should be getting; seeing the fear of death in the eyes of the parents, should I be caught

in their home; being able to give each family in return
for their hospitality only a note that Radio London
screamed would be honoured with food and help when
the Allies arrived, yet realizing too well the futility of it
all; sensing the joy of seeing my plans work or feeling the
ever increasing agony of a plan that failed – yes, these
memories are, to an escaped prisoner, the real meaning of
war – memories that will remain in my heart long after
the world has forgotten.

As I lay in my bed that first day in the Vatican, I wondered. Was it sheer courage that kept me going all those
months, or was I just a damn fool? It would have been
easier to stay a German prisoner – I knew that. The 'Jerries' had treated me well, and I didn't escape because of
fear of ill-treatment. I had lived in a free country twenty-
three years, and no one had pointed a gun at me there
and said, 'You do this and that or else!' No one at home
had made me hold up my hand and cry, '*Heil Hitler.*'
None of my teachers in school had ever taught me to
hate, deceive, and kill!

It was taking me all this time to figure out why I had
escaped – guess I never had time to think about it before.
I didn't like the idea of being behind barbed wire or being at the mercy of some damned arrogant German. All
my life I had heard about the Americans fighting for
freedom; and, here, I had been doing it all these months
– more out of instinct than anything else. ...

* * *

... This was Easter 1944. For the next few weeks Winton
Sexton lay seriously ill in the Vatican as a result of his
incredible feat of endurance. He finally got his freedom
when the American troops rolled into Rome at the beginning of June. He had certainly earned it.

CHAPTER TWELVE

Escape in Korea

AT the end of the Second World War Korea, which had been occupied by the Japanese, was divided in two. North of the 38th parallel of latitude was administered by the Russians; south of this line was administered by the Americans. As a result of this division, North Korea formed a Communist Government and South Korea a Republican Government aided by the United States.

In June 1950 the people of North Korea invaded South Korea. The United Nations' Security Council called on all member nations to come to the aid of the South Koreans and a small American force was at once sent there. Within a few months the reinforced United Nations Forces had not only pushed the North Koreans out of the south but had themselves occupied North Korea almost to its northern border with Manchuria (part of Communist China).

Now the Chinese Communists joined in and by April 1951 they had driven the United Nations Forces almost out of North Korea. In this month the Gloucestershire Regiment earned their nickname 'the Glorious Glosters' by making a gallant stand on a hill near the Imjin river. In this battle Captain Anthony Farrar-Hockley was captured by the Chinese Communists: for his gallantry in the action he was later awarded the D.S.O. (he already had the M.C. for gallantry in action in the Second World War).

Farrar-Hockley's first attempt to escape was during a river crossing, when he lowered himself into the water and allowed the current to sweep him away from the column. For several hours he drifted with the current, getting clean away from his guards. He was recaptured while making his way through the enemy lines.

He escaped for a second and a third time and each time had bad luck. The difficulty was not in getting away but in avoiding recapture in a land where his fair hair and blue eyes stamped him immediately as an enemy.

After his third attempt Anthony Farrar-Hockley was incarcerated in a hole dug in the side of a hill, its entrance closed by an oil-drum. He bored a tunnel through the earth from the back of his cave – and was free again. This time he reached the shore of the Yellow Sea before he was recaptured.

He was given a spell in a political prison before being taken to the combined working camp and interrogation centre where this story opens. . . .

*   *   *

. . . We made the final decision to escape while working on the hill one morning. After telling the story of my captivity to my new companions, very naturally the subject of another escape had arisen. With the rapid onset of the Korean winter, I had originally decided, after my discharge from Sinuiju jail, that I would take up winter quarters in a prison camp and make a fresh escape in the following spring. In any case I had Tom with me; and I had felt that I could not leave him alone with the North Koreans, knowing that he would suffer at least in part for my misdemeanour if I managed to get away. Now, talking to the two working with me – Jack, the young American flier, and Ron, the Australian – it seemed to me that circumstances had changed considerably from those on which I had based my former appreciation.

The first change had been that we found ourselves in a North Korean interrogation centre, and not in a prisoner-of-war camp. Though we had not expected to find any luxuries in the latter, we had anticipated sufficient food to maintain life throughout the winter. Here we were getting a diminishing ration of boiled millet daily with a very thin soup, containing a bean or a radish leaf to convince our stomachs of its authentic nourishment value. Worse, Tom, who was under intensive interrogation, was being punished for his lack of response by being starved. His rations had been cut off completely, and they were now threatening to cut off his water supply. Our efforts to feed him from our own meagre issue of millet had been circumvented; at mealtimes we were supervised to the point where the guard commander or a sentry actually watched us eat.

In the second place, the barn in which we were quartered was now bitterly cold at nights. The North Korean troops in the village had all been issued with warm winter garments, but the interrogators made it clear that they would not issue clothing to those who did not co-operate with them. We were not co-operating and had no intention of doing so. It seemed as if the bitterest phase of the North Korean winter would find us in what threadbare garments we still possessed. Jack was the worst off. He had been shot down in mid-summer, wearing only thin underclothing and a summer flying suit. Ron, who had parachuted from a Meteor shot down over Sinuiju, was only better equipped to the extent of a woollen shirt.

The staff of the interrogation centre were the most unpleasant and unscrupulous captors I had encountered up to that time, being either fanatical Communists, sadists, or a combination of both. The commander was a lieutenant-colonel of the infantry who spoke a little English. After our arrival, he had pointed out that, as war criminals of the worst sort, we could not expect a proper ration of food while awaiting our turn to be interrogated, unless we worked for it. This meant, in fact, hard labour, constructing air-raid shelters for his headquarters, digging and removing earth and rocks, carrying water for cementing over a long distance, and carrying timber and bricks up to the hill from the village. We were all weak from the privations of our captivity, and on our coarse, poor diet we were expending strength we could ill-afford. There were sometimes additional tasks in the evening. For instance, the officer who dealt principally with us was an infantry major – referred to by Kim, the civilian interpreter, as the Young Major. He hated us bitterly. Whenever possible, he would find us unpleasant tasks, such as cleaning out the filthy headquarters latrine – a huge stone jar sunk in the earth which had to be emptied with a small can by hand into a leaking bucket. What enhanced his pleasure in setting us this duty was that he could refuse us permission to wash afterwards, so that we must return to our quarters filthy with latrine matter. On other occasions, we had to work the crude machine that cut fodder for the cattle, or clean up the animal-stalls – jobs we minded less because we were sometimes able to steal a *diacon* (a cross between a turnip and a radish), which, though raw and unpalatable, filled our empty bellies for a short time. I protested to Kim on my first two initial interrogations about this treatment, without result. He excused himself by saying that it was no affair of his, but betrayed his feeling, by replying to my remarks about the Geneva Convention and its Prisoner-of-War clauses, with a comment that the Convention was an instrument of bourgeois reaction which, anyway, was inapplicable to war-criminals such as ourselves. Kim was a vain man, who posed as an ex-professor in political economy at Seoul University, but let it slip to Jack one day that he had really been an announcer on the Seoul Radio. He had a marked inferiority complex and, like the Young Major, was really a savage under a thin veneer of education.

These were the circumstances surrounding our captivity – with a prospect of deterioration. Before we met that morning to make our decision, however, one other important aspect had been considered: Tom's future as a lone captive in the hands of a group of men who hated him, as an American major of the regular service, perhaps more bitterly than the remainder of us. He was, to them, the epitome of all the power and abundance in life which they coveted so much, feared so much, and thus hated so profoundly. What had led me to consider leaving Tom at all was that our escape might make our captors afraid that the news of his treatment would become known to the outside world. If successful, we should actually institute such inquiries through Kaesong to ensure that he received the care a human being might expect. But both Tom and I knew that their fury on discovering our absence might be so unbridled that he would not survive it.

The night before we took the final decision, I rolled over on to my side and began to whisper in Tom's ear, putting to him the prospect as I saw it and the hope that escape held for us. Tom said:

'Of course you must go. As the senior officer here, I order you to disregard my safety, if you feel you have a chance of making it.'

I reminded Tom that he would be absolutely at the mercy of the Young Major's temper – a temper we knew to be demoniac in character.

'You must go,' said Tom, again.

Knowing him, I should not have expected any other answer. On the following morning we reviewed the position and made our decision: I would begin work that night.

*

Initially, my interrogations had been conducted by Kim alone. These had been of an entirely political nature, in order to sound me out as a possible convert to their cause – or, at least, a co-operator. They had a young soldier elsewhere in the village, who had ostensibly accepted their views and supplied them with a certain amount of information after a terrible sickness which had left him looking like a skeleton. We saw him twice and he begged us, in a voice that might have belonged to a very old man, to abandon resistance to our captors. To his knowledge, he said, one American who had resisted them had already been starved to death in the very building we now occupied. He was led away from us by U, his principal instructor, who urged him not to waste his time speaking to us.

On the very night that I was determined to begin work on breaking-out, I was called out after darkness for an interrogation by the Young Major, a Captain Li, and a lieutenant I called Poker-Face. Kim interpreted; the others spoke no English except for Li, whose vocabulary was extremely limited. As I followed Kim along one of the village paths to a hut just below the air-raid shelter on the hill, I wondered whether this was to be another political interrogation or military interrogation in earnest. If the latter, what would they ask me? I knew that the greater number of their questions to Tom were concerned with information he could not possibly have given them, even if he had been prepared to do so; for they had demanded all the details of the top-secret codes used by the Far Eastern Air Force Headquarters – insisting that he must know these as a major flying with an operational squadron in Korea! The questions they asked me that night were even more fantastic. When I was brought before the Young Major, he asked me through Kim:

'Give us the organization, means of recruitment and training, method of dispatch, and system of communication of the British Intelligence Services throughout Europe and the Far East.'

I was so amused to think that they believed me to be intimately in the confidence of the War Office that I smiled. Captain Li began to hit me about the head with a heavy wooden ruler. After an hour of threats, blows, and a warning to reconsider my attitude during the next day, I was taken back to the barn.

At that particular time, the sentry on duty outside the barn door was an unpleasant youth with pimples whom we called 'Hoju' because he used this term to Ron. We loathed him because he delighted in making our lives difficult. It was he who had caused the straw that we lay on to be removed; who had spied on us during meals and seen us hiding food to give to Tom; who prevented us from visiting the latrine. Whenever he was on duty, we were forced to talk in whispers, or he would get the guard commander to separate us in different corners, and insist that we neither lay down nor stood up, but sat up. At first, we had tried humouring, then ignoring, him; finally, we resisted his every command for as long as we could. I was glad to see him standing there on sentry, for I knew that before long he would be relieved. Though the attention he paid us was not directly intended to prevent us from escaping – it was merely a means of demonstrating to himself his power over us – his attention on this night might lead to disaster. I waited in the darkness until the new sentry came on, and then began my work.

I planned to cut a hole in the outside wall of the barn. The lower half of the wall was of brick and too hard for my poor tools; but the top half was of wattles and mud, running up between stout timbers from brick to roof. While working outside, I had picked up an old screwdriver and a rusty table-knife. With these tools and a Shick razor blade that I had secreted since the days at Munhari, I had to cut away the hard mud, bound with chopped straw, and to cut the wattles on which the mud was mounted. The sentry was fifteen feet away, at the far, gable-end of the barn, by the main entrance to the courtyard. To enter the barn, if his suspicions were aroused, he would have to come into the courtyard – a matter of five paces – unlock the door, and switch on the light. If I kept a careful watch, I might have time to assume a sleeping pose but, after a certain point in my work, I would not be able to explain why there was the outline of a hole in the wall above us! Knowing that I should probably fail to cut my way through completely in one night, I decided to reach a point on the first night which might be explained, if noticed during the next day, by a fall of mud from the wall. Of course, I could not begin to cut the wattles but hoped to be able to look at the few I had exposed in daylight, so that I should be able to make a work plan for the following night.

The next morning, when the guard commander opened our door to bring in our bowls of millet, we all came near to heart failure. Looking at the wall, we saw that a large number of the wattles had been laid bare, and that the main area of mud removed was just about the size for a man to crawl through! It seemed that the great dark patch shrieked at the guard commander and sentries to be noticed.

The day passed in the normal way. When we returned from work, we at once asked Tom if anyone had taken an interest in the wall. Apparently, it had remained unnoticed. We ate our evening meal, and settled down for the night, ostensibly to sleep. Hoju was on guard immediately after dusk that night, so we knew he would not be on duty again for six hours. Shortly after he dismounted, I began to work.

Tom, Ron and Jack lay back under the mats, listening to the talk of some of the officers of the interrogation centre, whose room was in the western half of the barn. Once I began to cut the wattles, we became absolutely committed to escaping that night, and I increased my speed as much as I dared. Every noise, however slight, seemed to echo through the room. I felt that, at any moment, there would be a cry of alarm from the officers next door, chairs would be thrown back, the doors opened, and a crowd of infuriated North Koreans unleashed upon us. Now and again the anxious voices of one of the others would reach me, asking for a progress report, and I would reassure them as best I could. I removed a complete section of wattles, after about two hours' work, and began to cut the hard mud away that lay beyond them. After about ten minutes, I made a disappointing discovery: there was another section of wattles between us and the outside. Though the room was very cold, the sweat ran from my forehead, face and neck, as I cut, prised, pulled and scraped as quickly as I could. Another hour passed before the second section was free. I pulled away the mud that remained on the far side, touched a smooth, flexible surface, pushed against it, and felt my hand slide through into the cold night air outside.

I returned to the floor, where the three were lying beneath their mats. Jack and Tom were talking in whispers. Ron had fallen asleep! Waking him, I went back to the hole and crawled through as quickly as I dared, dropping on to my hands on the far side. The wide ledge which ran along the outside wall was covered with empty bottles, buckets, tin cans, a motor-car tyre, and an old cast-iron wood stove. Standing on the ledge, I removed the bottles and the stove to one side to make way for Ron, who was the next to come out. His head appeared in the hole, his shoulders, his hips. Suddenly, he lost his balance. He fell forward, swept the ledge with his arms, and knocked the stove on to the track below. A loud crash rang through the village.

Near-by was an ox, lying in its stable. As Ron disappeared back through the hole in the wall, I ran across to the ox and lay down behind him, waiting for the reaction to the alarm. Several minutes passed, but no sound came above the heavy breathing of the sleeping ox. After ten minutes, I returned to the hole and called to Ron in a whisper. This time he managed to get right out of the hole before knocking a bottle off the ledge but I caught it before it could fall. Jack followed. The three of us moved, as planned, to a stack of dried corn-stalks about eighty yards from the barn. Here, Jack and Ron concealed themselves, while I returned to the courtyard. We had completed the break-out.

In a corner of the courtyard was a pile of old padded jackets and a pair of padded trousers. It was most desirable that we should have these, because of the lightness of Jack's and Ron's clothing – I was afraid that Jack, especially, might suffer from cold shock once we reached the coast. I crawled back into the courtyard through an opening in the wall, normally used to pass fodder through to the cattle-shed. Laden with clothing, I returned the same way to the corn-stalks.

Both Jack and Ron felt much better when they had donned their new clothing. I took the old black raincoat that Jack had discarded and we set off across the rice paddy on a course that led north-west to the mountains. Neither shots nor other sounds of alarm reached us as we crossed the main Chinam-po highway, and left the interrogation centre behind a hill – free men once more.

*

By morning we had put twelve miles between us and our prison; Pyongyang, a broad stretch of the Taedong river, and the fertile Taedong valley lay below us in the morning sun. Our hill-top gave us ample cover in which to rest from the night march. We ate our raw *diacons*, taken from the fields far back, as we discussed the route to the coast.

North of Chinam-po, we knew the seashore was covered with soft mud that often ran out for more than five miles, even at high water. But there were deep-water inlets northwards, and the port of Chinam-po would be about twenty miles south of the point at which we expected to find the sea. Ron and Jack agreed with me that we should turn north on reaching the coast, and seek the deep-water inlets and the fishermen's craft that lay in them rather than risk the sentinels of Chinam-po. Once we got to the sea, we could only hope that wind and tide would not be against us. The problem of water for the journey was one that concerned me most; for I felt that, in our present condition, we should not be able to handle the boat effectively, if we remained at sea for more than a week without water.

After a second careful reconnaissance, we descended from our hill at dusk, with a stream and valley to cross before climbing a range on the far side which led to the sea. The brown and yellow leaves lay everywhere, as we passed through the woods on the lower slopes. There had been plenty of chestnuts here, but the village boys had taken them all, leaving the spiky cases strewn beneath the trees. Reaching the rice-paddy in the valley, we made a detour round the first village that lay on our course. Beyond, the stream flowed fast and deep between high banks of soft mud. I was hoping that we should find a crossing-place higher up, for I was anxious that we should not get our clothes wet; the heavy night frost would certainly freeze them, and we could not count on a sunny day to dry them out before another night fell.

A young civilian came suddenly upon us from a tiny side-path, glancing curiously at us as we passed. We continued across the valley without looking back until he was out of sight, when we quickly ran back along the track we had crossed, changed our direction and took the small, disused footpath that led along the river bank. As soon as we reached good cover, I led the way into the bushes to see if we were being followed. Sitting there on the cold earth, we could hear nothing but the river noise below us. Only after ten or fifteen minutes did we hear light footsteps. Looking through the branches, I saw the civilian we had passed earlier coming along the footpath, looking carefully about him as he went. He passed without seeing us and I watched him take a path that led to the main track running to our right. Half an hour went by; he did not return. I decided to go on.

We made another detour to avoid the next village, and were about to descend to the stream again when we were challenged. I heard the action of a rifle-bolt close by, and as the moon emerged at that moment from the clouds, saw a sentry about twenty-five yards away, his rifle covering us. Jack and Ron were behind me. It was foolish of us all to get recaptured; their chance of withdrawal was better than mine. Signalling to them to crawl away along a rice-paddy bank near-by, I walked slowly towards the sentry, speaking in a normal voice, hoping to distract his attention.

Attending to me, he did not spot the other two. He halted me firmly when I was about ten paces from him.

Each of us stared at the other: he did not know what to make of me; I wondered how I could slip away from the weapon that covered me.

The guard turned out. I was led into the guard-room in a nearby village, which we had not observed in our day-light reconnaissance because it lay in a re-entrant. By this time I had decided to attempt a bluff and, in the friend-liest voice I could raise, I said, *'Tovarich!'* pointing delightedly at a coloured picture of Stalin on the wall.

The soldiers looked at me in puzzlement for a few moments. They regarded my black raincoat and the Chinese Communist cap that Tom had given me for the escape; they indicated my beard and blue eyes to one another as they discussed me amongst themselves. One of them came forward and said a few words to me in what I believed to be elementary Russian, and I replied heartily in gibberish, ending as many words as possible with 'ski', 'shi', 'ish', and 'off'. As their brown eyes grew friendlier, I began to indicate that I must be on my way, pointing to their watches as if asking the time. I really believed that I was going to get away with it; for they were smil-ing now and two men shook my hand. With luck, they might take me out on to the path and escort me to the edge of the village. I was about to light a cigarette offered to me, when the door opened and a North Korean police captain entered. He stepped towards me, speaking rapidly and apparently fluently in a language that was certainly neither Korean nor Chinese. After a couple more sen-tences I realized that the game was up: he was evidently a Russian interpreter. I took a good pull on the cigarette and said in English:

'I'm afraid there seems to have been some sort of mis-take.'

By the look on his face, I could see that he intended to rectify it. I left the guard-room with my arms bound tightly behind me.

*

I spent a very unpleasant night, being awakened every

half-hour or so by the guard, just to make sure that I had not slipped out of my clothes and crawled through a crack in the floorboards. Two or three hours after sunrise, the door of my cell in the local police-station opened and I looked up to see the commander of the interrogation centre standing above me.

'Ah,' he said, greeting me with a friendly kick. 'So it is you they have caught. I wondered which one it was.'

I was removed from the cell, still bound, and taken into another village, where Kim and a lieutenant-colonel of the police were waiting for me. As I approached, Kim looked up to say:

'You have been very foolish. You must be killed for this, I think.' His face was twisted with rage.

The whole party of seven or eight who had come out to fetch me breakfasted in a house while I remained outside. Their meal over, I was brought in for a preliminary examination. In order to infuse the proper spirit into all concerned, the police lieutenant-colonel cocked his pistol, brandished it in my face, and then began to hit me over the head with it. He had made sure that my hands and arms were securely bound before he began.

*

We had agreed on the tale to be told if any one or all of us were caught. First, we should insist that Tom knew nothing of our plans to escape; that we had cut through the wall and slipped out whilst he slept. In this way we hoped to save him any further retribution. Next, someone had to take the blame for devising and planning the escape, and, as the senior officer in the party, it was my duty to assume this responsibility. Finally, at all costs, we were determined to conceal from them that we had intended to seize a boat and escape by sea, as we were most anxious to avoid any special watch being kept on boats in the future.

This was the story I now told. I told it during my first examination in the village; and I told it again at the

Central Police Headquarters in Pyongyang in the afternoon of the same day. By this time I was sitting in an office containing three colonels of police, who, to my surprise, seemed to have nothing better to do than question a wretched escaped prisoner-of-war. It may have been, of course, that the prospect of losing prisoners who would report the conditions of captivity to the outside world was sufficient to command their personal attention. Whatever the reason, my interview with them that afternoon imposed on them at least a measure of responsibility for what followed.

Before I was taken from the room, an incident occurred which was typical of their irrationality. The first colonel seated at a desk, said:

'You say you tried to escape because we treated you badly, gave you no winter clothing, and so on' – this was part of our story. 'Well, we have no food, clothing, or medical supplies to spare. The inhuman bombing by the American aggressors in violation of all the laws of decency has withheld supplies from us. You must not blame us; blame your own side.'

No sooner had Kim translated this than the second colonel spoke. Without reference to the previous remarks, he completely contradicted them.

'We have plenty of supplies: the bombing of the American aggressors has had no effect on our war effort. But we only give these things to those who understand the truth and co-operate with us. If you co-operate, you will receive the same as any other person.'

As if this contradiction was not enough, the third colonel apparently decided that yet another was necessary.

'You can never have such things from us. You are a war criminal, and thus have no status except as a criminal. Only because of our goodness has your life been spared.'

Having translated these three statements, Kim led me from the room. Perhaps the colonels wanted to argue out who should have spoken and what he should have said. I

was taken to a square stone building near-by where the
Young Major settled down to question me himself. Poker-
face (the lieutenant) and Kim were with us. I had a feeling that the interview would not be a pleasant one.

Now, although we had agreed to tell a set story and I
had told this, I had refused to say in what direction Jack
and Ron continued when I was recaptured. At first, I considered giving them a false scent, but realized there was
really no point in this. I was not going to give them the
information and I might as well say so. At each examination I pointed out that I was a British officer and could
hardly be expected to provide them with details that
would assist them to recapture my comrades. The Young
Major now informed me that it was his intention that I
should do so. An argument that lasted for about half an
hour began. At the end, Kim was given instructions by
the Young Major, which he translated to me.

'You think you can trick us with your lies; but you will
never be able to do so. We are armed with the knowledge
of scientific Marxist Socialism and, scientifically, analyse
your words. Furthermore, your attitude reveals your in-
sincerity. You refuse to co-operate with us and show yourself to be our bitter enemy. The Young Major now gives
you your last opportunity to redeem your crime of making an escape and of forcing the others to do so by using
the rank you held in the forces of the aggressor. If you do
not take it, we shall have to adopt severe measures.'

When he had finished they all looked at me. I said: 'I
have told you how things stand. I have nothing more to
say.'

When Kim had translated this back to the Young Major,
the latter rose to his feet and said what I believed to be
the only English word he knew:

'O.K.,' he said, making for the door. 'O.K.'

His drawn pistol covering me, Poker-face intimated
that I should follow, and, with Kim, we left the room.

The Young Major had set off down a passage. Almost
at the end of this, on the left-hand side, was a steel door

which had two handles on it of the lever type – levers six
or more inches long, whose inner ends locked into recesses
in the door lintels. As we passed through this door, I saw
that it was very thick and that the greater portion between the two steel faces appeared to be packed with
fabric of some sort. Poker-face closed the door, locking it
with the two inside levers and moved round to join the
Young Major.

'Strip to the waist,' said Kim.

My mind could not conceive the truth that my senses
offered. We were all standing in a small square room,
with cement-faced walls and a concrete floor. High above
us, from a wooden ceiling, ropes trailed from metal rings.
There were two more such rings in the left-hand wall.
Under the right wall was a large barrel of water. One
little chair, such as a child might use at a kindergarten,
was beside it; across its back lay more ropes, in a tangle.
In the light of a single bright electric lamp that burned in
the ceiling, I saw that there were stains on the floor and
walls that looked very much like blood. As I stripped off
my filthy, lousy shirt and jersey, I knew that I was in a
torture chamber.

Yet my mind could not conceive it. I was living in the
twentieth century – the year A.D. nineteen hundred and
fifty-one. Surely these three men could never bring themselves to torture me in cold blood. Looking round at their
faces, I saw neither passion nor compassion in any one
of them. I threw my clothes to the floor, and Kim kicked
them into the corner as Poker-face tied my wrists again.
The Young Major spoke to Kim, who said:

'Kneel down.'

Kneeling there, looking up at them, still unable to comprehend that this was really happening to me, I saw the
Young Major's hand come round to strike me on the
temple, as the first of a series of blows that he and Poker-
face released upon me. Kim joined them when they began to kick; and it was he who covered my face when the
Young Major saw that I was anticipating some of the

blows and ducking. Just before the cloth came down over my eyes, I saw to my horror that the Young Major's face had assumed an expression of savage pleasure: he was really enjoying my suffering.

In my innocence, I had thought this maltreatment was to be either my punishment or a means of inducing me to give information about Jack and Ron. I discovered that it was merely the overture. The covering was removed and I was assisted by Kim and Poker-face into the tiny chair. I almost thanked them for what seemed to be an act of remorse or compassion. It was neither. They now bound my legs to the front of the chair, my arms to the two up-rights at the back. My wrists, still secured, were tied down with a second piece of rope to the cross-piece between the two back legs. The Young Major kicked me in the chest and the chair fell over, with me, on to its back.

Poker-face now produced a towel, as the Young Major threw two or three dippers of ice-cold water over my face and neck, drawn from the barrel in the corner. Still I did not understand, thinking, as I lay shivering with the cold, that I was to be chilled to the bone by repeated dousing. But Poker-face placed the towel over my face and, a second later, more water was thrown over me. When I tried to rise – a pitiful attempt in which I just managed to lift my head forward a little – the Young Major put his boot on my mouth and shoved my head back again. More water struck the towel, some running off on to my bare chest – but some was absorbed. I tried to blow out some of the water which had seeped through into my nostrils and mouth. If they are not careful, I thought, they're go-ing to choke me. And then, instantly, comprehension fol-lowed. That was exactly what they intended to do. I think I had never been so frightened in my life.

It was such a simple but effective torture. The towel completely covered my face, its ends resting on my chest below and on my hair above. The application of water provided just sufficient moisture to make the towel cling lightly to my flesh, and so hold it in place. Thus, every breath I drew was drawn through the towelling, the process of inhaling only serving to draw the material more tightly on to my face. While the towel was reasonably dry, I could breathe adequately. But as its water content increased towards saturation point, each successive breath provided less and less oxygen for my labouring lungs. My mouth and nostrils began to fill with water. I realized that I was dying as I shook my head from side to side in a last despairing effort to throw off the clinging towel-mask. Poker-face or Kim took my head between their hands and held it steady as the Young Major poured on more water. I suffered another short, terrible struggle to breathe before sinking into a delicious, shadow-filled tranquillity.

*

Of course, I had thought they meant to kill me. The violence of their treatment had been such that I had not hoped to live when I understood their purpose. But they were more experienced than I.

The Young Major must have known exactly when to stop – perhaps the moment I became unconscious. I came to, still lashed to the little chair but now upright, the water pouring from my nose and mouth down my chest. I had come round rather quickly because the Young Major was applying the end of a lighted cigarette to my back at frequent intervals. I saw that he was smiling. It was not a pleasant smile. He was good enough to desist when Kim began to ask me for the information they wanted. About ten minutes later the process began all over again: I experienced the same terror; my expectation of death was the same as before, yet concerned me less than the agony of finding my breath dying in my lungs. When, eventually, I was dragged from the room, they had tortured me in this way three times.

Scarcely able to walk, I left the building between two police officers who had been called in. They took me through the cold, overcast night to a concrete cell block about two hundred yards away, and handed me over to the warrant-officer who was on duty. The cells were constructed on much the same lines as those at Sinuiju; the prisoners were sitting inside in the same way. The only difference I perceived then or later was that this appeared to be more modern and more strongly constructed. Two warders took me down the long passage that led past the cells, opened a door at the end, and guided me along an extension by the light of an electric torch. Finally, almost at the end of the passage, we came to an unlighted cell. A push sent me to the floor, where my legs were bound and the knots on my wrists strengthened. Satisfied that I was securely roped, the warders departed. The metal rang, as the door closed behind them and the key turned in the padlock. Their footsteps echoed as they withdrew along the passage. The door to the main passage closed; the last vestige of light disappeared. For the time being, my tormentors were content to leave me, if not in peace, at least alone.

*

That was the first day. They came for me on the second day, but not on the third; again on the fourth day; again on the sixth. In between times, I lay on the concrete floor, taking refuge in a corner from the water that covered most of the cell. Each morning I was brought a bowl of boiled maize, but had no water to drink. So that I could eat, my wrists were released, but not my sore, throbbing ankles. Though I asked to go to a latrine, I was not allowed to do so. As I had contracted enteritis from either the *diacons* or the maize, my clothes were soon fouled; but the lice did not seem to mind. Day and night, as I lay there, they wriggled across my flesh, setting up considerable irritation wherever they feasted on my blood. Sometimes it seemed to me that my whole body was alive with millions of them, eating my flesh away. It was impossible to remain in one position for more than a few minutes at a time: the discomfort became almost unbearable; my joints seemed to be on fire. There was no light during those six days, except when I was led out to the torture chamber, or when my food was brought in. I lay for ever listening for the sound of footsteps that would take me back to the little room with the water-barrel in the corner.

When they brought me back on the evening of the sixth day, my spirits were lower than they had ever been before. I could not disguise from myself that my resistance was weakening. Now I was reduced to the state where I said that I would endure it for one more time; and when that time came, for one more time again. I experienced that night periods of light-headedness, due, I think, to the severe beatings. Periodically I began to hear voices in my ears, and have vivid dreams of being with my family again. That day Kim had said to me:

'If we do not find them, I think you will be tortured to death. We have many ways of killing you slowly.'

Some time on the seventh day I realized that I had taken almost all that my mind and body could take. I prayed very hard; and I think my faith in God was never stronger. Within an hour my circumstances improved.

The door to the main passage opened and I saw a flashlight coming towards the cell. Another was switched on as three men reached my doorway. For a moment I thought that I was to be taken out again: Captain Li from the Interrogation Centre came into the cell and stood over me, calling my name.

'You are very lucky,' he said. 'Tomorrow you will be shot.'

Such was my condition that I was glad – grateful that I was going to die a clean death that was in keeping with my profession, instead of dying vilely, in fear and agony in the torture chamber, with my own cries in my ears. I confess I am not of that breed of men who manage to remain silent under torture: I swore and shouted at the inquisitors each time, as long as I had breath.

Captain Li departed, but not the other two. I saw that a Korean police officer stood outside with one of the warders, watching me turning over and over restlessly,

seeking for ease that was never there. He spoke to the
warder, who entered the cell and, bending over me, un-
fastened my wrists and ankles; then departed, relocking
the cell door. Unsteadily, unused to this freedom of movement, I stood up. Two of my ribs were cracked from
kicks; my head, shoulders, and thighs were sore and
bruised; my back was covered with cigarette burns,
which smarted at the slightest touch from my filthy
clothes – but I was free to move again! If I wanted to
move a leg, I could move it! I could raise my arms and
lower them at will! For several minutes I experimented
happily under the eye of the watching policeman, though
I had forgotten him. He called me over to the barred window, where we stood face to face. He was a man of
middle height, clad in the uniform of a captain of the
police. In the torchlight, I saw that he wore spectacles.
'*Tambay, eso?*' he asked, after a moment. I shook my
head; he knew I had no tobacco. He drew three cigarettes
from his pocket and passed them through the bars and
found some matches to give me. As I stood in front of
him, smoking my first cigarette for many weeks, he shook
his head, smiling at me with obvious sympathy.

After all that had happened, this simple act of compassion was too much for my self-control. The tears rolled
down my bearded cheeks as we stood, in silence, regard-
ing one another.

*

When Captain Li came into my cell on the following
morning, my mind was at rest. The preceding hours had
been passed comparatively comfortably, on a piece of
matting that had been brought to the cell by another
prisoner – apparently permitted some measure of freedom
in return for doing chores for the warders. He was a
Korean national of Chinese parentage who had spent
some years at a high school in Harbin. His English was
quite good, and we had a whispered chat. It seemed that
I was in the political block of the jail – a bad block to be
in, because its inmates were made to work longer hours

than the ordinary criminals. Would the Americans rescue, me? I said that I feared they had other commitments of a higher priority. He brought me some old rags, and with these I endeavoured to clean some of the filth from my body. I scrapped my underclothing, feeling that I should not be requiring it very much longer. My greatest regret was that I had neither cap nor comb, so that I should appear rather an unkempt soldier before the firing-squad. As a great luxury, I sat down on my little rice-straw mat in the corner, leaning my elbows on my knees.

I now had a little light, which, however faint, made a great improvement to the cell; for, shortly after being unbound on the previous day, some covering on the roof had been removed, revealing a small shaft about the diameter of a penny. Gradually, my eyes took full advantage of it. Sitting in the corner, I went over my life, realizing how lucky I had been to have had so much happiness. I felt sure that I had had far more in my years than any other occupant of the block. I hoped my family would be informed of my death without too much delay, so that there would not be prolonged anxiety.

When Captain Li appeared, I rose, picking up Jack's black raincoat which had been thrown into the cell on the previous day. I thought it would cover my ragged clothes. 'Where you are going,' said Captain Li, 'you will not need that.'

He was probably right. I let it drop back on to the mat and preceded him through the door. We marched back down the passage, emerging into a fine November morning. The sun was shining from a blue sky; the wind was light; the air was keen but not too cold now that the sun was up. Beyond the doorway, standing at ease on a mud square, I saw a file of soldiers armed with rifles. I wondered how far I should march with this firing-squad before we reached the place of execution.

Captain Li said: 'Go on,' motioning towards the soldiers with his pistol. Saying the 23rd Psalm over to myself, I walked over to them, and was marched to the road that ran towards the centre of Pyongyang. At that moment I was astonished to see Jack coming out of a near-by building.

'Do not talk,' said Captain Li. Three soldiers with him separated us on either side of the road, before we could exchange more than a greeting. I was just wondering whether Jack was to be shot, too, and if so, who would be shot first, when everyone with us except Captain Li and the three men walking with him wheeled to the right and disappeared. We continued to walk along the sunlit road without a word, heading for the wooded hill which stands in the centre of Pyongyang City, overlooking the airfield across the river.

It was when we were crossing an open space of rice-paddy between one suburb and another, that an opportunity occurred to talk. Captain Li saw a friend whom he ran after, calling on him to stop. They began an animated conversation some distance away. The guards drew together in a group to light cigarettes and have a chat. Jack and I worked along the paddy bund towards one another and sat down.

'Where are we going?' asked Jack.

'I don't know,' I replied. 'Are you going to be shot?'

Obviously, he had not thought of this. 'Can't say,' he said, after thinking it over. As the guards continued to disregard us, we decided to settle a few more points. Jack told me that he had been caught with Ron two days before. After a short wait with their captors, they had been taken back to the Interrogation Centre, where they had spent a miserable time. Both he and Ron had been badly beaten up, in spite of 'confessing' to our story. In addition, Jack had been made to kneel for hours with a heavy board held up by his arms behind his back, receiving a rain of blows every time he moved. Tom was recovering from several heavy beatings. Apparently six of them had considered it safe to attack a one-legged man after removing his crutches, while two men had covered him with pistols, in case he leapt to his foot and overcame them. He was still very weak from this and through his former starvation – concluded two days ago – and from a fever, given him by being drenched with cold water and being left in a bitter wind. Both he and Ron had been taken off that morning in a jeep with the Young Major to an unknown destination. Kim had remained at the farm, while Li had brought Jack on foot to the Central Police Station. He was just telling me that he and Ron had turned south at the coast instead of north, when Captain Li returned. To my surprise, he did not seem annoyed that Jack was near me and obviously conversing. Instead, he made a remark that sent my hopes soaring to the blue sky.

'You understand,' he said, tapping his pistol and looking at me very directly, 'if you try to escape again, I shall shoot you.'

*

We had a long, hot march – the more fatiguing because we were both weak and had had no food that day. Southeast of the city we came to a small coal-mining town where we met a jeep at the main cross-roads. My spirits were not so high when I saw that the Young Major was sitting in it.

He was very affable, nodding and smiling at us; but we did not return his courtesy. After a few minutes' conversation, he got out and entered a restaurant, leaving us to climb into the jeep with Captain Li. I was very pleased to leave the Young Major behind us and continue the journey on wheels.

After some miles of open country, where we passed at intervals Chinese-manned 'flak' batteries, presumably defending Pyongyang, we drew up at the entrance to a disused coal-mine. Captain Li handed us over to North Korean soldiers at an office, suddenly became very friendly, and handed us all the cigarettes in his packet as he departed for Pyongyang.

'What do you make of that?' said Jack, as he disappeared. 'Two nights back that bastard was beating the hell out of me!'

*

We marched across the principal mine road to another office on the far side of the hill, where our names were taken by two North Korean Army officers. Then we were escorted towards a group of huts near-by. As we reached the doorway of the last hut, there was a great shout; welcoming words greeted us; on all sides friendly faces appeared; Henry, Spike, Mike, the South African, Ronnie our Gunner, Tom, Ron – and new friends, British, American, French. It was almost a second homecoming as we were borne inside. ...

*   *   *

... Although Anthony Farrar-Hockley continued undaunted in his attempts to escape, the odds were always against him and he was cheated of final success by the truce and the exchange of prisoners which followed it.

CHAPTER THIRTEEN

Through the Iron Curtain

FOR many people in Europe the end of the Second World War was not the end of oppression and suffering. In Hungary, for instance, the victory of Russia over Germany meant the creation of a new Communist system of government which is ruthless in its suppression of everyone who is not wholeheartedly in its favour. No opposition of any kind is allowed and all non-Communists who are not able to hide their true beliefs from the Secret Police are killed, sent to concentration camps or forced to flee the country.

It is not easy to escape. The borders between countries dominated by the Soviet Union and the rest of the world are the most heavily guarded in history, and form the barrier which Sir Winston Churchill christened the 'Iron Curtain'. Even the seashore of satellite countries is patrolled by armed soldiers night and day; all boats are guarded and no civilian is allowed on the beaches from seven in the evening until seven the next morning. The whole system of government is based on terror and force.

Christine Arnothy was only fifteen years of age when the Russians marched into Budapest, the capital of Hungary. For the next three years she hid with her family in the country. At last it became obvious that a free life would never be possible under Communism, and the family decided to escape through the Iron Curtain and the Russian Zone of Austria into Vienna.

For fear of being given away to the Secret Police by informers, the escapers could not carry any luggage: instead they wore as many of their clothes as possible and stuffed their pockets full with small possessions. ...

*　　*　　*

... Every one of our movements had been minutely studied for weeks. We knew exactly what answers to give if anyone questioned us. First of all, we were to go to the station. We were only to take tickets to the next station so that the booking-office clerk could not tell anyone where we were going. At the next station my father would take tickets as far as the frontier town. If, on the train, a patrol came and asked us what we were going to do in Ovaros, we should talk about Aunt Charlotte, a distant relative who lived there and who had invited us to visit her. When we arrived at Ovaros, we should try to get off the train as inconspicuously as possible and we should go to the house of the man who slipped people over the frontier, in an outlying part of the town. He would escort us to the station of the first Austrian village on the other side. From there, we should proceed to Vienna. We had enough money to pay the guide and to buy two thousand Austrian schillings. After that, we would see what happened. Such was our plan. There was nothing to do at the moment except to take care that everything went according to plan. Otherwise we might completely lose control of events and of ourselves. ...

We went slowly down the main road. It was only round about five o'clock but it was already dark. It was raining. The dog bounded along in front of us. He would run on, then stop and retrace his steps to make certain he had not lost us. My father walked with difficulty; he did not see well in the dark. My mother held my arm. I was perspiring. My layers of garments stifled me.

We arrived at the station.

In the distance the train was approaching with an ever-increasing din. At last it came into the station. We climbed up the steep iron steps to the compartment. The dog made despairing leaps to follow us and had managed to hoist himself up on to the lowest step when another passenger, an elderly man who was impatient to get in, brutally kicked him off. Not in the least discouraged, the dog jumped up again, but the doors were already shut. Standing in the corridor, I could not manage to get the window down; it was jammed, or too stiff. I pulled it with all my might and I felt one of the dresses I was wearing had split. Sweat was beginning to trickle down my back and I could feel tears running down on to my chin. I leant my face against the glass so that no one should notice I was crying, and, in despair, I fixed my eyes on the deserted dog, staring with blurred eyes through the misted pane.

The train was moving and the dog was barking; he began to run along the platform, beside the coach. His thin, ugly little paws carried him at breakneck speed and I had the impression that he was catching us up, that he was going to leap on to the carriage step. But he grew smaller and smaller; already he had stopped barking, he had only enough strength left to run. And then he was no more than a little speck. The train had left the station and was steaming along between the dark fields.

I went into the compartment. Three people were installed in it besides my parents: two men and a woman. The silence was complete: you could hear nothing but the rattle of the wheels. Before the war, these coaches had been enlivened by the chatter of the passengers. Nowadays no one dared to enter into conversation. Any sentence might be dangerous and it was impossible to know who might not be a police spy. This silent journey had something frightening about it. I hadn't brought a book with me. I shut my eyes and leant my head against the back of the seat. The gaze of the woman sitting opposite me burnt through my closed eyelids. I decided to gaze at her in turn; it was the only means of making her turn away her head.

The ticket-collector appeared. He punched our tickets without saying a word.

'How many minutes do we stop at Belatelep?' inquired my father.

'We don't stop there at all,' said the ticket-collector, suddenly becoming more talkative. 'It's two days now since they cut out that stop for the evening train.'

The woman with the piercing eyes began to stare at us again, with interest. This time it was my mother who extricated us from our tricky situation. She said to my father:

'Then it would be better to go and see them on the way back from Ovaros and not to break our journey now. You could take tickets on to there, couldn't you?'

'Is it possible to extend our tickets as far as Ovaros?' inquired my father.

The ticket-collector nodded his head and dug out of his pouch a block interleaved with sheets of carbon paper. How complicated it is to take one's ticket on the train! The ticket-collector had to make inscriptions in three separate places but, finally, everything was arranged and my father put the tickets in his pocket. We would have liked to take off our coats but we did not dare to, for the others would see our heavily padded shapes. There was nothing, perforce, for us to do but to remain sitting in silence, motionless with suspense.

'I don't believe it's raining any more,' said my mother, after an endless lapse of time.

My father nodded, and let his cigar-ash drop on his overcoat. He promptly brushed it off with scrupulous care. The train grew emptier and emptier the nearer we approached the frontier town. The disagreeable woman began to collect her things, so did the two men. It was only then that we realized they were travelling together. They had not spoken, any more than we had. At last we saw them get out.

My father consulted his watch.

'The train's on time,' he affirmed.

We went out into the corridor. The train slowed down and ran into the station of Ovaros. We were the only people who got out. This was far from reassuring. It was half past nine. Having sweated in the train, we now found ourselves shivering in the wind and the moonlight. A platelayer was running along the track, a red lantern in his hand.

'If they ask us anything ... Aunt Charlotte!' repeated

my father, and, tickets in hand, we made our way to the
exit. Finally, we found ourselves together again outside
the station, in an almost deserted street. Two policemen
were standing on the pavement opposite. They stared at
us.

'Don't turn round,' my father told me. 'Let's walk
faster.'

We followed him. He knew his way. He had prepared
our flight with the utmost care. We left the centre of the
town and went farther and farther away from it through
a maze of little, narrow, ill-lit streets. When we reached
the outskirts my father knocked on the door of a house
with dark windows. The door opened almost at once and
a warm, unpleasant smell assailed our nostrils. A woman
ushered us in and led us to a room lit by a blinding, high-
powered bulb. The curtains were meticulously drawn. I
gave a hasty glance round. On a cooking-stove, that gave
out an infernal heat, a saucepan exhaled a thick steam
reeking of onions. A fat man was sitting at a table, busy
eating. He did not even get up when we came in, but
merely signed to us to sit down.

'It's off for tonight!' he said, between two spoonfuls.
His chin was fleshy and I should like to have seen his eyes
but he kept them greedily fixed on his soup.

'But why?' asked my father, in consternation.

The man at last decided to look at us.

'Because of the moon, of course. Shines too much.
Lights up everything. Can't possibly set off like that. Anyway, I don't want to risk my skin.'

The woman put another dish down on the table. I
scrutinized the face of the guide. I listened so intensely
to his explanations that the meaning of the sentences
escaped me. I only understood one thing: it's off. Perhaps
tomorrow. . . . It was nothing to do with him: *he* had no
control over the moon. Then he gave us to understand
that we must go away and come back at half past nine the
next night.

'But where can we spend the night and the whole of

tomorrow?' asked my father. 'We can't go to a hotel — the police would be warned at once.'

He waited for the guide to suggest our spending the night in his house. But the fleshy-chinned peasant was positive and peremptory; he had undertaken to make us cross the frontier: full stop. There was no question of staying in his house; the police made too many searches and they'd been keeping their eye on him for some time. He would only make the trip once or twice again, not more. This kind of business was getting too dangerous.

His wife added in a toneless voice:

'You'd better go at once. Come back tomorrow night.'

We definitely had to make up our minds. But where were we to go? I was hungry.

'Could you give me a little water?' I said, in the hopes of being offered something to eat.

With a brusque movement, the woman ran some water into a thick-rimmed cup. She thrust it into my hands. I only took two mouthfuls of it. The water was warm and smelt of disinfectant.

*

A few moments later we found ourselves once more in the street. It was essential to start walking at once in a definite direction, as if we knew where we were going. Strollers were suspect, and if we were asked for explanations, all was lost. So we set off with a firm, decided step, like people afraid of arriving late at the place where they are expected.

'Where are we going?' I asked, panting.

The cold air I breathed in cut like a knife.

'There may still be one possible chance,' said my father. 'But if that does not succeed there's no other solution for us but to take a train again and to travel until tomorrow evening. Impossible to go to a hotel, and the station waiting-room is only too often raided by the police.'

We traversed unknown streets and arrived at last in front of a church. My father went up the steps and we followed him. The heavy door was not locked. We pushed it open. In the dense shadow the sanctuary lamp gave out a faint glimmer before the invisible altar. Utterly worn out, my mother and I sat down in the last row of benches. As to my father, he disappeared. Were we to remain sitting here till daylight? And what were we to do for the whole of the rest of the day? We could not stay in a church for twenty-four hours. I ought to pray now, but I had not the strength to. I was cold, I was hungry, I was sleepy.

My father returned and touched us on the shoulder.

'Come,' he whispered.

We followed him. We walked down the nave and went into the sacristy. It was completely dark in there. But a gleam that filtered through the crack of a door allowed us to see a priest who was standing in front of us. He shook hands with us and invited us to follow him. He told us in a low voice:

'Be very careful, I implore you, and crouch well down as you walk, the moment you get into the room we're going to. The window has no curtains and a street lamp shines in from the street. The house opposite is a police-station and the policemen can see everything that goes on inside. If we were to put up a curtain it would rouse their curiosity.'

I wished I could see this priest's features so as to judge how much charity and how much fear there was in his make-up, but he had no face. He opened the door for us and went into the room, bending down as low as possible. The lamp in the street outside swayed in the wind and its shadow swung to and fro on the wall. We sat down on the floor.

'We can stay here till tomorrow evening,' my father told us.

'However did you manage to arrange this?' asked my mother.

But the question remained unanswered.

'We must get undressed,' said I.

'Only our coats,' replied my father.

Never had I imagined it was so difficult to take off a coat while remaining squatting on the floor. We helped each other as best we could. My father was elderly and his blood-pressure was high, but he made no complaint. Outside, the wind redoubled its violence. The street lamp shot its beam of light on to the opposite wall, sent it dancing up to the ceiling, where it disappeared in a flash; then, a moment later, the whole process began again. I was seized with giddiness, as if I were on a ship. I shut my eyes but the light hurt me, even through my eyelids. A strange sensation of sea-sickness came over me. My sweat-soaked clothes were stifling me and my sick uneasiness was dragging me down to the land of nightmares. I wanted to open my eyes but the luminous pendulum that kept swinging ever faster and wider paralysed me. Then, in the dizzy vortex of anguish and drowsiness, a mouth appeared to me: a mouth with curving lips. To whom could that mouth belong and where could I have noticed it so clearly as to be sure I had seen it before? The mouth smiled and spoke to me, but I could not hear the words it uttered.

The night of torture dragged on. One moment we were crossing the frontier, but the oscillations of the lamp brought me back to reality. It was two o'clock in the morning. My parents were asleep. To whom had that mouth belonged? Sleep overcame me once more. I was running along a dark road. A dead man came to meet me, one of those who had lain in front of our house in Buda-pest. He signed to me and smiled.

'They've stolen the wedding-ring off my finger,' he told me, gaily. 'I'm going to reclaim it from the thief. No doubt he'll give me back my arm, too.'

I noticed then that he had lost an arm and that a flower was growing out of the wound and getting bigger every moment until it finally blotted out the dead man's face.

At last it was daylight. We recovered the dregs of our

strength as a wounded man does on the battlefield when dawn revives him enough to drag himself along, crawling, towards the village.

Crawling like that, we left the room.

In the passage we stood upright and walked along to a narrow recess where we found what we needed to make a sketchy toilet. We still had to keep all our clothes on. Soon afterwards we found ourselves squatting once more in the room where we had spent the night. An old priest, with an impassive face, brought us some coffee. He put the cups down on the floor as if that were the natural place to put them. He said nothing and behaved as if he scarcely noticed we were there. The time passed with atrocious slowness. Heaven grant there would be no moon tonight! So far, the weather was cold and rainy. The sky was muffled and grey.

We sat motionless for hours; then, once again, it was dark. The dance of the street lamp started up once more. Six o'clock. After an interminable time of waiting, at last it was eight o'clock. I hid my face in my hands to shield my eyes from the light. I had the feeling that I was pressing my face against someone else's hand. This feeling was not new to me, but whose hand was it and when had it stroked my face before?

At nine o'clock we crept out of the room. The priest was standing there in the dusk and nodded us good-bye. We went through the sacristy, then once again we were in the church. The wan light of the sanctuary lamp made a faint red haze before my eyes. Then we were delivered up to the night. As we made our way we kept anxiously scanning the sky. Thick clouds were heaped up so low that they looked near enough for one to touch them.

The door of the guide's house opened at the first knock. This time the couple were more amiable. The wife was preparing some mulled wine for us.

'Wine? At this moment?' my father asked incredulously.

'I make everyone have some before we set off,' said the

guide with a grin. 'Gives 'em strength and raises their morale. I can't undertake anything with people who are frightened. And everyone's frightened on an empty stomach, even me. So come on, let's drink.'

He emptied a great mug of steaming wine. I raised mine to my lips and tasted this liquid. It was spiced and scalding hot. But my palate soon became accustomed to it and I emptied my mug avidly and resolutely. This drink warmed up our tired and famished bodies as if new blood had been injected into them. The room suddenly looked bigger to me and the guide's face rounder.

'I've drunk it all up,' I said thickly, giving a broad grin.

I had the impression that my mouth was split to the ears and that I should never manage to be serious again.

'Well done!' said my father. His spirits had risen, too. Then, with an elegant, airy gesture, he indicated the door.

'Can we leave now?'

The guide took another draught.

'Too much,' said my mother uneasily. 'Too much. If you drink too much you'll lose your way.'

'And if he does lose it? What'll happen?' I said, with my mouth wide open as if for a guffaw. I wanted to cry, but I only laughed louder than ever.

The plump little peasant seemed suddenly to make up his mind.

'We'll be off,' he said, putting on his leather coat. He kissed his wife and gave us some instructions.

'Never walk one beside the other. Always in file, as if we weren't together. If I stop, you stop. If I lie down flat, you do the same. If I run, you run.'

My father interrupted good-naturedly:

'I'm sixty, my friend. It's not easy for me to run, you know.'

The peasant turned suddenly icy.

'Anyone who's running to save his life hasn't got any age,' he said, pulling in his belt. 'On your way!'

We went out into the blackness. The guide in front, my mother next, then myself. My father came last. We kept a

distance of six or eight paces between us. It was a quarter
to ten. The street was deserted. Our footsteps echoed as if
we were walking under an arch. Soon we left the town
and found ourselves in the vineyards. They were well
tended. But how difficult it was to walk there! The earth
was rough and slippery. It was very dark. The guide went
forward at a rapid pace and, at all costs, we had to follow
him. My father stumbled and uttered a stifled cry. The
guide growled:
   'Silence.'
My father was finding it difficult, walking in the dark;
he kept slipping on the clods of earth. I longed to give him
my arm but, among the vines, we could only advance in
Indian file. At last, we arrived at the foot of a hill. A
stream flowed in front of us and the rain had begun to fall
again. It protected us, for it made visibility very poor.
The frontier guards could see no better than we did.
   The darkness was dissipating the effects of the alcohol.
I stared at my feet and I listened to the dragging sound
of footsteps. I was past knowing whether I was frightened
or not. The moment was something beyond my grasp;
events were too overwhelming for me, and I felt as if I had
been swept beyond the limits of human comprehension. I
went on walking.
   The guide stopped abruptly and, with a motion of his
hand, gave us the order to squat down. Panting, we sat
down in the wet grass. How good it was to sit down for a
little! It was eleven on the luminous dial of my watch.
   Was it possible we had already been walking for an
hour and a half? The sweat began to chill again on my
back. I was thirsty.
   The guide came up to us without raising himself upright.
   'I don't know if they've already gone past,' he whispered. Then he added: 'I'm frightened.'
   It was more irritating than alarming to hear him say he
was frightened. What must we be feeling if *he* were
afraid? We lay down in the soaking grass. Not far from

us ran the main road. The asphalt showed pale and smooth in the darkness. It was nameless anguish to know that we would have to cross that broad, clear gap. How much longer should we have to stay here, waiting? The distant blast of a whistle rent the silence. Some instants later, a car went by. The shape of the guide reared up again.

'They've gone,' he said. 'We can try and get across.'

'Is the road the frontier?' I asked him.

He stressed his impatience with a little shake of his head.

'Of course not. The frontier's still a long way.'

Where was the frontier? What was the frontier like? We reached the edge of the road. The cemented surface spread before our eyes as if an invisible hand were widening it in front of us.

'Run!' ordered our guide.

My parents crossed the high-road as if it were a skating-rink. They wanted to run but all they could do was stumble. We were in the middle. An inner force urged me to run, but I followed the pace of my parents. The guide had already been on the other side for a long time. He gesticulated and muttered oaths.

'At last!' he said, when we arrived. 'Now there's a clearing – and then the forest begins.'

The road stretched behind us like a silver ribbon. We ran through the clearing and finally reached the trees. I leant against the first damp trunk and got my breath back, pressing my face against the bark.

The guide never stopped grumbling:

'This is the very last time I ever do this job with old people. It's impossible. They creep along like slugs.'

We continued on our way, plunging into dead leaves up to our ankles. It was very dark. From time to time, a wet branch brushed against my face. And it was then that, suddenly, during that crazy journey, I realized to whom that nameless mouth and that caressing hand had belonged.

To Pista. I saw him again as I had seen him one day

when he had said something to me, very close by the candle. I could not remember what he had said to me but I saw his mouth again and the gleam of his splendid white teeth. And the hand had belonged to him too, that hand that had helped me cross the plank above the drowned man. It was then that he had stroked my cheek. And I had only realized it at this moment. But, yes, at this very instant he was near me. He was holding my hand.

'Lie down,' hissed the guide. 'Lie down.'

We were lying full length in the leaves but, now, I no longer felt so abandoned. Pista was there to help me to surmount these last difficulties. The guide ordered us to go on. All I heard was his authoritative voice; all I felt was the contact of the wet soil; it was dark, I could see nothing. I could hardly hear the laboured panting of the two tortured elderly people. We walked on. We walked fast, making an agonized effort and I did not feel strong enough even to glance at my watch.

The forest was growing less dense; the guide was becoming more and more uneasy and hostile.

'You'll have to pay more. For old ones like you, I shall ask extra.'

'You shall have all you want, but get us across the frontier,' said my father, and his voice reached me from very far away. Yet he was only a couple of steps from me.

We came to a clearing when, suddenly, the moon began to shine with all its brilliance, with all its celestial coldness. Our guide started swearing again. I no longer paid the least attention to him. Water was running all down my neck, my hair was soaked and my damp clothes imprisoned me like a cuirass. The dazzling moonlight flooded the black landscape with white.

'That's the frontier,' growled the guide. 'And that infernal moon has to shine! We'll have to run. ... Go on – run – even if it kills you!'

Why had I always believed that a frontier must, of necessity, be a material obstacle? A barrier – or a wall like the ones that border certain mountain roads. And now

I saw, as I ran, stupefied, and sobbing with the effort, that the frontier was only black grass and moonlight. I walked in the light as if drenched in a bath of silver and there where it shone most intensely, there where my hand and my hair and my heart were whitest – that was where the frontier lay.

I swathed myself in those enchanted rays.

Darkness suddenly asserted itself again, after the clearing. And I heard the voice of the guide, relaxed now:

'You can sit down; we're in no-man's-land.'

I collapsed beside my parents. I pressed one cheek against the earth, against that earth which belonged to no one and which was mine. This was where I was at home: here where spirits met again in the luminous void that stretched between the two parts of the world.

'Let's go on,' said the man, after that brief repose.

We were treading on Austrian soil. But the station we had to reach was still a long way off. My mother took off her shoes and wrapped her feet up in her silk scarf which she had just torn in two. She walked the rest of the way like that. My father lurched along, staggering, but his courage remained unshaken.

Dawn found us in a little Austrian station. Street vendors and men in short leather breeches occupied the waiting-room. They spoke a language I did not understand. It was the first time in my life that I had been in a foreign country. If I had begun to speak, people would have looked at me with astonishment. Our guide withdrew in company with my father; when he returned, he held out his hand to us.

'You're in luck. For the present, you're safe. Your train to Vienna leaves in ten minutes.'

And, having made this farewell, he disappeared into the crowd.

Here we were, alone together once more. My mother put on her shoes again. My one craving was an inexpressible longing to drink a cup of boiling-hot coffee.

'I bought two thousand Austrian schillings from him,'

explained my father. 'He let me have them at a fair rate of exchange and he's taken tickets for us as far as Vienna. A thoroughly decent fellow! I only hope he gets back without any hitch.'

I asked:

'How long will these two thousand schillings last?'

My father considered.

'About two months. At least, I hope so.'

'And after that, what will become of us?'

'After that, we shall have to begin our life all over again. . . .'

The waiting-room was becoming more and more animated. The women loaded themselves with their big baskets and bustled out on to the platform. We, whose limbs were quite benumbed, dragged ourselves along like half-unconscious survivors of a shipwreck who struggle against the undertow and reach dry land at their last gasp.

Stiff with sleep, we managed to sit upright on the wooden benches of the little local train. A sullen ticket collector punched our tickets with complete indifference. Opposite me, a man lit his pipe with ritual care. The nauseating smell of cheap tobacco turned my stomach. It began to rain again. The landscape melted into the grey sky. In the distance, factory chimneys went by, one after another. So did ruins, and still more ruins. I had the impression that I had been in this train for years, as if fate had nailed me to this hard wooden seat and forced me to travel unceasingly past endless ruins, in the company of silent beings. I had believed that, beyond the frontier, beyond Hungary, in the countries they called Occidental, the sky would be blue and the people happy. I had thought they would surround us joyfully and that their smile of welcome would make us forget the past. But, in this train, nobody smiled at all and the tobacco smoke became thicker and thicker and more and more unbearable.

We were getting near Vienna. I looked avidly out of the window. My heart beat fast. How many times my parents had talked to me of that enchanted city, always sparkling with gaiety. The train stopped in the midst of ruins. This must be the station, since everyone was getting out. We, too, got out. The rain trickled down the charred walls and dripped off the broken gutters. In a few seconds we were soaked to the skin. The crowd swept us along with it towards the exit. My coat was getting heavier and heavier and I would like to have split through that cocoon of wretched clothes I had worn for three days without being able to take them off. Suddenly I felt the fastenings that kept up my nightdress giving way. Impossible to stop it from unrolling its full length! There I stood, with the rain running down my face on to my grey coat, whose hem showed several inches of silk nightdress. I felt impotent and ridiculous. That light blue contrasted so sharply with the dingy grey that it was beginning to attract stares. People stopped and looked at me without the faintest smile. I rushed forward, in tears, towards a near-by hut. The nightdress hindered my running, clinging to my ankles; the muddy water soaked through my shoes and splashed my clothes. When, at last, I got under cover, I had to wait till my hands stopped trembling. At first I wanted to tear the silk that had come down at such an awkward moment, but the material resisted. It was stronger than I was. There was no other solution but to pin it up. At last I was able to rejoin my parents and we left the station. The curtain of rain blocked our view. Where, oh where, was Vienna?

We set off walking at random. Chance brought us to the door of a café. We went into it. The waiter gave one glance at us, then resumed his chat with a customer. At another table, a couple was drinking coffee. The man occasionally spoke a few words; the woman never answered.

We sat down. The waiter came up and flicked a duster over the table.

'Three coffees and something to eat,' my father said in German.

We were so utterly exhausted that we could find

nothing to say to each other. We sat, motionless, looking out into the street where wind was now making the rain swirl. A stout old lady pushed open the door and entered, carrying a very fat dachshund in her arms. That reminded me of our own dog. Perhaps he was still running despairingly in pursuit of the train and of his faith in human beings.

The waiter brought the coffee and three minute grey rolls. I bent my head over the cup and closed my eyes. I drank. The beverage was only coffee in name, but it was scalding hot and it warmed both body and heart. Already, the street seemed to me less hostile. I devoured one of the little rolls. At that moment, I caught sight of myself in a mirror opposite me and I noticed that I was smiling. ...